PRAISE FOR *APPETITE*

"Sheila Grinell's debut novel *Appetite* takes us into the heart of a family being torn apart by conflicting beliefs about what constitutes love, marriage, and success. Do parents have the right to try to stop an adult child from marrying if they see disaster looming, or should they back off and wait to pick up the pieces? In this tight, well-written novel, Grinell highlights the conflict between youthful idealism and adult disillusionment in ways that are both moving and thought-provoking."

—Mary Mackey, author of the *New York Times* bestseller *A Grand Passion*

"*Appetite* is the story of the conflict between a boomer couple, Maggie and Paul Adler, and Jenn, their millennial daughter, over the daughter's impending marriage to an Indian guru. It is an engrossing account of a struggle to find common ground about how life should be lived. Long-held principles can be lost, debased, and degraded over time, sometimes to disastrous effect, while hopeful and idealistic plans for the future remain untried. This intergenerational drama of relationships, both long-established and newly formed, makes for a gripping journey—not only for the characters but for the reader as well. Sheila Grinell has done a splendid job in this fascinating first novel."

—Mickey Friedman, author of *Hurricane Season*

"In her debut novel, Sheila Grinell weaves a rich and sensual tapestry of individuals held together by devotion and duty. Taut and sexy, *Appetite* is a story about finding your own way and the magnetic appeal of youth, ambition, and freedom. A fun read that will leave you hungry for more."

—Gina Gotsill, co-author of *Surviving the Baby Boomer Exodus: Capturing Knowledge for Gen X and Y Employees*

APPETITE

A NOVEL

SHEILA GRINELL

swp

SHE WRITES PRESS

Published 2016
Printed in the United States of America
ISBN: 978-1-63152-022-8 pbk
ISBN: 978-1-63152-023-5 ebk

Library of Congress Control Number: 2015954338
Cover design by Julie Metz Ltd./metzdesign.com
Interior design by Tabitha Lahr

For information, address:
She Writes Press
1563 Solano Ave #546
Berkeley, CA 94707

She Writes Press is a division of SparkPoint Studio, LLC.

This is a work of fiction. Names, characters, places, and incidents either are the product of the author's imagination or are used fictitiously. Any resemblance to actual persons, living or dead, is entirely coincidental.

To Niko and his parents

I'm gonna keep my skillet greasy if I can.

—Mississippi John Hurt

FALL

ONE

There are two kinds of people in this world, Maggie Adler thought, those who eat when anxious and those who can't. She stared at the bran muffin on her plate; two plump raisins poked through the crust. She picked at them like a scab and sipped her tea.

A year ago her daughter, Jenn, had quit her job and taken off for New Delhi. At first Jenn had written letters. Then she switched to emails that occasionally mentioned a man. Then the man's name, "Arun, rhymes with moon," appeared. Then the emails stopped, leaving Maggie in the dark. So she began to worry. Worry welled up whenever her concentration flagged; worry flavored her days.

Across the table, her friend Ellen said, "So, you don't like Zumba?" They were at brunch after a two-hour class.

"I liked the music."

Zumba was Ellen's latest aerobic exercise. Every six months Ellen launched a new campaign for self-improvement, but she never took herself too seriously.

Maggie said, "I'm worried about Jenn."

"Oh, that's what's bothering you? For a minute I thought something was wrong." Ellen spread a glob of butter on her scone. "Come on, Mag. We've been over this. Jenn is twenty-five years old and she can take care of herself. Besides, you said she's coming home."

Last week Jenn had sent a one-line email saying she'd be back before Christmas, not one word of explanation. Despite Ellen's logic, Maggie couldn't shake the thought that something *was* wrong. She sipped her tea.

Ellen chewed as she talked. "You people blessed with a roaring metabolism just don't appreciate what life is like for the rest of us."

Maggie let the comment pass. It suited Ellen to put her in a separate category, to ignore the hours Maggie spent walking the neighborhood, the years of healthy cooking, the continual abstention. When they'd first started exercising together, Maggie had made a point of complimenting Ellen's lovely skin, such a contrast to her own premature wrinkles. Ellen had tossed the compliment aside, saying she didn't need flattery. They had been easy together ever since.

Ellen said, "Time for some fun. What are you doing this afternoon?"

"I'm doing the books for All Saints'."

"Again?"

"Every month."

"You are a good soul," Ellen sighed, licking sugar off her fingers.

Maggie swept crumbs from the table into her empty teacup and rose. She didn't wait for Ellen to gather her things.

"See you next Friday."

"Mag, call me."

"Sure," she said, turning away. She pushed arms through

the sleeves of her sweat suit jacket, making another dim mental note to fix the zipper.

She had parked beneath an oak, one of the eight-story trees she so admired in downtown Pelham. A few yellowed leaves lay on her car's hood and windshield. She brushed them aside mechanically, planning the route she would take to the supermarket, the post office, home. No one waited for her there. No deadline except her own. Service to the church would bring balance to her day, or maybe the right term was "ballast." She would finish the September books by four and take the accounts to Reverend Stevens before he left at five.

Behind the wheel, she fished her cell phone out of her gym bag and placed it on the passenger seat. All week since the email, she had been keeping her phone at the ready. New Delhi was ten and a half hours ahead, so if Jenn called in the evening, as she used to do from college, the call might come around now. She pulled onto the street and into the right-turn lane, heading toward the parkway. She drove fast, too fast her husband, Paul, always said, but she knew every turn by heart. They had lived in suburban Pelham since Paul had gotten his own research lab in lower Manhattan and Jenn was in grade school. Maggie had always liked the way the parkway snaked between the trees, between the low, stone fences alongside the roadway. She used to play a game, from home to Jenn's school without stepping on the brake, using only the accelerator and the clutch and her sense of rhythm to cover the five miles. Of course, she never played it with Jenn in the car. A mistake would have been disastrous.

Ahead, the stoplight turned yellow, same as the leaves overhead. How many other parkways in the world were

lined with trees and stoplights, she wondered for the ump-
teenth time as she braked. No clutch in a Prius, or at least
none you control. So many things were different now. She
and Paul used to be coconspirators, figuring things out together, like how to pay for his education, where to live,
how to school Jenn. It had been fun to get by on her salary
while he earned his degree; they had been a team up against
the odds, plotting the plays.

Maggie pressed her lips together. Little remained of
their conspiracy. Now they might not converse for days
at a time. She still made meals for two; he ate the leftovers
when he came home. Sometimes when she entered the
kitchen to greet him, she would find him standing in front
of the fridge, door open, using the fridge light to eat from
the plate she had left for him. She would ask him to sit
down, offer to heat up the food, or bring him a drink. He
usually told her not to bother. Sometimes she didn't get up
when she heard him in the kitchen, keeping her nose in her
book. Sometimes she found him asleep in bed when she
returned from an evening walk. At night in the king bed,
they didn't need to touch. And to think they once happily
shared a single mattress. She yearned to turn the clock back
to a simpler time when love enveloped the three of them,
and Paul's research didn't interfere.

The light turned green. She stepped on the accelerator and the car advanced soundlessly. Still hard to get used
to the electric mode, much as she appreciated it. Ah, that
could be her motto: how hard it is to get used to things
that should be appreciated. Little things, like the bouquet
of peonies that arrived on her birthday, sent, she suspected,
by Paul's assistant. And big things, like Jenn's taking off
for India. Jenn, who'd had a hard time settling in after col-

lege but became reanimated studying Vedantic philosophy. If only she hadn't hooked up with that guru, or lover, or whatever he was. Icy fingers rose up from Maggie's belly and squeezed her heart.

The phone chirped. She clutched it, squinting to read the display. Not Jenn. She replaced the phone on the passenger seat and looked up. A van loomed in front of her, taillights flashing. She stomped on the brake, heaved the steering wheel to the right. The tires gripped and screeched.

The rear of the vehicle ahead zoomed bigger. She couldn't push the pedal any harder. She couldn't turn the wheel any farther.

Bang—she lurched sideways as the Prius's left wheels lifted off the pavement.

She felt the car hurtle forward, bouncing and shivering. Metal cracked and crunched. She couldn't breathe. She couldn't see.

Then everything stopped.

She sat still, taking stock. She felt dizzy. Her heart pounded; her face and chest burned, but no sharp pain. The now-deflated airbag spread in front of her over the steering wheel. On the floor on the passenger side, her gym bag and purse lay overturned, contents spilled. Releasing the seat belt, she opened the door. Slowly, tentatively, she climbed out of the car. The Prius had jammed into the guardrail; the passenger side bore horrible gashes across both doors, and the safety glass in the windows had crazed into hundreds of segments, like a malign spiderweb. Ahead, a van was parked, right rear fender collapsed, left blinker on. A man approached.

"Are you all right?"

"I think so."

He stopped in front of her. "I saw it in the mirror. You slid along the rail. I called the police. They're sending an ambulance."

"I don't need an ambulance. I don't want to go to a hospital."

"Yeah, but you should for the insurance."

"Insurance?"

"You're gonna make a claim, aren't you?"

Maggie's legs trembled. She leaned against her mutilated car and tried to clear her mind. Her neck and shoulders were beginning to ache. She tasted dust in her mouth, saw it on her shirt. No way would she sit for hours in a cold emergency room. She would go to her own doctor if necessary. But first the police would come. And then?

"May I use your phone?" she asked. "Mine's in my car."

"Sure. Here."

Maggie turned away. The man walked around to the front of her car and squatted, examining the damage. She punched in Ellen's number, got her answering service. She punched in Paul's number, expecting to reach his assistant, but Paul answered.

"I've been in an accident. No one is hurt, but I can't drive my car. Can you come for me?"

"What happened?"

"I'm not sure. I glanced down and a car cut in front of me, and I couldn't stop. I'm on the parkway. The police are on the way."

"Are you sure you're okay?"

"Please come."

"When did it happen?"

"Five, ten minutes ago."

"How about the other car?"

"Paul, just come."

"I'm tied up here right now. I'll get someone to take over. I should be there in less than an hour if there's no traffic. It'll take you that long to finish with the police. Okay?"

She cut off the call, not surprised at his nonchalance, but disappointed nonetheless. He wouldn't care about the damage to the car, a practical matter he'd delegate to her, but he should care about her discomfort. She didn't want to stand around for an hour on the parkway. Her shoulder, the one that had been beneath the seat belt, throbbed. Against her will, she began to cry.

The other driver approached. "Looks worse than it is."

She fished a tissue from her pocket and dabbed at her eyes. Her legs would not stop trembling.

Lights flashed in the distance. "Would the police give me a ride home?" she wondered out loud.

"They're not allowed to. Live around here? I'll take you."

"No. I'll call a cab."

"Hey, it's the least I can do. No problem."

A fire engine pulled up, siren squealing, and then a squad car. A wave of embarrassment swept over Maggie; one moment of carelessness had caused so much commotion. But who was to blame for the accident? Maybe the other driver was at fault. She looked at him: under forty, clean-shaven, relaxed. He stepped aside when the officers approached.

A fireman asked if she was hurt. She said she was fine, truly. Then a policeman stood before her with his back to the roadway, outlined against the midday sun. Automatically, she read the name on his badge: Sergeant Hernandez. She wanted to cooperate perfectly. Well, she *really* wanted Sergeant Hernandez to tell her she wasn't at fault. He handed her a form and a pen. She squinted at the paper. It asked for vehicle and insurance numbers. She leaned into her car from the driver's side, barely reaching the glove compartment, to retrieve her insurance card. She copied the numbers into the appropriate boxes and signed her name. A routine, predictable thing, filling out a form and signing your name. It soothed her. She had stopped trembling.

While a junior officer paced off the skid marks, the sergeant turned his attention to the driver of the van. When they finished speaking, the driver approached her again. "I'm Brian," he said, offering his hand.

She didn't take it. "Aren't we adversaries?"

"We don't have to be. No one was hurt."

She had never been in an accident before. Was this how to gauge it—whether people were injured?

"There's no problem," he said, "as long as you're okay."

Maggie shrugged her shoulders, testing her body.

"I'm sore but I'm whole."

"Glad to hear it. Two weeks in a rental car and everything will be back to normal." He put his hands in his pockets and leaned against her car, an arm's length away.

A perfect stranger, yet she wanted to believe him. Her shoulder burned and her stomach stirred; she needed to keep calm. She looked around her. It was a beautiful day, sunshine overriding the autumn chill. Birds called in the woods behind them, audible over the noise of passing cars. A breeze fanned her cheeks. How ironic that an accident gave her occasion to be still outdoors.

"No offense," he said, "but your car won't be hard to fix."

"How do you know?"

"I used to fool around with cars. Your wheels and chassis are straight. You only need bodywork. The car, that is."

Could this man be flirting with her while the police car lights flashed? At another time she might have felt flattered, but now the police commanded attention.

Brian said, "You should get a pro to check it out."

"I intend to."

He turned on his heel and jogged to his van. He loped back, tight bodied like a runner, holding a knapsack. Opening the sack, he withdrew a tablet and fiddled with it.

"Okay, I've got a connection. Take a look." He held the tablet so that she could see the screen: a Prius like hers was pictured in the middle. As he touched it, its outer layers disappeared, revealing the frame. Then the parts zoomed together, and the dealer's ad spread across the screen. "Prius is pretty tough. So long as the chassis's not twisted, you can fix the rest, and it'll drive fine."

Maggie felt uncomfortable standing so close to him. She could smell his sweat, feel the heat generated by his muscles. A lean, musky male, less than an arm's length away. Much younger than she.

"Why are you being so helpful?"

"I'm a sucker for sad women."

She couldn't respond; was it so obvious to a complete stranger? She didn't dare ask how he could tell.

After a beat, he turned off the computer. They stood in silence as a spate of cars sped by in the far lane.

The policemen stood talking together, gesturing and nodding their heads. Holding a clipboard, the sergeant approached them. He addressed Maggie. "Looks like you were going pretty fast when he cut in front of you." Turning to include Brian, "I'm not going to give either one of you a ticket. There are no witnesses." He separated the layers of a form and handed her the bottom, pink copy, pointing to a long number he had written. "This is the report number. We've called for a tow. You'll need someone to drive you home." He turned to Brian. "Here's yours. The report will be ready within twenty-four hours."

Maggie looked at the pink page. It read "Brian Sayler," followed by an address, vehicle identification number, insurance company name—all the information she had provided on her form. And the sergeant had given her information to Brian Sayler. She saw him study it.

"Is it Ms. or Mrs. Adler? Your house is on my way. Sure I can't give you a ride?"

"No thanks, my husband is coming. From lower Manhattan. I'll just wait."

In fifteen minutes she could be home, taking a shower or contemplating the damages over a cup of tea. Why not cut herself some slack? And what if she were to ride with this man whom chance had tossed her way? An attractive man, a pleasant enough person. Jenn would accept the offer. Jenn, who used to pick up strays and find them brilliant. Jenn, who might call at any moment on the landline at home.

"Want me to wait with you?"

"No thanks. I'll be fine."

"Well, you know where to reach me." He tucked the tablet into the knapsack and walked toward his van.

Maggie touched her injured shoulder gingerly. Traffic had picked up, probably the after-school crowd. There was aspirin in her gym bag, and she wanted to get it before the tow arrived. She regretted summoning Paul now that she was calmer. A cab would have been quicker. And Paul would tell her to stop worrying about Jenn and keep her eyes on the road. As if she could.

TWO

Sunlight seeped around the edges of the blinds and Paul Adler woke, feeling like fortune's darling. Soon he'd have new money for the next phase of his research; soon his world-traveling daughter would come home. He lay quietly in his mistress's bed, happier than he had a right to be, savoring his success, and his luck.

Cancer, Paul had long thought, was beautiful. But he never said so, not even to his scientific colleagues. People couldn't think about cancer dispassionately, and he didn't want to challenge them. Where others saw monstrous distortions, he saw an orchestra of tiny alterations in biological mechanisms that let tumors strike out vigorously, crowding ordinary life out of the way. For decades, he had been trying to understand its magic. And now, at last, he was close.

He dressed quietly, let himself out of Irene's apartment. Although his belly flared the front of his sweatshirt, he walked like a younger man, upright, pressing ahead. Even at 6:00 a.m., energy oozed out of the city. A truck pulled up in front of the grocery midblock, and the driver got out to deliver a tray of breads. Paul looked past him to the deli next door, where the owner used a hose attached to a spigot beneath his plate-glass window to force dirt and paper into the gutter. Should he grab a sweet, greasy corn muffin, the kind that sits in your gut and makes you feel satisfied for an hour? God, he loved New York—best food in the world, twenty-four hours a day. He inhaled deeply and the October chill caught in his throat. He exhaled and watched the vapor condense. Soon the streets would heat up and his breath would disappear. Nothing like the early morning with its endless promise.

Walking fast, he reached the hospital that housed his lab in twenty minutes. He took the elevator to the suite of rooms he captained at the end of a corridor on the ninth floor near Administration. He had a tiny, cluttered office; another windowless room next to his contained a desk, copy machine, cabinets, and Sandi, the lab manager. Four industrial refrigerators in the anteroom held reagents and experimental material. There were three wet-lab rooms, where the research staff practically lived, their computers perched on desks jammed under shelves that held books, bottles, tubes, specimen trays. Photos of spouses, dogs, and scenes from home sprouted from the edges of shelves and monitors. Paul hired grad students who didn't mind the cramped quarters, or at least didn't complain.

He stepped into his office, intending to check email before the staff meeting called for eight. As he sat to boot his machine, Sandi appeared in the doorway holding two mugs of coffee. She passed one to him and leaned against a file cabinet to drink from the other. She was Paul's age but looked older, tired. It wasn't a matter of muscle; she could heft boxes of supplies as well as he. But her short, mousy hair drooped, her unadorned face sagged, and she made no effort to dress, wearing the same sky-blue smock over her street clothes every day.

"How come we're meeting on a Friday?" she asked. Sandi had worked for Paul for all the years he'd run the lab, and she spoke her mind. She had tended to him in so many ways, keeping the books, writing his monthly staff reports, soothing the young researchers, arranging his travel. Lately, he had been depending on her for dry cleaning.

"I got a call yesterday from the foundation. They want some fine-grained detail. You know that pretty much means that we got the grant. You'll get to push me around for another three years." He grinned.

"Well, I expected that."

"You're pretty casual about your paycheck."

She raised her brows. "You always find a way." She turned to leave and then turned back. "I almost forgot. Stamford wants to see you right away. I told him you had a meeting, but he said it can't wait. I'll tell the others."

He rolled his eyes and reached into his in-box. He glanced at the papers one at a time without concentrating, sipping the hot, black brew in Sandi's best mug. Of course his peers didn't understand the groundbreaking implications of his work. With one more suite of experiments, he would prove that he could destabilize one type of brain cancer cell in a matter of days. On his fingers he counted the months until he could start spending the grant money, when the paperwork would be finalized, processed, and the funds would hit the bank. He reached up to smooth his hair, a vestigial gesture from when thick hair used to spring from his scalp. These days, the mirror showed a receding hairline, but to his satisfaction, not one touch of gray. Ten fresh samples of glioma tissue from the hospital's neuro-oncology department lay waiting in the lab to be processed.

cxÓ Ócw

Halfway down the ninth-floor corridor, Provost Robert Stamford stood in front of a glass door etched with the hospital logo. As Paul neared, Stamford opened the door and gestured toward his office down the softly lit interior hall-way. Stamford was a short, stocky man who wore round-rimmed glasses and a bow tie. He was known, and mocked, for speaking in paragraphs where others would use a sentence. He and Paul had been scientific colleagues years back but had diverged professionally, Stamford moving into administration while Paul wrestled with research in the lab. Stamford oversaw the hospital's research portfolio; Paul refused to kowtow.

Thick carpet muted the sound of voices, a telephone, their footsteps as they made their way to Stamford's office. They passed Stamford's assistant and entered the room. At the far end, a wooden pedestal desk with a glass top glinted in the light from the windows. Behind the desk, framed photos on a credenza showed Stamford shaking hands with politicians and portly, white-haired men and women whom Paul understood to be donors. Three framed diplomas hung on the wall. Stamford sat in an armchair and beckoned Paul to the couch.

"I understand congratulations are in order."

"How did you hear?"

"You played handball last night. Everyone in the locker room heard your conversation."

"Nothing is official," Paul said, sitting, "so I'm not prepared to discuss it."

Stamford's face remained neutral. He crossed his legs.

"Comes at an opportune time, doesn't it?" He paused. "I'd like you to think about something. When you're ready to staff up, I have a candidate for your new position." He folded hands in lap and leaned back into the chair, a faint smirk on his face.

Paul felt annoyance rise. Stamford irritated him more quickly and more thoroughly than anyone else. He thought Stamford a parasite, a stuffed shirt who exploited other people's creativity to elevate his own standing. Twenty years Paul had struggled to develop his lab while Stamford manipulated the wealthy. Stamford was just a landlord, but he acted like a lord.

"I'm pretty sure that you will need to hire someone to gather the data for your next experiment. Your team just gets by as it is."

"We do good work, Robert."

"But you do need my help. You know you need me to cover the overhead on staff. For every salary dollar you spend, my department kicks in a quarter."

A siren sounded outside, growing louder as the ambulance pulled up to the emergency entrance in the courtyard below Stamford's windows. Paul sometimes forgot that he worked in a clinical setting.

"I'd like to introduce you to someone. She's a master's candidate at NYU, cancer biology. She's also the niece of two of our hospital's good friends. Her aunt and uncle are in a position to make another donation."

"Do you expect me to hire somebody's niece to help you make your numbers?" He was proud of his team of compatible people whom he could trust. No interference welcome.

"Paul, you're a fine researcher, but you need to take a broader view. We've been good to you here, through thick and thin." Stamford waited a beat. "Just take a look at the girl. We can talk again after you meet her." Stamford rose and went to his desk to push a button on his phone. "Eric, would you please give Dr. Adler Ms. Caldwell's contact information? He's on his way out." Paul rose and they moved together to the door, Stamford cupping Paul's elbow as he would a woman's.

"I'm confident that you will appreciate Ms. Caldwell's gifts and that you'll be an excellent mentor." They moved into the hallway. "She's very bright and capable. She's also very attractive, you know." Stamford opened the glass door to the main corridor and its fluorescent glare. "Again, congratulations."

Footsteps squeaked on the linoleum floor as a pair of orderlies pushed an empty stretcher and a couple of IV stands ahead of them. Chatting loudly in a foreign tongue, they moved aside as Paul passed. He strode down the antiseptic-tinged corridor and charged into his warren, past a startled Sandi. Nothing like five minutes with Robert Stamford to kill his joy. He punched his phone.

Irene, a nurse three floors below, his mistress for nearly a decade, answered. "What's the matter?"

"Why do you say that?"

"Why are you calling me at work?"

"Want to meet for lunch?"

"You could have asked me this morning."

She had a point. His voice softened. "How about it? I can't get to your place again until Thursday night."

"I'm on duty. See you Thursday."

He replaced the phone in its cradle. He knew she didn't like to be interrupted at work. So why had he phoned? Because she would understand his pique without his having to explain. She disliked Stamford nearly as much as he did.

He refocused on the manila folder on his desk. Inside, a neat stack of papers, courtesy of Sandi. Report from the tumor biology conference to which Alicia, his lead researcher, had gone to represent the team. Next: letter to Alicia's former advisor. Next: request to a correspondent lab in Stockholm to send more tumor tissue. None of the issues grabbed his attention; he closed the folder.

He stepped into Sandi's office and over to the vertical file jammed against the rear wall, where she kept paper copies of important documents. He opened the drawer labeled "Grant Proposals." As he thumbed through the files, he heard someone behind him.

"What are you looking for?" Sandi said, coming toward him. She stood frowning, arms akimbo. "Before you make a mess, tell me what you need."

"I want the foundation proposal."

"I figured. Here." She handed him a wedge of paper squeezed into a black metal clip.

"Atta girl."

"I'll bind it properly when you're done."

Paul opened the clip and spread the papers on his desk, looking for the budget. He found the salary items in year one, year two, and cumulative. He subtracted the dollars that his current team cost, rounding quickly. There was enough to pay a level-one research assistant. He could go up a level if Stamford kicked in the overhead. Paul added numbers in his head: if he rolled the three years together and didn't give raises, he could add a few grand to the position. Still not enough. He didn't want a level one; he needed more. Stamford had the advantage.

He picked up the phone to call his wife, his ultimate resource.

THREE

And there was Jenn, coming through the international-arrival doors, dark curls surrounding her head, layers of cloth flaring from her shoulders and obscuring her figure. She hobbled, a bandage around her ankle. She had phoned Maggie from Frankfurt close to midnight the night before, asking to be picked up at JFK at one in the afternoon. She was all right, she had assured her mother, but couldn't talk because her flight was boarding.

"What happened?" Maggie took Jenn's backpack with one arm, embracing her with the other.

"I twisted my ankle in the hotel lobby, day before yesterday."

"Is that why you came home suddenly?"

Jenn laughed. "Sort of. We stayed at a deluxe hotel in Delhi, and I tripped going up the marble staircase. Up! My usual graceful self." She adjusted the mirror-cloth bag over her shoulder.

Maggie ignored the reference to Jenn's history of bumps and bruises. "Are you sure you're all right?" She searched her daughter's face, browned and smooth beneath a patina of fatigue. She scanned her body: Jenn had always carried more flesh than was fashionable, and she looked solid, normal; no foreign parasites had wasted her, thank goodness.

"I'm fine. But I'll go for an X-ray tomorrow; not to worry." They started down the long, concrete corridor, Jenn stepping carefully. "This airport is almost as ratty as Delhi, but without the smells. You can't imagine how many smells there are."

"Should we get a wheelchair? Where's your friend?"

Jenn's voice brightened, "Arun's staying on until Thursday. He has the luggage. We decided it made sense for me to fly yesterday. Better than hanging around a dirty clinic in Delhi."

They rode the elevator to the parking level. Maggie offered to bring the car around while Jenn waited on a bench, her foot elevated. It had been over a year since Jenn had left her job and apartment in Brooklyn. She used to say that she didn't mind working at a halfway house because philosophy majors like her appreciated existential problems. But she wasn't happy. Then one day she called to ask for her immunization records, saying she needed to get booster shots and renew her passport to go to India. Maggie had been taken aback and pressed her for details, to no avail. Now that Jenn was home, Maggie counseled herself not to bombard her daughter with questions.

Maggie pulled the Ford Focus to the curb. Jenn hefted her backpack onto the rear seat and sank into the front in a cloud of cloth. The woolen shawl encasing her shoulders fell open, exposing silver-threaded sari cloth bunched around her neck. She wore no makeup. Filigree earrings dangled against her cheeks; she smelled faintly of cloves.

"Gave up the Prius, Mom?"

"This is a rental. I had an accident a couple of days ago." Sergeant Hernandez's scowl loomed in her mind's eye. Shame flashed through her. She didn't want to discuss it.

"What happened?"

"Nothing serious. No one was hurt. The car only needs bodywork."

"Are you okay?"

"I'm fine, I'm fine." Maggie reached for the dashboard. "How about some heat?"

"No thanks. But make yourself comfortable. Still wearing the leather jacket with the ink stain I made in junior high, I see."

Maggie's left hand went to the stain.

"Now I know I'm home." Jenn removed the shawl from her shoulders. "I've gotten hardy, Mom. You spend so much time outdoors at an ashram. We moved around a lot. Arun is in demand."

"He's coming on Thursday?"

"Uh-huh. Not to our house. He's going to see some colleagues first. And he has family in New Jersey. He'll spend time with us afterwards. I want you and Dad to get to know him."

"Of course." Maggie didn't want to share Jenn with this man, but she would. And she'd figure out how he had managed to captivate her. Studying the road signs, she pulled out of the parking lot.

Jenn leaned her head onto the seat back and closed her eyes. "I need a nice, long, hot soak. Then I'll be fit for company."

"I think there's some Epsom salts under the sink."

They threaded their way along the web of highways

that cross Long Island, heading for the bridge to Westchester County and home. When Jenn was little, she and Jenn used to love crossing the bridge for the view: Manhattan skyline in the distance, jagged shoreline beneath. From the top of the long arch, you could see for miles, Long Island Sound lapping into nooks and inlets, all kinds of boats making their way through the channel. Maggie would marvel at the great port city that had grown in this place, and Jenn would ask if they could stop to catch a fish. They had gone fishing once, trolling for flounder from a motorboat that bounced in the currents. Maggie had been miserably seasick. Paul and Jenn had had a fine time, and Jenn had reeled in the only catch of the day. For years afterward, she'd ask her father for another fishing trip. Paul had been too tied up at work to produce one.

"I've had a good year, Mom. Being with Arun in India was better than I expected. You would have approved."

"Why do you say that?"

"Because you care about what's important. You taught me to ask tough questions about character and conduct. I found answers in India. I couldn't find them in Brooklyn."

As Jenn adjusted the seat belt, a breath of clove wafted toward Maggie. She glanced toward the woman Jenn had become. She couldn't help but recall every other Jenn she had transported in the passenger seat: curly-headed kid going to nursery school, chubby preteen going to the orthodontist, sullen-faced adolescent fleeing to a friend's house. Every Jenn she had loved had telescoped into this unknown Jenn, sitting here now.

They traversed the long, high bridge. Approaching the toll plaza on the far side, Maggie steered around an eighteen-wheeler braking into the exact-change lane. The rental, so much lighter than her own car, seemed to float from one lane to the next. She gripped the wheel, aware that she was being unnecessarily cautious. Too much caution could be as dangerous as too little.

As the car slowed, Jenn sat up. "Tell me about your accident."

"There's not much to tell. It was on the parkway. A car cut in front of me and I couldn't avoid it. No one was hurt." She shuddered inside, hearing the sound of metal crunching, seeing the squad car's flashing lights, seeing Brian Sayler's lean frame crouched beside her car. How annoying that he came to mind. Much as she disliked it, he had made an impression.

Jenn reached a hand out to touch her mother. Bangles on her wrist tinkled.

Warmth spread from Jenn's fingers into Maggie's arm. She loosened her grip on the wheel. Jenn could always soothe. As a child, she used to bring home mangy dogs and cats, and they would turn sweet under her care. When she got older, she brought home mangy teenagers. Jenn would feed them grilled cheese sandwiches and play their favorite music. Unkempt, rude kids who never looked Maggie in the eye, gawky boys and dumpy girls, one after another. Jenn thought them beautiful, or talented, or misunderstood. She never seemed distressed when they stopped coming to the house, when they dropped out of her life without a word of thanks. Maggie would ask about the latest missing person, and Jenn would flick her hand in exuberance and say, "She's fine. I'm so proud of her!"

And now Jenn had Arun. Or Arun had Jenn. She feared Arun might spirit Jenn away before her mother had time to find out how she had grown.

Ahead, brake lights glowed red. Rush hour had crept up on them. Maggie turned off the highway onto a boulevard to take back roads into Pelham. As the car stopped at an intersection, Jenn looked out her window at the single-family houses nestled in lawns sprinkled with dried leaves.

"It's so tidy compared to India. You can't imagine the view alongside the road from Delhi to Agra. People crowded together, living out in the open, unprotected, unloved." Jenn paused. "Is Dad coming home tonight?"

"Yes, later. He wants to hear about your . . . adventure. He's going to wonder why you're injured and traveling alone."

Jenn flicked her hand. "Actually, this was my best trip yet on an Indian airline. Arun knows the system. We had to change my flight, and he put me in a wheelchair and told me to cry in the airport office. So I cried while he talked. We got the flight we wanted and the service was super all the way to Frankfurt. Arun said they probably bumped some unlucky Indian woman who'd been waiting a month for a seat. But it made the airport manager feel important."

"And that didn't bother you?"

"India is many things, but fair isn't one of them. I've learned to accept the world as it is, not as I wish it to be."

Maggie looked at Jenn's face: no sign of irony. That was change.

They pulled into the driveway, and Jenn limped upstairs to draw a bath. Maggie went to the kitchen to make tea. The All Saints' account books lay on the kitchen table. They would have to wait. She gathered the ledgers and printouts into a pile and placed them on a shelf in the pantry. Then she sat, sipped, listened for Jenn's footsteps overhead.

Yellow ceramic tile covered the walls and even the ceiling of the 1920s kitchen; a crooked web of crazing had accumulated in the glaze, a gentle reminder of its age. No cabinets attached to the tile walls; everything had to be kept in the pantry: onions, potatoes, bread in a bread box, dishes, pots, brooms, detergent, newspapers, napkins. When they bought this old house, they told themselves they would modernize the kitchen as soon as they could afford to. But they hadn't. Paul worked all the time, and Maggie raised Jenn and a succession of dogs, and she grew herbs in the rickety mudroom with its tall glass windows. As time passed, Maggie had grown fond of the mudroom, the yellow tile, the simplicity of tucking everything into a pantry. It pleased her to live deliberately, like her great-grandmother but with a better icebox. She respected the integrity of the old house. She wondered what Arun would make of it.

The mudroom door banged open. Paul walked in carrying a briefcase.

"You're home early."

"Where's Jenn?"

"Taking a bath. Washing away her flight. Can I get you something to drink?"

"No, I need to do some paperwork later. What's up with her?"

"I'm not sure. She injured her ankle and wants to go for an X-ray." Maggie rose and opened the fridge: Was there enough lettuce for three?

"Where's the boyfriend?"

"Coming Thursday, but not to our house. He's going to stay with us later."

"I'm gonna make a few calls. Call me when she finishes

her bath." He disappeared down the hallway stairs to the basement.

They had finished half the basement, building an office that Paul used when he didn't need to go into the lab and a guest room with a TV. They nicknamed the basement suite the Lion's Lair because Paul roared when his favorite hitter got a run, or a pitcher threatened a perfect game. The only daylight entered from two clerestory windows; Maggie found the basement gloomy and worked at the kitchen table instead. She'd put Arun in the guest room, and she'd make it hospitable.

A moan, a wheeze, another moan, emanating from the living room, then a woman's voice holding one long, clear note. When Paul and Maggie arrived, Jenn was fussing with the sound system.

"What's all that groaning?" Paul asked.

"It's a present for you guys," Jenn said, turning down the volume on the CD player. "This style of singing grows on you. I'm really fond of it now." She sat on the couch, long skirt trailing. "Hi, Dad. You look great."

Paul kissed the top of her head. "You're a sight for sore eyes! Are you home for good?"

"Of course not," Jenn laughed. "But I'll be here for a while."

"You brought a sick cow with you?"

"It's a hand organ. You pump it like an accordion. It takes a few pumps to get going and then it resonates behind the singer. Like the drone on a sitar. Street musicians carry them around."

Paul sat beside his daughter. "Is that what you've been doing this year? Busking?"

"I wish. No one would pay to hear me sing." She squeezed

his knee. "But I've learned a lot about Indian music. There's always singing and chanting at the kirtans we go to. Kirtans are like workshops."

"What do you do at these workshops?"

"I help. Arun gives talks, and people want to meet with him, so I take care of them until he can."

Paul frowned. "What does that mean?"

"I listen. I take notes. If they don't know Arun's work well, I give them an orientation. I'm not adept at his philosophy yet, but I do what I can."

"Doesn't sound like fun or profit."

"You just wait. Arun bridges East and West better than anyone. We'll be rich and famous one day." She opened both arms with a flourish.

"Now that's more like it." He raised his hand for a high five, and she met it.

Maggie stood at the kitchen threshold, watching. Seeing them on the couch, bandage on Jenn's ankle, took her back to the three months after Jenn broke her leg in ninth grade. Paul would come home from work, on the days when he came home early, and plunk down next to Jenn and make her laugh. It was Maggie who dragged Jenn to the doctor and physical therapy, all the things that caused Jenn pain. Sitting on the same couch a dozen years later, Paul and Jenn looked as comfortable as before. Jenn seemed ready to tell Paul whatever he wanted to hear. But he didn't ask the questions that agitated her mother's heart. Paul, out of tune with her heart, in so many ways. She turned into the kitchen to make dinner.

ᘓᕲ ᕬᘔ

They ate at the dining room table so that Jenn could prop her ankle on the fourth chair. Jenn asked about Paul's work. He told her about the biochemical he was testing, something that works one way in normal cells and the opposite way inside a tumor. Maggie didn't want to hear about cancer; she wanted to hear about the ashrams and Arun and what made Jenn happy so far from home. Twice she tried to interject a carefully worded question, but Paul was on a roll, explaining his new research grant, and apparently Jenn wanted the details.

They moved to the living room for baked bananas, one of Jenn's favorites. Digging in, Jenn made happy "yummy" sounds. Maggie pampered her girl, cushioning her ankle, fetching tea, then honey. Paul asked about Delhi, and Bangalore, and Mumbai. Then he asked about Jenn's plans but didn't get an answer. Jenn stretched and yawned, arching her back extravagantly.

Maggie jumped in, "Should I make a doctor's appointment for you tomorrow?"

"No thanks, Mom. I'll take care of it. There's a bunch of things I need to do." She looked at her lap and smoothed a fold in her skirt. "I have to tell you guys. I wanted to wait for Arun, but I can't. We're going to get married. Here in the spring, and then we'll go back to India and get married there."

Maggie gasped.

Paul smacked his hand on his thigh. "You're pregnant."

"There are other reasons to marry, Daddy. I'd like you to get to know Arun. Then you'll understand."

"What if I don't like him?"

Jenn flicked her hand. "I think you will. You both will. Give him a chance."

"I'm surprised," Paul said. "I thought you'd be more

practical. What are you going to do for money? You can't keep traipsing around India crashing at ashrams." He rose, shaking his head no, and left the room.

Maggie felt a weight descend from her chest into her gut. There was no sense in protesting, and at least the picture was clearer. Or was it? She needed time to think. She picked up the dessert plates and forks. "I'm going to do the dishes. You must be exhausted. You need to sleep. We'll talk tomorrow."

Jenn gathered her skirt and limped to the foot of the stairs. Maggie watched her climb; yes, indeed, something was terribly wrong.

✺ ◌

She had almost finished loading the dishwasher when hand-organ music blared again. It stopped abruptly, and Paul appeared in the doorway behind her.

"If that god-awful sound is a taste of things to come, watch out."

"Jenn's gone up to bed. Be careful she doesn't hear you." Maggie poured detergent into the cup in the dishwasher door.

"I don't care if she does. She needs to know what I think." Crossing the kitchen to the mudroom, he retrieved his briefcase, stopped. "I don't get it. She's got brains and guts. She could start anywhere and rise to the top. I don't want her banging a tambourine for a huckster. Squandering her advantages."

"Neither do I, but she wants what *she* wants."

"Don't tell me you approve."

"We should hear her out." She reached for the pots from

the stove. "Maybe we can all talk about this tomorrow? Can you skip the Thursday seminar and come home for dinner?"

"I'm scheduled to make a presentation. It's important."

"So is your daughter's future."

Paul grunted and turned on his heel, heading for the basement. Over his shoulder, "I'll make it work."

Maggie lowered pans and a baking dish into the soapy water in the sink. She turned on the hot-water faucet. A mound of bubbles rose beneath the spigot, swelling and tipping toward the edge of the sink, threatening to fall to the floor.

This was what she'd feared: a man who might be twice Jenn's age, a demanding man who spirited her away. Something must have happened in India. She turned off the hot water and dried her hands with a dish towel, leaving the pans for tomorrow. As she flicked the light switch, her eye caught on a photo on the refrigerator: Jenn, with short-cropped hair, wearing jeans and hugging the dog, just before graduation two years before. It seemed like much longer.

She climbed the stairs, passing Jenn's bedroom. Light leaked from under the door. She rapped softly, and Jenn invited her in. Jenn sat propped up in bed with old scrapbooks and photos spread on top of the covers. An empty shoebox lay to her left—left-handed, like her father. Paul and Jenn had teased Maggie for years about being to the right of them or always being right. She was neither.

"I'm making a slide show for Arun to email to his parents. You and Dad made a handsome couple. Not that you still don't. We'll have to take some photos to get up to date."

Maggie sat on the foot of the bed, reflexively smoothing the chenille throw beneath her hand. "Are you comfortable?"

"I'm fine. *You* don't look comfortable."

True, but of course, Jenn meant no harm. Maggie's brow furrowed as she weighed her words. "I'm concerned. You want to marry a man your father and I have never met. And go halfway around the world."

Jenn pulled herself straighter. "You're going to have to trust me. I'm making a good decision. It's not what you or Dad would do, but it's right for me. Haven't you always encouraged me to follow my conscience?"

"But you can't build a life around conscience." Although, Maggie realized, she herself had been doing so these last few years. How many, actually?

"I'm not talking about good deeds and right action. I'm in love with a virile, passionate human being who understands the universe better than anyone else walking the planet, and he loves me."

Maggie remembered herself at Jenn's age, inspired by the grandeur of Paul's vision, his determination to beat cancer. That vision had remained elusive for both of them. "But what about you? You need to find your own way."

"I *have* found my way. It's miraculous. Everything Arun says, everything of consequence, I think, 'Yes, exactly so.' I get so happy imagining a lifetime with him. We'll make a difference."

Back then, what could anyone have said about Paul that would have dampened her desire to marry him? She looked at her daughter's glowing face.

"Tell me about Arun."

"He has an amazing mind. He thinks everything is part of one consciousness splintered into a gazillion fragments but still one. So everything contains its opposite. You wouldn't have day if you didn't have night—there would be no need to distinguish day. Do you get it?"

Maggie nodded slowly. "Sounds like metaphysics."

"Yeah, I thought so at first. It seemed too formal. But he knows how to apply his philosophy to everyday life. He helps people see where they're tripping themselves up, tripping over illusory opposites. He frees people."

"From what?"

"From their cares. First-world cares and third-world cares. Kids love him. I love him."

Maggie found it all too abstract. Frustration tightened the muscles in the back of her neck.

Jenn said, "I think you'll grow to appreciate Arun, but it may take some time."

Jenn locked eyes with her mother and held steady. The girl's confidence gave Maggie pause. Still, she had to ask. "How are you going to raise children when your cultures are so different? Won't you be torn?"

Jenn laughed. "Arun and I are world citizens, and if we have kids, they will be too." She began to pack photos into the box. "I'm starting to crash, Mom. Can we fight about Arun tomorrow?"

Maggie leaned forward and squeezed Jenn's good ankle. She rose and left the room, closing the door behind her. The door to the master bedroom was open, meaning Paul was still downstairs. For the first time in what seemed like years, she thought about asking him to come up and sit with her awhile, rub her contracted neck. She felt as frightened as a child in the dark. She couldn't banish the thought of Jenn vanishing into an alien world with no way back.

FOUR

Senior year at Ohio State, Paul had made two decisions: he'd gotten into cancer research and he'd snagged Maggie. Neither move was planned. He'd spotted Maggie in a literature class—he'd needed one more nonscience credit to finish his biology major—and, on a whim, asked to borrow her notes. She blushed, which he found refreshing compared to the hard-edged radicals and ponytailed jocks on campus. She seemed like a sweet, approachable sort of girl. So he asked her out for coffee a couple of times; she was a good listener. He took her to the movies; her comments revealed a good brain. Then he asked her to his professor's Christmas party, which turned out to be the clincher.

Growing up, Christmas had always meant disappointment. His father would drink and get meaner as Christmas Day unfolded. His mother would shrivel up. One year, he and his older brother, Lenny, escaped from the house to roam the streets of Indianapolis in Lenny's ancient car. The only other people visible were winos and cops. A squad car pulled them over—the police had spotted two motley teenagers for troublemakers—and warned them off. Paul realized there was no getting around Christmas. At least not until you reached eighteen.

Growing up, the brothers had been close out of necessity. Both their parents were inaccessible, their father soaked in alcohol, their mother sickly. Lenny was a garrulous, pushy kid, often in trouble, while Paul, two years younger, hung back and watched the fray. Lenny stood up for Paul against their father and the neighborhood bullies. Paul felt grateful even as he resented Lenny's superior strength. He longed to be as bold as Lenny and as admired by peers. Sometime during high school, Paul grew taller than his brother—and most of his classmates—and his perspective changed. He stopped idolizing Lenny and withdrew into himself, taking solace in baseball. But something happened to his arm; over three seasons they had to move him from third base to shortstop to second to first—hypermobile shoulders, and no coach caught it before the damage was done. He couldn't talk about it at home, of course. He learned to hide from his old man rather than risk abuse, and it disgusted him. After high school graduation, Lenny lived at home fighting battles with their father over girls, money, booze. Paul got drafted and was glad to go.

The war in Vietnam was winding down by the time he finished boot camp. Paul had wanted to see what the fuss was about, not trusting what he heard from Lenny or at school or on the news, but the army stationed him in Texas. He passed a test and they made him a medic. He had been an indifferent student in high school, but the army taught him the value of work: if you wanted something, figured out the system, and you worked for it, it came.

There was logic to it and justice in it. He adapted quickly. When he came home, he used his newfound smarts and the GI Bill to enroll in college in a different state, working part time to pay the rest of his bills. He spent vacations and summers on the job, not looking back. By senior year, he had caught the attention of his biology professor, who employed him as a research assistant, tending rats. It was Professor Kaufmann's Christmas party and a dead rat that led him to his future wife.

The afternoon of the party, he headed across the frozen campus toward the lab, where twelve rats waited to be fed. He would take their temperatures, sample their blood, and measure their droppings. He earned $7.50 an hour running a twenty-four/seven metabolism experiment. Mindless work, but enough to live on, carefully, until he finished his degree. As always, the ag building smelled of fertilizer, but it was warm. He took the stairs. A coworker was exiting the fourth-floor alcove where they hung their lab coats. Gordon grunted at him and raised an eyebrow. With stiff fingers, Paul removed his jacket.

"When are you going to get a decent coat? I'm tired of seeing you shiver." Gordon pulled a stocking cap over his ears.

"Haven't had the time."

"Nah, you're just cheap. Never met anyone as cheap as you." Gordon picked up his coat. "Paperwork's done."

"You're good for something after all."

Gordon slapped his back as they passed. "Later."

Paul hung up his jacket and threaded arms into a rumpled, stained lab coat. He didn't mind doing early-morning and late-night feeds, but he'd be dammed if he'd pay for laundering an apron. Gordon was wrong. He wasn't cheap; he'd had to fight for every buck, and he wasted nothing.

The lab coat didn't reek yet, so he buttoned it across his chest. In the next job, he'd have better; there'd be a regular supply of clean white coats for everyone.

He opened the door to the animal room, even warmer than the hallway, and smelled the familiar mix of kibble, excrement, and disinfectant. Most of his rats hunkered in the corners of their individual plastic bins on a rack along the far wall. Paul worked his way along the row, picking up a rat in his left hand and inserting a needle with his right, then bottling the blood sample. He put a precise measure of meal into the feeding trough, picked up the droppings, and moved on. He would enter the data when he finished the round.

Halfway down the row, one of the rats lay still, four pink paws curled in the air. Shit, he thought, one less data point. At the last feed, had it looked sick? Could he have made an error? If he had screwed up, wouldn't more than one have croaked? He chalked up the death to chance, the engine of life, destructive half the time. Putting on fresh latex gloves, he held the six-inch corpse in his left hand, sliced open the whitish, hairy skin of its belly with a scalpel. He reached into the slit and slid his fingers beneath the slippery tube of gut. He worked it loose from the surrounding membranes, then yanked it free from its attachments at mouth and anus. It was yellow but intact. The other organs looked normal too. He boxed and labeled the body and gut, shelved the box in the refrigerator across the room, and went back to tend the next specimen.

So the dead rat had a yellow gut. He had seen other rat guts that were pink, or brown and white. Just like humans—so much variety within the same functional frame. The so-called radicals on this campus didn't understand that variation was a good thing. They wanted everyone to think the way they did and fall into line behind their placards. They didn't understand the natural order of things. He had tried to tell Maggie the ways in which the radicals—on the left and the right—were wrong. But she hadn't agreed; she listened to the crap her snotty, lefty roommate spewed. He was convinced he'd win her over in the end because she was smarter than the rest of them. Looking around to check that things were in order, he left the animal room, eleven labeled vials in hand. In the lab next door, he deposited them in a drawer. Someone else would analyze the specimens. Kaufmann's outfit ran like a machine, parts functioning independently, smoothly. He didn't mind being a cog, for now.

A few hours later he stood behind the dissecting table, now covered with a red cloth, to serve eggnog to the partygoers, lacing it with rum for the over twenty-ones. Kaufmann's wife had decorated the lab and hovered near the Christmas tree in front of the fume hood, presiding. Kaufmann stood just inside the door to welcome his guests. Paul watched him greet colleagues and students alike. He wore a red corduroy Christmas jacket, no doubt bought by the wife, that looked at odds with his khakis and sneakers. Paul liked him; he was shy and evenhanded with his technicians. He knew his stuff. And he left you alone most of the time. At five to eight, Paul signaled for Gordon to take over the bar and stepped into the hall to wait for his date to arrive.

Maggie emerged from the stairwell at the end of the hall looking flustered, cheeks red from the cold. She never took elevators. Quaint, but he liked the result, a tight little body with good legs. She wore a long sweater that hinted at her shape and a lacy collar, of which he approved. Feminine but not delicate; she wouldn't turn into one of those demanding women who suck up a man's energy. Hanging her coat in the alcove, he ushered her into the animal room. She wrinkled her nose at the odor.

"The party's in the lab. I want to show you my charges first." He walked her over to the rack with its twelve plastic bins. "I take their temperatures every eight hours. One of them died today." He lifted a mottled gray-and-white rat out of its bin and placed it in her outstretched hands. She caught her breath but held the wriggling rat steady, cupping her hands over it to make a cage. The rat tried to escape, but she held on. It pleased him to see her so stalwart.

"What should I look for?"

"Feel how active it is. Burns more calories than the next one. Yet they're both normal."

"I don't want to hurt it." Her brow furrowed. "Why do you have to measure them all the time?"

"Professor Kaufmann thinks every rat has a slightly different metabolism . . . a different way of utilizing food to make energy. Metabolism changes after a meal, or exercise, or sleep." He could almost see her thinking. "We're looking for formulas that apply to any animal in the species, any time."

Maggie handed back the rat carefully. "What makes one rat different from another?"

"We have ideas about enzyme production and some other physiological stuff." He replaced the rat in its bin. "We need proof."

She rested her hand lightly on his arm. "I didn't realize your work was so important."

She looked so interested. And pretty, brown hair nestling in waves on her shoulders, hazel eyes wide as she scanned the animals. He wondered if he could cop a kiss.

Maggie walked along the rack, looking at each rat, stopping at the empty bin. "Is this for the one you lost? I'm sorry."

"Doesn't matter. We'll have enough data to finish the study."

"But you lost a living creature." She lifted her chin.

"One rat is as good as another. It all amounts to electrical energy in the end."

"No," she said softly. "It amounts to a lot more."

He busied himself straightening the feed containers on the table behind them. He didn't tell her that she had just scored, that no one else made him see virtue in the ordinary. Her thoughtfulness impressed him; her respect touched a nerve.

"Let's join the party. It smells better in there." He ushered her into the hallway.

At the door, Professor Kaufmann beamed at them, and Mrs. Kaufmann bustled over. She took Maggie by the arm and pulled her into a circle of graduate students' wives near the tree. Paul could see Mrs. Kaufmann chattering as Maggie smiled courteously. He drifted over to the bar, wanting to take the edge off the social hour. Gordon handed him a glass.

"Hey, man. So that's why we don't see much of you anymore." Gordon lifted the pitcher of eggnog to pour. Paul stopped his arm.

"Just rum. The conversation is cloying enough."

Gordon poured himself a shot, took a sip, and grimaced. "This stuff is awful. Wanna go get stoned?"

"No, I've got company."

"So I see. Pretty, but too virginal for you."

Paul refused to take the bait. He poured himself a shot. Gordon laid a hand on his arm.

"I've got enough weed for everyone. Good stuff. I'll meet you and your date downstairs in half an hour."

Paul shook his head no. Gordon shrugged.

Sipping the too-sweet rum, Paul surveyed the room. Kaufmann had attracted a bunch of creeps. Not one cool soul in the laboratory, which made Paul like him all the more. The few biology faculty who had stopped by the party hovered near the entrance, waiting their turn to shake Kaufmann's hand and make an excuse. Petty people—they couldn't see that Kaufmann was the only one of them with original ideas. Paul looked around for his date. Maggie appeared to be listening intently to Mrs. Kaufmann. He was pretty sure she didn't care about the woman's stories, but she would say something appropriate. Maggie had good manners. It pleased him to see that she could handle society when she needed to, society for which he had no patience. Gordon nudged his shoulder.

"I guess you have better things to do tonight."

In Gordon's shoes, his army buddies would have been unmerciful. They would have demanded to know how and when he got into Maggie's pants, teasing him, bragging about their own exploits. Paul had always played along, not believing a word the other young guys said, replying in kind. He'd learned a few things about his fellow soldiers, like never challenge the little guys because they'll do fifty push-ups to your twenty-five, and, more important, that you earned prestige by scoring. He had lost his virginity at nineteen with a town girl at a beery dance, but he hadn't liked her. Now he had a classy girl with whom something might be at stake.

"Can you take over for me tonight and tomorrow? I'll work all week Christmas."

Gordon grinned. "Sure. You can return the favor when I get an old lady." He raised his cup in toast.

Paul walked over to the tree, circling behind the knot of women. Mrs. Kaufmann spotted him.

"Paul, I hear that you haven't yet proposed to this lovely girl."

"We've only known each other two months, Mrs. K. Can I borrow her a minute?" He placed his hand at the back of Maggie's waist and curled her toward him. Blushing, she stepped out of earshot of the others. Her eyes darted right and left.

"I'm so embarrassed. Please believe me. I didn't say anything personal."

"I know. I came to rescue you."

She raised her hand to shield her mouth. "What an annoying woman! She wouldn't leave me alone. I hope you don't have much to do with her. Your rats are better company."

He suppressed a laugh.

"Oh, have I offended you?"

"Not at all. I think we can leave now. How about you tell her good-bye?"

Paul walked to the window overlooking the quadrangle between the science buildings. He leaned his forehead on the cold glass, peering through the bare branches of the elms below. Only a few pedestrians crossed the quad—no protesters in the cold and dark. He pulled his forehead away from the pane as Alvin and the Chipmunks began to squeal. Time to go. He had met his obligation to Kaufmann and his wife. With luck, he would spend the next thirty-six off-duty hours with Maggie. As a rule, he didn't bring girls back to his room. But if he could persuade her to stay, the rule was going down.

This girl could be a prize. With her on his arm, he could fool the world. They'd accept him in graduate school as a solid citizen; she'd serve as camouflage for his disgust at their small-mindedness. She could help him make his mark. So pretty, and intelligent, and receptive. He hoped to hell she liked sex.

FIVE

On the last day of class of her sophomore year, Maggie decided her future belonged to Paul Adler. It was, she realized, the first grown-up decision she'd made, and she hoped it was right.

She had been a diligent, if uninspired, student in high school. As a shy only child, she didn't do the social scene. The one crush she developed senior year on the dreamy boy in French class hadn't born fruit. Some people in her church youth group pointed her to Ohio State, and her parents agreed to pay in-state tuition if she earned room and board. So she enrolled and got a job waitressing. Coming from a small high school in a small town, she felt lost freshman year, confused by the protests, the pot, the promiscuity. If not for her roommate, she most likely would have gone home and to community college. But Sarah pulled her along, introducing her to people, teaching her how to take exams, sharing her music and clothes. Sarah seemed to know more than other freshmen: She had a diaphragm; she'd read the classics in prep school; she'd been to Europe more than once. But she was no snob, except for her politics. You had to agree with her or she cut you down. A gap had opened between them at the end of the school year when Maggie refused to go on a protest march to protect dolphins from trawlers. She told Sarah that she didn't know enough about the fishing industry to judge; secretly, she feared getting into trouble and being sent back to an angry mother. When Sarah asked her to room together again, Maggie was surprised and, preferring the devil she knew, relieved.

On her first date with Paul, just a walk in the park after work, he told her he wanted to do research in biology and asked about her interests. She said she'd been told that she was good with numbers, and a woman could always fall back on accounting. He asked her whether she *liked* accounting, because you should like what you study. She could hear her mother scoff at the notion of picking a major because you liked it. Her mother had told her to pick something "reliable" that led to a job she could do for a few years before settling down. Then he said that someone as pretty as she should be having fun. No one had ever called her pretty. In the mirror, she saw an ordinary girl with many imperfections. Paul didn't seem to notice.

They began dating regularly, strolling campus and sitting in coffeehouses to watch the crowd. At first she had been embarrassed by the fierce way he put down protesters and hippies. He'd said that the army had given him a bullshit detector, and he used it aggressively. As the weeks went by, she learned to trust his opinions. When he called her a truth-teller, she basked in the praise. In the spring she consented to sex. He said that he'd wait until she wanted to make love, and one day she did.

They were sitting on the steps outside her dorm in the

dark. He had walked her home after work, and she laid her tired head on his shoulder. Slowly he leaned in and kissed her forehead. He took her head into his hands and kissed her neck. He lifted her face toward his and kissed her lips. And she kissed him back, and then she wanted more and he could tell. They went to his room and he undressed her slowly, and then they were both naked in his bed, and he asked her to trust him and she did. She'd been relieved at how simple it was, giving pleasure and learning to be pleased.

But then she suffered. She could hear her mother's voice, icy with contempt, calling her foolish for believing in a young man's tenderness. Her mother had told her so many times that extramarital sex debased a woman, because that's all men wanted. She'd told Maggie to hold herself to a higher standard, as defined by church and state. She said nothing else, letting Maggie learn about sex on her own. Outside her home, people talked about making love, not sex. She felt confused, and she let the confusion lie until Paul changed her. She was surprised at how much she wanted him. Over the months, despite fear of maternal shaming, her desire had grown with each date.

On the last day of class, Paul met her at her dorm. He seemed anxious, toying with his keys. She sat next to him on the top step of the porch, wanting to touch his jeans-clad thigh with her bare flesh, but afraid someone might come by. Instead, she absorbed his scent and his heat, feeling as if all the separate cells of her body were drawn to his.

"Kaufmann found me a job." He looked at his feet. "Research assistant to a colleague of his working on cancer. Same kind my mother had. They want me to start right away." He fiddled with his key chain. "It's a sweet deal. All the way to a PhD, if I want it."

"You don't sound happy." She tried to read his face.

"Here's the catch. It's in Michigan. I've got to move by the end of this month."

Her chest squeezed tight.

He turned to face her. "I'm asking you to come with me. You can take classes there." He placed his hand on her thigh. "I've never felt so close to anyone. Nor have you. I don't want to lose that. Do you?"

She couldn't untangle her thoughts. Yes, she wanted to stay close to him; something animal in her wanted to live in his skin. Could she pick up and leave? It had taken two years to get comfortable at State. What would her mother say?

He stroked her hair. "I'm not asking you to marry me. Just come with me. Try us out. I've never said that to any other girl." He lowered his voice and leaned into her ear, "Pretty good experimental design, huh?"

She couldn't speak, but the tightness in her chest eased an inch.

He meant for them to live together. Could she move into an apartment with Paul? The only person with whom she'd ever shared a room was Sarah. She'd managed to figure out how to live with a roommate, but a boyfriend? "I need to think about this."

He laughed and pulled her close with one arm. "That's what I would expect." He kissed her temple, held her tight. "You won't be lonely. Knowing you, you'll make friends soon enough. And I promise not to work all the time." He released her, scrutinizing her face. "Do you want to meet later at the café?"

"No. I have a final tomorrow." She stood slowly and gathered her things. She wanted to laugh and she wanted to cry.

"I'll call you." He rose, kissed her hand, and walked down the steps.

Maggie pulled the dorm door open and climbed the stairs to her room, heart pounding. Sarah lay prone on her bed with an open book. Maggie changed into the baggy cotton shorts in which she studied and sat on the edge of her bed. Tomorrow's final didn't seem important; she needed to think.

"Why are you sitting there like that?" Sarah asked. "You're giving me the creeps. Go study something." Sarah sat up and brushed back her long hair. "I'm going to put on a record."

Maggie hesitated. Talking to Sarah meant risking a barrage of violent opinion, especially about Paul. Sarah had disliked him from the moment they met. They were both the kind of person who uses up all the oxygen in a room, both tough-minded, neither willing to back off for the sake of harmony. But Sarah was a friend, and worldly. Sarah could fly where other people walked; Maggie often imagined wings fixed to her back, like a dragonfly's, iridescent in the sun.

"Paul is transferring to Michigan, and he wants me to go with him."

"Well, that's a shocker. Do you want to go?"

"I think I'm in love with him. But I don't know. And my parents . . ." An undercurrent of fear surged through her.

"Your parents are irrelevant. This is about you." Sarah sat beside her.

"Paul wants us to live together. He has a job. He said I could go to school."

"Do you want to live with him?"

"My parents would never approve." Disingenuous: her

mother would roundly criticize anyone she brought home, and her father would hardly notice.

Sarah reached for a pen and a notebook. "Let's not worry about your parents. You don't need them. With your grades, you might get a scholarship. Let's make a list of the conditions for cohabitation."

"What do you mean?"

Sarah wagged her head as if to say, "Isn't it obvious?"

"Like who pays for what, and who does which chores. Sort of like a contract for the relationship." She sat cross-legged on Maggie's bed and held the pen poised.

Maggie stared at the floor. This wasn't about chores.

"Believe me, you need a contract. Otherwise you'll get exploited."

Maggie pictured Sarah's latest beau, a bearded, skinny guy all too willing to carry posters and armbands to rallies for her. "I don't think you have contracts with your boyfriends."

"I don't have boyfriends. I see guys who are into the same things I am, and we communicate, mind and body. Which is fine for me. You're the marrying kind. You'll take a load of crap."

"Paul doesn't want to marry. He said he wants to try us out."

"That's dandy, but you need to protect yourself. You need to be clear about what you expect."

Maggie didn't want to hear Sarah's theories about equality in domestic relationships. She wanted to know how to think about what Paul said. "I don't know what to expect. I'm not sure I should even switch schools."

Sarah put the pen down. "If it were me, I wouldn't transfer. If a guy wants me, he has to help me do my thing, and my thing is the movement. You could use some conscious-ness-raising, my dear." She uncrossed her legs. "Think about what you want."

What did she want? She'd always assumed that she'd get a modest job after graduation and concentrate on doing well. In time, she'd marry a decent man and raise children much better than her mother had raised her. Paul made her think differently. So smart, so dedicated to science, so certain he would do great things. A life with him might be exciting in ways she couldn't imagine. If she could keep up.

"I want to get a degree. And Paul wants me to."

"You can study accounting anywhere," Sarah said. "The issue is the deal with Paul."

No, Maggie thought, the issue is responsibility . . . to Paul, to her parents, to her future. She stood and reached for her keys. "I'm going for a walk. Thanks for listening. I'll think about what you said."

The warm air felt soft, so welcome after the hard Ohio winter. Maggie could smell the new leaves and the sap run-ning through the trees along the path that led away from the dorm. She hurried through the quadrangle opposite the ag building, afraid Paul might exit and see her. He'd caress her and she'd want to kiss him, and then she'd cry. And then he'd get that gentle look on his face and ask her what was wrong and listen to her babble through her tears with-out judging her. And that would be the end of thinking.

Her mother might accept a transfer to Michigan be-cause of its reputation, and her father would only care about the cost. But living with a boyfriend? Her parents would be appalled. They'd think radicals on campus had perverted her and would insist that she come home. Could she follow Paul and lie to her parents? She couldn't compromise her principles. Would sharing an apartment with Paul work out? What if he got frustrated with her cautious ways? Did she know enough about housekeeping to live with a man? Would it be smart to make a contract, like Sarah said? Would Paul respect her more or less for wanting one?

The bell tower chimed, breaking into her thoughts. She walked briskly, trying to concentrate. Rooming with Sarah, she had learned to think beyond the obvious. When Maggie needed help with a paper, Sarah asked pointed questions that led to new ideas and additional paragraphs. When they talked about issues on campus, Sarah opened new dimensions. She made Maggie read Betty Friedan, although, according to Sarah, the book was old and the women's movement had already moved on. Maggie thought Sarah had moved on, to the environment and dolphins caught in tuna nets, while she still struggled with being both feminine and strong. The "feminine" girls in high school had seemed trivial, talking boys and clothes. The "strong" girls Sarah collected were unkempt and belligerent, snubbing Maggie for her lack of political muscle. Sarah was the only girl who seemed to achieve both. She chose her clothes carefully and used lemon juice on her dirty blond hair. She grabbed the megaphone at rallies to exhort the crowd, sure of herself and her ideas.

Maggie came to a crossroad where the path led off toward the stadium. Realizing how far she'd walked, she turned to retrace her steps. Sarah might be close to the ideal girl, but Maggie could not hope to equal her. Sarah might think Maggie a mushy-minded sellout if she followed Paul to Michigan. But maybe staying at State would be, for her, selling out, picking security over possibility. As she headed toward the dorm, her mind resolved. She knew what to do. She would find a way to follow Paul to Michigan and hitch onto his dreams. Her dream for a good life would fold neatly into his. Sarah would have to understand. The hardest part would be convincing her folks.

ೕ๏ ๏ಌ

In the end, she stayed in Ohio because Michigan didn't offer her a scholarship. But she doubled her course load, graduated in eighteen months, and moved into Paul's apartment. They married shortly after. Her mother heartily disapproved.

SIX

" I can't add one more thing," Alicia protested. "I have to maintain the quality of my work, and everyone else's for that matter." The lead researcher removed her glasses and stared unblinking at Paul, then Tim and C. K. The four of them sat around a Formica table in the hospital's ninth-floor employee lounge, which they used for staff meetings. It was just before lunch hour, and the place was still quiet except for the buzz of the Coke machine and the fluorescents overhead.

"Whoa, I'm not asking you to do any more," Paul said. He could have predicted her response to hearing that the grant had come through. Poor, diligent Alicia. She hardly smiled, and the tight bun fastened at the back of her head made her look even more severe. Now in her late thirties, she had worked for him for her entire career. Meticulous, persistent, and unoriginal, she oversaw the research agenda and kept the others on task. He appreciated her work ethic, and the research team had gelled around her, prissiness notwithstanding. He watched her close her laptop and cross her arms in front of her chest. Could be attractive with a little work.

"I'm gonna bring in another person. Sandi posted the job a couple days ago. I'm relying on you, Alicia, to integrate him or her into our process."

Alicia uncrossed her arms. Her voice softened. "I hope you get someone who knows what he's doing. I don't have time to teach."

Tim poked C. K. with his elbow. "Harmony restored," he said in nearly accent-free English.

Tim looked like an elf—slight build, earth-colored clothes, and pointy shoes—and he acted the imp. Born in Germany, he had learned his science in the Stockholm lab with which Paul had been corresponding for the past three years. He shared an apartment in Queens with another foreigner, C. K. from Singapore, who was also willing to work for the salary Paul offered. They were an odd couple, Tim quick and sharp, C. K. slow and round. In the lab, they ganged up on Alicia like little boys. She scolded them in return. Paul didn't mind a little fun as long as the work got done and done well. Surrounded by women and foreigners, he made the rules, and he made sure they were fair. Everyone deserved to catch a break.

"I'm interviewing today. You all carry on with what you're doing. The new guy will start with a new cytokine as soon as possible."

"Where will he sit?" Tim said.

"Sandi is gonna make room in her office for a desk. I expect you guys to clear up some bench space. Or else I'll come in and clean out your junk," Paul teased. Tim feigned a shudder. The last time Paul had reorganized the wet lab, they couldn't find their slides or reagents for days. "Any other questions?"

Tim shook his head no. Alicia sighed.

Satisfied, Paul pushed his chair away from the table. He figured it would take a month or so for the expanded team to settle into their new routine. He could wait. Patience came easy with the crew. He liked feeling responsible for their livelihoods. It felt like wearing a thick blanket around his entire body that no one else could see; it warmed him despite the weight.

"Enjoy your lunch," Paul said, rising to leave.

The others stood, chair legs scraping on the linoleum tile. Hugging her laptop, Alicia walked quickly down the corridor. Tim and C. K. made for the elevator. Paul considered joining them to go get a greasy corn dog from the push-cart they patronized outside the hospital's main entrance. He liked to stand around at the curb, eating and watching human behavior—fancy fauna, after all—and root for the secretaries gesturing urgently for taxis, their skirts riding high up their thighs, hoping to squeeze in a visit to the dentist or a shrink during lunch hour. But a corn dog might give him heartburn. He'd better get Sandi to order a tuna sandwich while he wrote up the cytokine protocol. Years before, Sandi had asked if she could donate sick days to one of the secretaries, a friend of hers with a serious illness. Paul had said yes, and then donated extra days of his own. A small thing, he had thought, but to Sandi consequential. She'd catered to him ever since.

A cluster of nursing trainees spilled into the corridor outside the employee lounge, chattering about the class that had just ended. Paul walked past the elevator bank, between them. This particular bunch of would-be technicians—black, white, brown, mostly female—looked good to him, not overstuffed and bedraggled like so many others. He tipped an imaginary hat. It amused him to think of their printed scrubs as pink and lavender and aqua flowers blooming against the faded green walls. Indoor flora on a gigantic scale. He loped down the corridor.

As he opened the door to his lab, Robert Stamford stepped out.

"Ah, Paul. I've brought you a candidate for your new position. Your lab isn't easy to find, and I feared she might lose her way. She's the young woman I mentioned the other day, Hope Caldwell. I trust you'll give her a good hearing." Stamford jingled keys in his left-hand pocket.

Paul frowned. "Actually, Robert, I'm going to lunch. She should make an appointment with Sandi, like the other applicants."

"Yes, certainly. But Ms. Caldwell happened to be visiting, and I thought you might be able to interview her now. I hope you won't hold my informality against her?" Stamford's chin tilted upward, eyebrows arching above a little smile.

"I doubt this is a casual visit." A metallic taste developed in Paul's mouth. "I take it you're leaving?"

"Yes, of course. I'll expect to hear from your office when the search concludes. Good luck." Stamford bustled away down the hall, his round behind bouncing like a woman's beneath the tails of his sport coat.

Paul contemplated heading for the hot dog cart. Nah, he should get the interview over with. He strode into his office and sat at his desk, buzzing for Sandi and pulling a handful of forms from a folder. He would handle the interview by the book—ask the right questions, in the prescribed order, take precise notes—and write the standard rejection letter.

Sandi entered, grinning, and handed him a résumé

printed in purple on embossed letterhead. "She's in my office," Sandi said. "When do you want her?"

"I don't want her. Stamford's pushing me. An interview is all he'll get." He fished reading glasses out of his top drawer. "Give me a minute to read this." He waved the résumé at Sandi.

"Don't jump to any conclusions." Sandi placed hand on hip, which hitched up her habitual blue smock and exposed beige capris underneath.

"What's that supposed to mean?"

Sandi turned on her rubber heel and withdrew, closing the door behind her.

The purple text, to Paul's surprise, showed that the girl might be qualified to work in a lab like his. She had a biology degree from a credible school and one year's graduate work in a zoology program a few years back. He picked up a pen and was about to call Sandi when the door opened and Hope Caldwell walked in. Tall, athletic shape, blond hair sleeked behind her ears into a knot, all pink cashmere and pearls. A Grace Kelly type, expensively groomed. But not pretty. He shook her outstretched hand.

"I'm really pleased to meet you. I've read about your work." She sat in the folding chair beside the desk, crossing muscled legs beneath a soft pink skirt, clasping her hands in her lap. She leaned toward him, waiting. He guessed she was pushing thirty.

"Which part of my work interests you?"

"I'd like to learn about the genetics of cancer. Isn't that where the answers lie?"

"Not entirely. The environment of the cell counts too." He riffled through the folders in his bottom drawer, pulling out a set of dog-eared, black-and-white photos. He spread them across the desk for the woman to see. "These are cells from a single brain tumor we analyzed decades ago. Look at the genetic material."

The photos showed nuclei in each of six cells, with chromosomes standing out like dark lines against a lighter background. In one nucleus, the chromosomes looked like an array of tiny tubes poised in orderly fashion. In the other nuclei, the arrays looked successively messier—in the sixth, multiple tubes extended wildly in all directions. She pointed to the sixth photo, saying it looked like trouble.

"That's the easiest cell to recognize as cancer and kill. The deadliest one is the closest to normal." He picked up the first photo, ready to give his usual spiel about the mutability of cancer and the interaction of genome and environment.

She interrupted, "Is every tumor all mixed up or only in the brain?"

"We think, more or less, every tumor. But it's hard to generalize without longitudinal data."

"Now I see why you want to work in a hospital. You can get lots of samples from the same patient." She leaned back in her chair. "It would be a privilege to work for you. I'd learn a lot."

She caught on quick, he thought. But he felt vaguely discomforted. She had somehow taken charge, as if she were interviewing him. Replacing the photos in their folder, he picked up the purple résumé and removed his reading glasses.

"I see that it's been a few years since you studied biology. What are your career goals?"

She uncrossed her legs and cupped both hands over her knees. "Well, my undergraduate program was unexceptional, and I wasn't sure what I wanted to do, so I went to work in my parents' art gallery. It was exciting at first, meeting the people they represent and their clients." She gazed off into the distance for a beat. "But I realized that I couldn't really make a contribution, and biology was my first love. So here I am, looking for a fresh start." She smiled. "And I wouldn't mind not having a window. I've spent enough time behind plate glass."

A little jab? A veiled complaint about the lab's being windowless? Or was he overreacting? Job applicants don't try to piss off the boss. Maybe her manners came from the art world, where you're supposed to be coy.

Someone knocked hard on his office door. Recognizing Alicia's urgent rhythm, Paul invited her in to buy time. She looked surprised to see Hope Caldwell and took a step backward. He introduced Alicia as his lead researcher and asked her what was up.

"I had an idea, but it wouldn't be appropriate to discuss now." Alicia stood in the doorway, shifting her weight from one leg to the other like a nervous adolescent. She stared straight at Paul.

"If you'd like privacy, I'll be happy to wait outside. But I'm interested in your work, so please feel free to discuss your idea. If you don't mind," Hope said, smiling sweetly. "I probably wouldn't understand anyway."

Alicia nodded. No one moved. Alicia said, "No thanks. I'll send an email," and turned to leave.

Hope stood and extended an arm to shake hands, saying, "It was a pleasure to meet you. I hope to be able to assist you." Alicia nodded again and hurried away.

"Don't take it personally," Paul said, "she's not long on social graces, but she does an excellent job."

"I'm not the least offended. I don't mind difficult people.

You have to be thick-skinned when you work in an art gallery. But that's another story."

Hope resumed her seat and crossed her legs. She folded manicured hands on top of the pink cashmere skirt. "Can I answer any other questions?"

                        ⁕ ⁕

Paul laid the platter of chicken on the dining room table and sat down opposite Maggie. Jenn, still wobbly on her sore ankle, sat at her customary place on the long side of the table between them. This would be the earliest he'd eaten dinner in weeks.

After Hope Caldwell had left his office, he had wanted to talk to Irene about Stamford's move, but she'd been on duty. So he'd taken an early train home, surprising Maggie at four forty-five. She had seemed annoyed, furrowing her brow and fussing about not having enough chicken. So he had gone to the supermarket. Returning with another bird and two bottles of wine, he'd hung around the kitchen, his shoulder wedged against the cool yellow tile, while she prepared the food. Such a silly, inefficient kitchen. No cabinets; the fridge out in the hall. Every time he went into the pantry to search for something that should be at hand, he'd rip the kitchen apart mentally and rearrange the fixtures. More than once he'd threatened to hire a handyman to install cabinets, but Maggie claimed that she liked the kitchen as it was. So crazy tiled it remained.

Leaning on the doorframe, he watched her practiced movements: cutting, chopping, sautéing, while pots hissed on the stove and a timer clamored for attention. Maggie glided from stove to counter to fridge, her forehead wrinkled in concentration, talking all the while about Jenn's new interest in vegetables. He didn't really listen, his mind spinning tasks for the research crew plus one. A gingery smell rose from a pot on the stove. You could always count on Maggie for a good meal. She spooned a lumpy brown concoction from the pot into a bowl and arranged chicken parts on a platter. He carried the platter to the table, just as he had done when Jenn was little and he came home at five from a less demanding job.

"How come so early, Dad?" Jenn asked as they passed the bowl of brown whatever.

"It was a different kind of day. Administrative stuff. I couldn't make it into the wet lab, so I came home to see how you're doing."

"My ankle feels better every day." She smiled a real smile, eyes crinkling at the corners. "Arun called from the city. He's coming next weekend. Will you be home?"

"Count on it." He wanted to say more, but Maggie looked daggers at him. As they ate curried potatoes—the brown goop—and chicken sauté, Jenn talked about learning to cook vegetarian at one of the ashrams she'd visited. She offered to prepare the meals when Arun came, promising they would like the flavors. Paul grilled her about getting enough protein. Jenn patted his arm and told him to have faith in her knowledge of nutrition. When they finished eating, Maggie cleared the plates and Paul gathered the bowl and platter, telling Jenn she was off KP until she stopped hobbling.

Paul followed Maggie into the kitchen and placed his load on the countertop. He waited as Maggie consolidated the leavings and scraped them into the trash. As the sink filled with water, she turned to face him. "Why are you standing there?"

Paul grunted. She had such a nose for trouble. He might as well lay it out. "Your buddy Stamford is interfering again."

"Oh. I thought you were worried about Jenn's guy." She began loading the dishwasher, but he knew she was listening.

"He's pushing me to hire the niece of one of his donors, and he's threatening to hold back the overhead unless I do." He could feel the adrenaline enter his bloodstream.

"Tell me more."

"There's nothing more. He's an unethical SOB."

Maggie wiped her hands on a dish towel. "Robert wouldn't want to jeopardize the work. Maybe this person could do the job."

Why, he thought, does she always take Stamford's side? Irene would stick pins in his effigy. "Yeah, but it's my team. The chemistry's damn good, and I want it to stay that way."

She turned back to the sink. "Do you have someone else in mind? You could convince Robert the hospital would be better off with your person."

"No one yet. I just started to interview."

"Surely he'll wait while you search. Have you contacted all your colleagues? They'll know someone good who needs a job." She poured detergent into the cup and closed the lid.

He considered her suggestion. Perhaps he could steal someone from another lab, someone with enough experience of the right kind to justify the hire. But he would need to offer a bigger salary and word would spread like plague, pissing off the rest of his researchers. Then there was the question of Hope Caldwell herself. She could probably do most of the job if he supervised closely—and she could handle Alicia with one hand tied behind her back. Pushy broad. Hard muscles under soft cashmere. Attractive all right. But he didn't need complications now that the definitive experiments lay just ahead.

"I'll look into it." Paul headed for the hallway and the door to his basement office. A solution to the Hope Caldwell problem might lie among his contacts. He'd deal with Jenn's boyfriend later.

SEVEN

T he man who stepped off the train on Saturday afternoon looked more like a banker than a guru: medium height, stocky build, wearing a navy blue blazer over golf shirt and Dockers, indeterminate age. He gave Jenn a chaste kiss, then reached out to shake Paul's hand. Another surprise: a corporate handshake, strong and almost too long. Untidy black hair, skin a few shades darker than Paul's, large brown eyes looking steadily into his. Not a great physical specimen, Paul thought, but Jenn had never cared about looks.

Paul hefted Arun's suitcase and pointed toward his car parked in the station lot. As they walked, Arun tucked Jenn's arm into the crook of his elbow. Paul thought the gesture far too possessive. He hadn't coddled Maggie when they were courting. Then again, Jenn still limped a bit. She seemed to like hanging onto Arun's arm. And his every word.

They made the drive back to the house in ten minutes, Jenn asking about Arun's week in New York, Arun replying in a soft voice, rolling his *r*'s. Paul couldn't quite follow the conversation. It seemed they were speaking in code, like a long-married couple. He stopped listening. Too painful.

Maggie stood on the front steps, waiting to greet them. Paul lifted Arun's bag from the trunk and followed the others into the living room. Maggie bustled: seating them on the sofa, asking about drinks, mumbling about Arun's not having an overcoat should the weekend turn cold. Arun said that living in India had acclimated him to all kinds of weather, and he assured Maggie that he would be comfortable. Paul's hackles rose; he didn't trust any man who made small talk. He sat silently while Jenn laid out plans for the weekend and Maggie went to get drinks.

It was warm for November. A few dry leaves drifted in through the open porch doors. Paul had wanted to enclose the porch years earlier, but Maggie liked the way the breeze flowed through in summer. The house was her turf; she picked the furniture, she bought the groceries, she entertained his colleagues and his brother the few times he'd come east. She could do whatever she wanted with the house, Paul thought, but she shouldn't coddle this oily guy leaning on their daughter. He hoped the weather would turn nasty and show Arun up.

As Maggie finished serving coffee and tea, the phone rang and she left the room. Paul leaped into the conversation.

"Where are you from?"

Arun placed his teacup on the table and folded hands in his lap. "My parents are both physicians in India."

"No, I mean where are *you* from?"

Arun smiled, his round, brown cheeks bunching into balls. "Ah, the better question. I was born in Bangalore and went to school in California. I am a naturalized American citizen, but I've spent the last nine years in India and Nepal, and something of the culture there has transfused me."

Oh lord, Paul thought. He talks like Robert Stamford.

"I studied economics in college, but I minored in Eastern philosophy, to learn more about the stories from Hindu mythology my mother used to tell us. I confess that I found Kabir far more alluring than Keynes." He paused, glancing at Jenn. "I've been lucky to find my calling. And to be able to share it."

"What's your calling exactly?" Paul saw Jenn reach for Arun's hand. She settled back into the couch, an expectant look on her face. He noticed how unusually still she had become. Maggie emerged in the doorway, laid a plate of cheese and crackers on the coffee table, and slipped into the chair opposite his.

"At the basic level, I translate the wisdom of the ancient Hindu into concepts accessible to everyone. Many others have done this, but my system seems to work for young people. I take a technical approach."

"So you only use a hundred forty characters at a time," Paul said.

Arun and Jenn laughed together. Jenn said, "Not technological, Dad, technical. Arun turns philosophy into science."

"That's not possible."

Maggie interjected, "Can you give an example? We'll understand better." She leaned forward, picked up the cheese plate, and offered it to Arun, who shook his head no. She replaced the plate. Paul knew she wouldn't touch the food herself, never did between meals. Queen of willpower. He helped himself to a chunk of cheddar.

Arun crossed his legs, the khaki cloth pulling tight over his thick thighs. "Certainly. For millennia the sages defined human character as having two components, the physiology with which one is born, and the accumulation of one's actions in the external world, karma. Nature and nurture, one would say today. The sages had methods for balancing the two that predate modern psychology. Some would say they improve upon it."

"That's not science," Paul said. "Science makes predictions and tests them. All that *I Ching* stuff looks backwards, not forwards."

Arun tipped his head in acknowledgment. "Indeed, Dr. Adler. I hope to see the day when biology can predict the details of human character. But in the meantime, the sages have something to offer."

Jenn said, "Just because science hasn't caught up with them doesn't mean the sages are wrong."

Maggie spoke up, "So it's like acupuncture? It works even if we don't know why?"

"You can measure the results of acupuncture," Paul said. "It's testable."

Arun said, "We measure the results of our work in terms of the improvement our clients make in the conduct of their lives."

Maggie said, "What do you tell them to do?"

Arun said, "We don't tell them to do. We help them to be. When I first began to study the sages, I could not imagine how their wisdom could translate into practice, especially for young people, some leading very harsh lives indeed. But I discovered that I could formulate a series of questions that can be applied to most forms of human experience. I was equally astounded and delighted when children began begging to talk with me."

Jenn said, "You'd be amazed at how much happier they get."

Paul replied, "I'd be amazed if it made a lasting difference."

Maggie cut in, "How is what you do different from psychotherapy?"

"It is not based on the concept of the ego asserted by Western thinkers. We see the human spirit in rounder terms." He sat straighter, as if preparing to teach. "We believe that people must respect themselves as embodiments of the divine, or the laws of nature, if you prefer, in order to respect others, and nature itself. That respect is the source of all morality and also of happiness, in the highest sense. We help people appreciate the simple, wonderful fact of existence, and that liberates them."

Maggie rose abruptly. "You must want to unpack and settle in. We can talk more at dinner. I'll show you your room." The men stood. Maggie picked her way around the coffee table and Arun followed, retrieving his suitcase from the foyer where Paul had left it. Jenn beckoned to Paul to take Arun's place next to her on the sofa.

"Arun's very subtle, Dad. It'll take you a while to understand his thinking. Believe me, he makes wonderful sense. People who follow him live good lives. Including me." When Paul did not sit, she stood to face him. "Please give him a chance."

"He's your guy. I'll get to know him." He laid his arm across her shoulders and gave a reassuring squeeze. "But science is my bailiwick."

"I'm the one who said 'science,' not Arun. It's one of the ways I explain his ideas to people. Don't hold my wording against him." Jenn's voice pleaded, but her eyes were steady.

"Okay, kiddo. I'll keep an open mind." He suspected he wouldn't though. Couldn't, in the face of the mumbo jumbo–rhubarb rhubarb bound to come. Jenn's adolescent fascination with punky kids and nerdy kids had amused him. This was different.

"Arun graduated at the top of his class at Cal Tech. He could have taken one of the cushy jobs he was offered, but he's too much of a humanist. He followed his heart to India. He's one of the few people I've ever met who's going to change the world."

"Fine. You can tell me about it later. I'm gonna do some work. Call me for dinner." He headed for the basement, grabbing his sweater from the rack by the door to fend off the underground chill. No one was scheduled to work in the lab that night. Too bad. He would have enjoyed sparring with Tim on the phone. In the lab, with the crew, he felt at his best, did the best. He could use a dose of lab right now. This guy was poison. He needed to make Jenn see.

≈≈≈

They played tennis for a couple of hours Sunday morning while Maggie took Jenn to church. Arun returned serves hard, with surprising strength. The guy appeared to be enjoying himself, bouncing around the court in Bermuda shorts, admiring the weather and the surroundings. Paul won most of the games on finesse—that is, if Arun hadn't let him win. To his chagrin, Paul tired first. When Arun declined a beer, Paul suggested lunch at the club. He wanted time alone with him to scope him out.

They took a table by the window in the dining room. Maggie had joined the club when Jenn was small for the swimming; she kept the membership current to please her book club, or so she said. Paul no longer knew anyone there. He sat running hands idly across the white tablecloth while Arun read the menu. When the waitress appeared, Paul ordered a cheeseburger, rare. Arun ordered a salad and folded his hands in his lap, looking relaxed. Only a few other tables were occupied and the room was quiet.

"Why are you a vegetarian?" Paul asked. "Plants and animals are made of the same stuff. In fact, plant DNA is heftier than ours."

"It's a habit. I grew up omnivorous like my parents, but when I started traveling across India, I discovered that the vegetarian food was better. Tastier and less likely to be spoiled. Now I simply enjoy it."

"Do you play tennis in India?" Paul asked.

"No, I don't feel the need. There is so much else to do. I played in college. I'm very glad I could still give you a game."

"That's not what I mean. If you took my daughter to India, what would she do besides cook vegetarian?"

"I was not aware that Jenn wishes to play tennis. She told me she didn't care for sport."

Annoyance mounting, Paul concentrated on the creases in his napkin. "I'm asking a bigger question. What's there for her?"

Arun sat straighter. "Ah. Yes. Dr. Adler, I appreciate the opportunity to tell you about my dreams and my dreams for your daughter." He leaned forward and spread fingers wide on the tablecloth. "I plan to set up a system of instruction for teachers in the schools. They will learn through guided practice to bring light into burdened young hearts. And we will celebrate, one heart at a time."

Paul rolled his eyes. "You're gonna have to be more specific with me. Where will you live?" He had never challenged Jenn's boyfriends before because there was no need. "What's Jenn supposed to do while you're instructing teachers?"

Arun unfolded his hands and leaned toward Paul. "Jenn has told me that she wants to work with me. As you know, she has a generous nature. She sees how my system helps so many young people. She is learning how to guide them. In time, she will be able to assist them herself."

An image of Jenn in a noisy, crowded Indian tenement, shooing flies off the faces of dirty, malnourished children overtook Paul. "I don't want her spending her time wiping up filth and exposed to disease."

"Rest assured, our work is sanitary. We don't practice medicine, although we are healers. Metaphor and music and meditation are our tools. I would be honored to share our literature with you."

The waitress approached with laden arms. Paul took the cheeseburger platter from her, and she lowered Arun's salad to the table. She pulled a ketchup bottle from her apron pocket, and Paul grunted approval. Dousing his burger, Paul picked it up in both hands. He bit in, dripping juice and ketchup onto his plate. He tried to imagine what attracted Jenn to this guy. Not his looks or his prissy style. Must be the sex, something exotic he picked up in an ashram. A knot developed in Paul's chest; he didn't want to think about Jenn twisting and sweating beneath Arun's thick brown body.

When she was little, Jenn had been his buddy, always game to try new stuff. She used to go to the lab with him on weekends and play scientist with his tools. When he started publishing in high-impact journals and got noticed at the hospital, he stopped bringing Jenn along. As he got busier, he pretty much left Jenn to Maggie's care. He had always assumed that Maggie, so conscientious, would do a good job. She must have screwed up about sex. Maybe she had avoided talking about it. Maggie could be a prude.

Arun said, "Jenn assures me that helping has always been her philosophy. She wants to work with me." He looked at Paul, who kept chewing. "I must respect her decision." Arun picked up his knife and fork and cut into his salad, carving the vegetables into bite-sized portions. He lifted the fork to his mouth, then slowly lowered it. "I understand that it is difficult to accept one's daughter's living half a world away. But we have work to do in the U.S., too, and we will visit often. Jenn cares so deeply about you." Arun smiled and raised the fork.

Of course she does, Paul thought, glad to hear the words even if he was being played. What would they do in the U.S.? Wheedle donations from the gullible? Did he expect Jenn to raise money? Paul chomped his burger, waiting for Arun to say something that would confirm his suspicion. Arun ate steadily, working his way from right to left across the plate. He kept his eyes on his food, stopping every few minutes to wipe his mouth with the edge of his napkin.

"Tell me," Paul said finally, "how you expect to make a living. You and Jenn."

"We charge a small fee for our workshops. Even now one can live simply in India."

"What happens when life gets more complicated? Jenn's accustomed to comfort."

"I know you have offered her every convenience. But she tells me material things have never been her focus."

Burger done, Paul started on his fries, twirling them one at a time in ketchup, licking the grease and salt from his fingers, watching Arun's face for a reaction.

Arun continued, "I admire Jenn's commitment. She often says she learned the value of discipline at home. I must

thank you and Mrs. Adler for raising her so beautifully."
Arun wiped hands on his napkin and placed it, folded, on
the table.

Everything Arun said rang false. Jenn was no fashion
plate, but no one would call her ascetic. She liked gobs of
chunky jewelry with her secondhand clothes. She liked her
pie à la mode and two sugars in her coffee. Evidently, she
liked Arun's brand of sugar. Paul pushed his plate away
and stood.

"We'd better get back. Maggie will wonder what I've
done with you." He picked up the check, intending to leave
a magnanimous tip.

⚬◠◠⟋ ◠◠◡⟍

As they climbed the steps beneath the portico, Maggie
opened the door to greet them. She looked wilted despite
her Sunday clothes.

"Arun, Jenn is waiting for you upstairs. She wants to
show you something." Turning to Paul, "I gather you've
had lunch? You've been gone a while."

"Yeah, we ate at the club."

Arun nodded thank-you and went inside. Maggie
beckoned and Paul followed her through the living room
onto the porch. They sat in plastic chairs with floral-print
cushions—a housewarming gift decades before. Sunlight
warmed them, although the breeze was cool. Paul glanced
at the weathered wooden swing set at the back of the yard.
They'd had a lot of fun with it when Jenn was young, and
the neighborhood kids had come round.

"Well?" Maggie said.

"I didn't get much. He said Jenn wants to go to India

with him to work in schools. Doesn't sound like a winner to me." Paul didn't want to be grilled. He didn't want to spend an hour going over the lunchtime conversation in excruciating detail, as Maggie would want. He rose. "She's too smart to fall for flimflam. Maybe it's temporary, the lure of the exotic. She'll get over it."

Maggie leaned forward and hugged her chest with both arms. "I don't think so. Have you noticed that nothing riles her? Her sauciness is gone. She doesn't argue with me. It's like she's floating above things."

"That's because she's a vegetarian."

Maggie didn't smile. "I don't think that's the explanation." Her eyes searched his face.

"I'm gonna go do some real science. Inoculate myself against what we'll hear over dinner. If he plays poker, after dinner I'll clean his clock." Paul turned into the house.

"Be careful, Paul," Maggie said to his back.

Picking up the briefcase he'd left at the top of the stairs, he descended to the basement. He turned on the lights and fired up the old computer at his desk. When the blue screen appeared, he opened a browser and searched on "Hindu sages." A mess of pages appeared—some in curlicue script with a line along the top; some studded with links to long words in which all the syllables contained the letter *a*. The articles read like gibberish, strings of long names that referred to one another. Too much to swallow. He'd take this guy on later.

He clicked over to his email. There at the top of his inbox stood the name Hope Caldwell. He deleted it.

EIGHT

Maggie pulled up outside the two-story colonial that housed the domestic shelter for which she volunteered, Arun beside her in the passenger seat. She parked beneath the bare branches of an oak, and they walked to the front door, painted deep pink against the light pink of the facade. Maggie explained that the original population of battered women had wanted a color that signaled safety. Arun replied that his mother was one of the first to sponsor breast cancer awareness in Bangalore, and he understood the value of pink. He opened the door for her to pass and followed her into the foyer.

In an imperious voice—the voice of the adventurer who had gone off to India—Jenn had insisted that Arun accompany Maggie on pet therapy duty. Maggie had demurred, but Jenn said it would be a great way for them to get to know each other, since helping was a value they shared, and Arun joined his palms in front of his chest in what Maggie took to be a gesture of supplication. So she'd called the shelter to ask if she could bring a man with her, just this once, just to observe. When she told Paul the plan, he asked if she'd enjoy Arun kissing her ass. Maggie told him to stop talking testosterone and resolved to make the best of the visit.

The house smelled like an elementary school, like sweaty children and cafeteria cooking. Kids' drawings covered the foyer walls; the furniture and paint were nicked and scuffed. They could hear a radio playing and dishes clinking somewhere in the background.

Two boys about waist high tumbled downstairs from the second floor and ran around Maggie's legs, exclaiming, "Jupiter, Jupiter." She laughed and lifted her tote bag to safety overhead. Arun looked at her with raised eyebrows.

"The dog's name is Jupiter. The kids can't wait to see him." The boys ran to the door, pushing each other aside to grab the latch handle.

"I too. I look forward to seeing the therapy a dog can provide."

"Jupiter's just a dog. These kids don't have pets, so he's special to them. Louise and I do the therapy part. Someone from the shelter sometimes sits in with us, mostly to control the kids."

"And have you been trained to give therapy?"

"No, neither of us. But it's not hard to see what to do. The kids need so much, and so many of them are scared."

A chubby girl who looked to be about ten approached from behind and circled arms around Maggie's waist. Maggie twisted shoulders to face her. "Hello, Britney. Are you excited to see Jupiter?"

The girl nodded. "Can I hold the leash?"

"Sure. In fact, we're going to need your help today with the younger kids. Miss Louise has a tough project. You'll be the leader."

Britney let go and skipped over to the door, taking charge of the handle. The boys gave way and disappeared around the foot of the staircase. Britney smirked and waved at Maggie, as if to signal her command of the situation. Maggie waved back.

"The young lady seems to know you," Arun said.

"Louise and I bring the dog here every Monday, and we get to know the long-term kids. The shelter tries to move the women into permanent situations as quickly as possible, but it's not always possible. I've gotten fond of Britney. In another setting, she'd show a lot of promise."

"But she has already shown promise. To you." Arun inclined his head two inches and joined his palms.

Maggie didn't know how to reply. He must have understood her meaning, yet he had turned it around into a comment about her. She felt her guard rise. She didn't want to banter with Arun. She wanted to stay objective, the better to protect Jenn. She took off her old leather jacket and hung it in the closet beneath the staircase while Arun waited in the foyer.

The front door opened and Britney squealed. Jupiter trotted in, Louise right behind him. In a flash, the two little boys reappeared. The three children hugged the dog, a big, reddish retriever who stood patiently. Louise, a lean woman in her sixties wearing an orange sweatshirt and carrying a big turquoise bag, clapped her hands and said, "Everybody into the playroom. Britney, take the bowl out of my bag and bring Jupiter some water, hon. Isaac, go get your brother and sister."

They followed Jupiter into what would have been the parlor when the building was a home, a bright, bare room with a linoleum floor, shelves along the walls holding books and bins of playthings, and a round table with plastic chairs. Louise smiled hello at Arun and ushered the children into a circle around the table, placing her bag in the middle. Arun stayed back while Maggie fished pencils out of her tote. Without warning, Isaac rushed past Arun, followed by two smaller children holding hands, looking wide-eyed at the dog.

"Who knows what holiday is coming up later this month?" Louise asked in her "take charge" voice.

"Thanksgiving," Britney said. "Everybody knows that."

"Right. And we're going to get Jupiter ready. Last week you helped Miss Maggie and me give Jupiter a bath. And he liked it, didn't he? It feels good to be clean."

Still holding hands, Isaac's siblings inched closer to the dog. Jupiter's bushy, wagging tail swiped their chests. They stepped back and giggled. Together they reached grubby hands toward the tail. Maggie bent down to ask them to join the circle at the table so they could take part in the activity. They hesitated, then went to stand on either side of Isaac, who leaned so far over the table that his stomach crunched on the edge as he fingered the brushes, papers, scissors, and ribbon that emerged from Louise's bag.

"We're going to groom Jupiter. That means brush his hair and look for any bad spots on his skin, like a sore. And then we're going to make him a Pilgrim hat." Louise held up a photocopy of a Chihuahua wearing what looked like a fedora with a buckle above the brim. "It fits over the ears. Isn't it cute?"

"Can I use the scissors?" Isaac said.

"You're too little," Britney said.

Handing her orange construction paper, Maggie said, "Britney, why don't you show Isaac how to use them properly. I'll make sure everyone stays safe."

ɞ ɷ

Maggie backed the car out and headed for the boulevard
while Arun sat silent, hands folded in his lap. It had been a
good visit: Britney and Isaac had gotten along better than in
past weeks; she'd taken a charming photo of Louise and the
kids crowding around Jupiter wearing the dumb hat. She'd
email it to the shelter for their newsletter. Perhaps she'd
print it large, frame it, and bring it next time. She smiled,
thinking about the commotion it would create among the
kids. They'd be so proud.

Arun's voice intruded. "The children seemed to enjoy
themselves. May I ask, Mrs. Adler, why you do this work?"

"Louise needs another person to help. Things can get
out of hand pretty fast." She checked the mirror and steered
the car into the left lane. She didn't want to share confi-
dences with this alien man, but it would be churlish not
to explain.

"I met Louise years ago when we had a retriever. She
and I used to exercise our dogs together. After we had to
put Silly down, I kept in touch. When she started doing
pet therapy, I agreed to help." At the time, Maggie had
guessed that Louise wanted to work at shelters to expiate
her own past abuse. But her brassy bravery struck a chord;
the two women volunteered together without belaboring
the past. Over time, pet therapy had become just as important to Maggie. The kids needed all the mothering they
could get. She wanted to be the stranger whose gratuitous
loving kindness made an impact, if ever so slight, like the
fairy godmother she'd read about as a child and wished she
had. She couldn't alleviate poverty, but she could give hugs.

"I think we make a difference. It takes a while though. There's so much working against these kids."

"What is the difference you make?"

"The kids open up. We teach them to give. It's easier to give to the dog than to each other." She toggled the turn signal for a left. "The dog disarms them. My husband would say it's genetics, biophilia. Humans evolved in nature and so we love it. I'm not sure why it works, but when we tell them, 'Treat the dog the way you would want to be treated,' their faces soften and they treat each other better." She completed the turn.

"And does this carry over to the rest of their lives?"

"Louise thinks so. The shelter staff thinks so. The board thinks so. I hope so." She thought about the kids they had just seen. "Isaac's mother has three kids under the age of five and no money and no education. She's twenty-four, works nights, and her boyfriend is in jail. Her kids don't trust the world, and can you blame them? You can already see how wary and tired they are in their eyes. They seem to know they're in for more grief."

They stopped at a red light. Maggie looked at Arun, who sat with fingertips touching in front of his chest. He turned to her.

"Perhaps the children will discover there's opportunity in grief."

The light turned. Maggie stepped on the accelerator, and the rental car lurched forward. "Are you saying adversity builds character?"

Arun spoke softly. "People build character. But they can be helped. Wise men and women over the ages have examined the human condition. I have studied their wisdom, and I've shared my findings with your daughter. Mrs.

Adler, Jenn and I wish to help children like Britney, whatever their circumstances. We believe the path to greater happiness is available to everyone."

"Isn't happiness elusive when you're a homeless kid who sees his father beat his mother?"

"I think you will find that true happiness and misery are equally distributed among all classes and castes."

Maggie stared straight ahead at the traffic. The conversation was going nowhere. What a pedant! And wrong. Crappy parenting damages children. Period. She took two deep breaths to loosen the tightness forming in her chest. Jenn must be listening to this cant. How much did Jenn actually believe? She would stick to small talk with Arun, or no talk at all.

The Adlers' driveway was almost bare of fallen leaves. As they left the car, Arun thanked Maggie for the opportunity to observe pet therapy. She returned thanks for his interest in the visit. Jenn met them in the foyer, all smiles.

"Did you make friends with the dog?"

Arun laughed. "No, there was no time. He was occupied. Your mother's work is very like ours."

"I thought you'd think so." Jenn leaned in to peck his cheek. She looped her arm around his and drew him toward the living room. "Come sit with us, Mom. I want to hear all about it."

Maggie mumbled something about seeing to dinner and moved toward the kitchen, her turf. As she hung her jacket in the mudroom, she caught a glimpse of the two of them seated on the couch, his hand stroking her cheek with such evident tenderness. She scurried into the kitchen.

Late-afternoon sun slanted in through the window, warming the oak flooring and the crazed yellow tile. Early evening was usually Maggie's favorite time of day; she would imagine everyone hurrying home or to a restaurant or a class, where something cheering and orderly would happen. This evening she took no comfort from the kitchen's glow. Arun's presence in the house, and in Jenn's affections, darkened her mood.

She took vegetables from the fridge, and onions and a cookbook from the pantry. She forced herself to concentrate on the recipes. She turned pages to *e* for eggplant and began to organize ingredients. Jenn limped into the room and took a seat in the breakfast nook, propping her sore ankle on the bench opposite. Her long skirt fanned out, smelling faintly of patchouli. Perhaps it wasn't patchouli. Perhaps it was some Indian thing even more potent.

"Arun's doing his email. Can I help? I'm pretty good with spices."

Maggie handed her the book. "Find an eggplant dish Arun will like. I'm broiling some fish, if that's okay."

"Sure. I like fish. Oh, I forgot. A man called about your car. He didn't leave a message. Said he'd call back."

Maggie caught her breath. This was the second time since the accident that Brian Sayler had tried to contact her. She would have to talk to him to make him stop. If she wanted him to stop.

"Do you have a more modern cookbook, Mom? The only decent thing here is ratatouille."

"I've used that recipe. It's good. I think I have enough tomato. Would it be okay for Arun?"

"Of course. If you like it, he will too. He's not from another planet." Jenn lowered her leg and faced her mother. "Did everything go okay at the shelter?"

Maggie hesitated. "Yes. Louise gave a good lesson. She

dressed up the dog in a Pilgrim hat. Corny, but the kids loved it." She placed a cutting board on the counter and reached for a knife and sharpening file. Hands raised to sharpen the knife, she paused.

Jenn said, "But?"

"I'm not sure Arun approved. He said something odd in the car. About opportunity and adversity. As if there's no difference between the shelter kids and the kids who go to Pelham Country Day."

Jenn stood and brought the cookbook to the counter. "He told me he thought you and Louise did a great job." She leaned on the counter. "Arun's approach is different. He doesn't believe that evil is a force. What we call evil he calls the lack of good. He believes everyone can manufacture *more* good, but some people need help. I'm not doing his ideas justice. You have to hear him explain things. He makes it work, Mom. He makes things better."

"And do you agree with him?"

"I still think some people are evil. But Arun's philosophy works at least as well as Reverend Stevens'." She straightened up. "Can I help?"

"You can peel the eggplants. They're a little tough. In the sink."

Jenn half-limped across the room to the sink through a slanted column of golden light. She ran a hand through her curls, pulling them back off her face, and surveyed the vegetables.

Maggie angled the knife blade on the sharpening file and drew it hard across. She took a dozen fast strokes, then wiped the blade on a dish towel. Her mother had taught her how to sharpen a knife decades before, and the scene flashed through her mind every time, even now when she was distracted. She picked up an onion, sliced off the bottom of the bulb to get a purchase on the skin.

She had never heard Jenn criticize Reverend Stevens or their church before. In fact, she'd seemed receptive to its teachings. True, she had brought home disrespectful young men and women one after another, but she had never adopted their bad manners or selfish habits. Maggie had been proud of Jenn's generosity and her ability to respond to the best in others. But now, Arun. A missionary without a church. No, a swami, and Jenn under his spell.

She peeled the outer layer off the onion and began to slice. What did Jenn see in Arun? What does it mean, "more or less good"? How much can a twenty-five-year-old understand? In the same situation, hadn't Maggie herself said next to nothing about Paul? Her mother would never have understood. Yes, Paul had beguiled her. She'd admired his strength of character and single-mindedness; she'd thought his noble ambitions more than enough for both of them. She never imagined he wouldn't be satisfied with a respectable career and a normal home. Looking back, her naivety embarrassed her. Choosing Paul had been playing with fire. But he hadn't asked her to follow him halfway around the world. It was the enormous distance that made the thought of Jenn's marrying Arun unbearable.

The knife slid on the top of the onion and sliced into Maggie's knuckles. Bright red blood welled in a straight line across three fingers. Maggie gasped and stepped to the sink to run water over her hand.

"What happened?" Jenn said.

"I wasn't holding the onion properly. You know, fingers tucked under. It's not serious."

"Let's see."

Jenn turned off the faucet and took her mother's hand in hers. The cut was clean and bleeding steadily. "Let me get my first aid kit. I can bind this for you. Do it all the time in India. Keep your hand over the sink. I'll be back in a minute." She limped away quickly.

Blood leaked out of the cut and down into the sink, staining the pale green flesh of an eggplant. Maggie flexed her fingers and the wound began to sting. She felt foolish. She should have paid better attention. She would need flexible fingers to do her chores: the elaborate dinner for four, the tax forms for All Saints', tomorrow's Pilates class with Ellen. Then her date for lunch. She would ask Jenn to minimize the bandages.

Jenn's footsteps, joined by Arun's, sounded overhead. Maggie considered getting the bottle of alcohol beneath the downstairs bathroom sink to disinfect the cut. But Jenn had told her to stay put. She waited, wanting to show Jenn that her mother listened to her, whatever the circumstances.

❧ ❧

Maggie looked over the edge of the restaurant balcony onto the hustle in the atrium lobby of Grand Central Station. People made beelines across the marble floor to pick up food from vendors doing a noisy lunchtime business. Across the table, Robert Stamford waited patiently while she, embarrassed by needing to talk to him and disturbing his busy day, toyed with her salad.

She'd summoned Robert to lunch because he was good to talk to in a crisis and because she knew he'd come. They'd first met when Robert and Paul were in graduate school. She'd realized soon after that he had a crush on her.

He was either too good a friend to Paul or too insecure to chase her. He hadn't married, and over the years his crush had gentled into a friendship, which she gladly returned. Their encounters, when Paul's business threw them together, pleased and gratified her. He was attentive and clever. And reassuring: when Jenn broke her leg and Paul was out of town, Robert arranged excellent care at the hospital and talked her through the procedures. She sighed and returned to the conversation.

"Bottom line, Paul hates Arun and Jenn adores him, and I'm trying to be objective, but he throws up a philosophical smokescreen." She looked into Robert's friendly eyes. "I'm stymied."

"To be honest, I don't really understand why you and Paul have disqualified the young man. Perhaps you simply need more time with him."

"I'm so on edge it's painful."

Robert reached into his sport coat and withdrew his phone. He fiddled with it a moment. "I've sent you contacts for one of the senior physicians. He's an Indian and a good man, and I'm sure he will be able to clarify questions of philosophy. Use my name." He replaced the phone.

"Thank you. That's very kind," but, she thought, unsatisfactory. The problem transcended philosophy.

"Have you tried talking to one of Jenn's friends to get the younger generation's perspective?"

She considered talking to Ellen's son, a little younger than Jenn but plenty worldly. "Good idea. Maybe dating Indians is the new trend. You are giving me hope." She smiled at him to signal gratitude for his trying to cheer her. She hoped he couldn't see that he hadn't.

In an uncharacteristic move, Robert laid a hand on her

arm. "I must ask. Why have you come to me? Are you and Paul at odds?"

How to respond? Yes, they were at odds, circling each other like suspicious dogs. Wasn't that why she wanted Robert to comfort her? But if she told the truth . . . Did she want him to close up the proper distance between them? She had never found Robert physically attractive; it was his kindness that endeared him to her. But perhaps that could change.

"No more than usual. We're both so busy we don't always talk. You are so sensible. I treasure your advice." She willed his hand away.

Robert released her arm. She could count on his behaving well. She picked up her purse.

"I should go. My train's ready to depart. Service to Pelham is spotty in the afternoon."

"Shall I accompany you?"

"Oh, no. You have a hospital to manage. Thanks for lunch." She gathered her jacket as he called for the check and sped away. He would notice her haste but make no remark, and his courtesy would appease her conscience.

The New Haven Local slid north along its rails, and Maggie indulged in fantasy. If she had chosen Robert over Paul, would she now live in a penthouse and entertain on weekends? Robert would need a different kind of wife than she had been, more of a social animal. Would there have been children? Would they still have sex? She shied away from the image of a naked Robert, soft and rotund, ever so carefully palming her breasts. No, no children with Robert, not even in fantasy.

But perhaps a different lover.

She'd had no real boyfriends before Paul. In the early years, he'd been lusty, and good at making her lusty. Without alcohol or weed, just the two of them in daylight or in dark, plain vanilla, good sex. Then she'd gotten pregnant, recovered, and grown more demanding, hotter and quicker. Paul said the change was due to residual vasculature from pregnancy. She thought she'd grown into womanhood, which meant owning her desires. And then he stopped coming home every night. Their lovemaking grew less frequent. She stopped expecting him to climb into bed beside her, hungry for her. She suspected he didn't always sleep alone the nights he stayed in the city. But they had Jenn and the dog and a reasonable life. At some point, she realized she didn't miss sex with Paul all that much, but she missed the intimacy. She wanted sex with intimacy. Could she have sex without intimacy?

If she were to take a lover, he would be the opposite of Robert, a man of the flesh, not the mind. A man who enjoyed simple animal sex. A hard, lean man like Brian Sayler.

ഛ൙ ൙ഛ

Sitting at her desk upstairs, Maggie sorted through the letters Jenn had sent from India, looking for clues to the hold Arun had over her daughter. At first Jenn had written on airmail stationery.

Dear Mom and Dad,

I am sitting in a restaurant where I had lunch with an Italian guy I met on the train. He didn't speak much English, but he knew German and I remembered some from college, so we actually had a good time, gesturing away. I follow advice to eat only hot things (I stick my finger in the food and if I can keep it in, the food's not hot enough). So far, so good, I am well. Right now two American girls are walking by wearing miniscule shorts and T-shirts with scoop necks showing their bras. They are oblivious to the stares and leers they provoke. I watch their insensitivity and lack of caution, and I shudder because they reinforce the bad name American girls have here. Thank goodness I'm not that kind of American. But if there's anything I've learned so far, it's how American I really am. For example, you go into the bathroom in the restaurant and there's a neat-looking marble sink. But when you turn on the faucet, water spills onto the floor because the marble basin wasn't sealed onto the marble counter. Why bother to seam the sink, or to check the seam, since the tourists won't be back anyway? (My Italian friend said someone paid off the building inspector.) I know I sound finicky, but the sink is a symptom of a kind of fatalism that I encounter all over the place. People don't seem to want to deal with issues, big or small. I suppose most people in old societies with rigid hierarchies are acting rationally when they throw up their hands and walk away from intractable problems. But I want them to do something about problems, even if they're tough to fix, because I'm a can-do American. My ancestors were frontiersmen, and pioneers are nothing if not self-reliant. I try to imagine how I would feel if I had grown up here—no can do! Seriously, growing up in relative riches and security, I am in no position to judge any Indian's attitude towards fate. . . .

She riffled through the short stack, looking for the more telling bits.

Yesterday, as I climbed down the temple wall (there were no barriers or fences to protect the ancient artifacts or to stop tourists from falling and breaking their necks) a dark-skinned man, not old but wizened with gaping teeth and tattered clothes, walked up to me and asked if I was American. When I said yes, he asked how I felt about India. I said, India is wonderful, and he burst into a huge smile. I was touched that my American opinion mattered so much to him. I couldn't tell him everything I feel about India because that wasn't what he wanted to hear. India IS wonderful. AND terrible. Wonderful for the beautiful colors (even poor women have lovely saris), and the spicy smells, and the chaotic mix of old and new (donkeys, pedicabs, motor scooters, and BMWs barrel down the street together), and the profusion of life in so many forms. Terrible for the crowding, the beggars, what they do to baby daughters they don't want, and to girls with insufficient dowries, and to widows. Suttee has been illegal forever, but women still throw themselves on their husbands' funeral pyres. In the twenty-first century!!! The contrast between wonderful and terrible tears at my heart. Life is so vivid here (death, too, I guess). It makes me feel that so many of the philosophical concerns I had in college, the words we used and the way we would rationalize things "at another level of analysis," just don't apply. I feel like academic philosophy is a luxury. They need something more fundamental here, as do I. It's beginning to jell for me, I think, but I'm not ready to say. . . .

These seemed like the musings of the daughter she knew. But then Jenn switched to email. Maggie powered up her computer and opened the "Jenn" file.

TO: maggieadler@gmail.com
FROM: jennadler@gmail.com
SUBJECT: My school

I'm writing from an Internet café about a mile and a half from this school attached to an ashram in the countryside north of Delhi. Sorry you haven't heard from me in a while, but I've been busy, and it's hard to get to the café. I have a job! Volunteer because I can't get paid, but a job, teaching English to children whose families don't have the money to send them to the public school, which is free but far away. They don't have transportation or books or uniforms and they (the children) need to work. But the ashram made friends with the adults and set up the school on the side (of course it's part time but some schooling is better than none). It's fascinating. My teaching is pretty rudimentary, but I'm getting close to the kids, and starting to understand the parents' lives and the value the ashram brings. My head is full of ideas! There are several foreigners staying here, including a Brit married to a half-Chinese woman who grew up in the British compound in Shanghai and went

to Oxford, of all places. So I have some remark-
able people to help me sort out my overflowing
head. This is why I came to India, to get experi-
ence that clarifies my life.

All's good. Love to you and Dad.

TO: maggieadler@gmail.com
FROM: jennadler@gmail.com
SUBJECT: Catching up

Sorry to be so sporadic. It's a long way to the café
in this heat, and the cell service here sucks, and the
ashram's satellite phone is only for emergencies.
My teaching is going well, I think. There's no way
to judge, not that it matters, I'm satisfied with the
work. And the kids are teaching me Hindi! Spoken
Hindi, in their dialect, with a child's vocabulary,
which covers the essentials and so suits me fine.

The ashram invited a new guy to talk with the
adults. He's an odd little Indian, but I like his aura
(don't worry, I'm not turning New Age on you).
This guy seems at peace, even when we're jok-
ing around—maybe because he went to college in
America—so we share a lot. It's nice to have some-
one solid to talk to about the people we work with.
The children's resilience continues to amaze me.
Arun (his name, rhymes with moon) says some of
the adults can still bounce back. He says he can re-
store resilience to some of the others. I am eager to
see his results. If there's anything India needs (and
the world needs) it's a formula for restoring health

after crisis, individual or planetary. As you see, I'm still interested in ideas, and being in the boonies helps me concentrate.

All's good. Love to you and Dad.

The rest of the emails were short. Maggie typed "ARUN" in the search function.

TO: *maggieadler@gmail.com*
FROM: *jennadler@gmail.com*
SUBJECT: *Our little community of seekers*

Since I last wrote (sorry it's been so long) our work has really blossomed. Arun and I have figured out how to link our activities so we get at the whole family. I get the kids talking, and he discusses what the kids say with the parents. He says it's the best way to stimulate authentic conversations. He spends a lot of time in the villages around the ashram, then he comes back and tells the monks and the foreigners and the school teachers (we now have a second volunteer) what's going on. I love these meetings. People have such different takes on the problems, although our goals are compatible. I've learned that there are no easy solutions in developing countries because everything is connected in ways outsiders can't predict. Villagers think differently. People without the tools money can buy have to depend on each other more than we do. I like it, although of course life would be far better and more comfortable with more infrastructure.

Do I sound like a policy wonk? Relax, no World Bank in my future. I think that kind of "aid" does very little to alter people's lives. The kind of work we do is better, helping people develop their own resources to accomplish what makes sense to them.

All's good. Love to you and Dad.

TO: maggieadler@gmail.com
FROM: jennadler@gmail.com
SUBJECT: Bangalore and more

Arun offered to show me Bangalore (he had to visit his parents and suggested I come along—we flew Air India, which is another story). Walking around his parents' neighborhood I thought I was in southern California, clean streets, modern stucco buildings, tended semitropical gardens. As unreal as Disneyland to someone coming from the countryside.

The best part was meeting Arun's family. His parents are both such warm, gentle people. You wouldn't know they have demanding professional lives. Both of them are doctors and they run a clinic together, but they seemed so unhurried when we talked. Of course they have servants for cooking and cleaning and the like, everyone middle class here does, but I don't think that explains their poise. Especially Arun's mom. You can see how lovely she must have been as a girl. She's still beautiful in a "mature" way and she seems so wise about the world. I hope I get to see her again. I so enjoyed her presence.

When we got back to the ashram, we got bad news. The head monk wants to decommission the school, not sure why. So Arun and I are making plans to continue our work elsewhere. He has many contacts. I must admit I'm a little concerned, but I trust him to figure it out. I'll write again when I know our next address.

All's good. Love to you and Dad.

TO: maggieadler@gmail.com
FROM: jennadler@gmail.com
SUBJECT: I am a new woman

We have landed on our feet so well that I feel like I'm dancing. Arun was invited to take over a community that an NGO started, and I am running the school. I have free rein to design my program, in consultation with Arun and the other teachers, and, of course, the kids. It gives me such joy to live my philosophy rather than just think about it. This is everything I'd hoped for, and more. Can't wait to make our dream happen!

All's excellent! Love to you and Dad.

The remaining emails were perfunctory, with Jenn claiming that she was too busy to write more. Maggie turned off the computer, still in the dark, too uncomfortable for words.

NINE

Jennifer was born on May 20, and three months later, on a red-letter day in science, Paul fell in love with her. He hadn't wanted a child so early in the marriage, at a time when his research had just started producing results, but Maggie had conceived and life took over. Falling in love had come as a surprise. He felt more like a teenager with a crush than a father, or at least the father he imagined he would be when responsibility descended on them. He found himself inventing a hundred nicknames—Jenny, J-girl, Jennipooh, Kidlet, Baybarooni, Midget, Missy—as the months passed and his affection blossomed.

Paul's own father, a bitter, drinking man, had taken his family to Indianapolis fifty years after the Adler clan had moved to the Midwest to farm. The older generations had been successful but eventually sold out to a big company. Paul's father worked in a Lilly factory for a decade, until his job disappeared and his wife took sick—Paul was ten, Lenny almost thirteen—and then he turned sour, punishing Lenny for nothing at all, bullying both sons whenever he drank.

He blustered continuously and lost his welcome at church, among relatives, and in the men's fraternal organizations. The boys feared their father but at the same time defended him to their friends. In secret, Paul swore he'd never be like his dad; he would be successful and admired. No one would mock him behind his back, least of all his family.

The day Jenny was born, Paul resolved to take proper care of her. Duty, not love, motivated him. He expected Maggie to provide the soft nurturing—she'd be Harlow's terry-cloth monkey. Maggie had worked all through the pregnancy; she'd set up an office in the corner of the second bedroom so she could do her bookkeeping from home while the future baby slept. Paul had suggested that she take a break from work, but they needed the money, so he went along with her plans. She was as efficient at pregnancy as she was at everything else: collecting hand-me-downs from friends, reading Lamaze books, massaging her nipples months in advance so she could nurse. Three weeks after Jennifer was born, he was taken aback when Maggie burst into tears and declared herself incapable of bearing one more sleepless night. He thought she was joking and made light of it. She flew into a panicky rage. The OB nurse they called advised Paul to give the baby a bottle at eleven so that Maggie could rest. He did, and it helped. Maggie began to smile a bit more, to accept half a glass of beer in the evening after the eight o'clock feed. She grew calmer as the baby slept more regularly. But the baby's routine kept changing, and Maggie continued to look frazzled. He didn't recognize the self-sufficient woman he knew to be his wife. Her distress unnerved him.

Then, at three months, the baby contracted the flu. Her temperature spiked to 104 degrees. The pediatrician said there was no danger and to comfort her while the fever burned. All night long, Paul and Maggie took turns trying to console the red-faced, whimpering infant. At four in the morning, Paul found himself pacing back and forth in the living room with the baby against his shoulder while Maggie dozed. He bounced her gently, cooing her name, feeling heat radiate from her little body to his cheek and down his chest. The back of his head and neck ached, but he was wide awake; the baby needed him.

Maggie appeared in the doorway, tying back hair in a ponytail, then stretching out arms to receive the still whimpering child.

"How is she?"

"Exhausted. Maybe a little cooler. She's dry though." He handed Jennifer to her mother. "If you're okay, I'll nap a bit."

"Hope you can sleep. I didn't."

She wouldn't have slept well on a normal night, he thought, or what had become normal since Jennifer's birth. He took off jeans and T-shirt and lay down. In the quiet he heard the kitchen clock tick and Maggie singing softly in the living room. He closed his eyes.

A voice blared next to his head; "6:30" glowed on the clock. He moved quietly to the bathroom to shave and dress. At 6:45, he stepped into the living room. Maggie lay on the couch on her back, eyes closed, holding the sleeping baby on her breast. He whispered her name. To his great relief, neither mother nor baby stirred. He tiptoed to the apartment door, then stopped to glance back. Maggie's chest rose and lowered softly; the baby's cheeks were rosy but not feverish, and her lips formed a pink, little O of content. How beautiful and vulnerable his wife and daughter looked. In that instant, he succumbed. He would gladly give up a night's sleep to keep them safe.

On the bus to campus, Paul visualized the scene at home when mother and child would awake. Maggie would be tender and businesslike, smiling through her fatigue while changing the diaper and offering her breast. Much as her weepiness had irked him, her devotion comforted him. He felt bound with her in a net of passion to protect the little life they had created. The urge to nurture his daughter deepened within him, unexpected and undeniable. Like mother love.

His own mother may have been attentive to Paul and his brother, but Paul couldn't remember. He could vaguely remember playing games and laughing with her around the time he first went to school. As time passed, her light-heartedness faded. She did the household chores—cleaning, cooking, washing, scolding—but she never smiled. And then she stopped doing chores. Lenny sometimes filled the gap. Paul made himself a peanut butter sandwich to take to school for lunch every day—which later killed his taste for peanuts. At the time, he attributed his mother's negligence to the fact that she didn't care about him and Lenny. Then she died, and the boys had to contend with the old man on their own. Paul channeled his anger at his father, never Lenny, silently opposing his every word. Only much later, while he was in the army, did he learn that his mother had suffered from stomach cancer for years, without complaint but lacking energy to nurture or to subdue their father. Lenny, it turned out, had known all along. Lenny, nearly three years older, had gone along with their parents, believing Paul, at ten, too young to understand. He was still angry at having been left out. He was still angry at having been left behind.

The bus stopped in front of the science building. When he entered the office that he shared with the other junior researchers, his buddy handed him a magazine. While his computer booted, he looked at *Science*, picking up a pen to check off his initials on the routing slip. He put a check next to P.A., thinking the initials suited him all right, and flipped to the table of contents. He saw two titles that might have implications for his own work. He turned to the first article, ignoring the squeeze of tension in his chest. Every time he picked up *Science,* he dreaded discovering that someone else had scooped him on his big idea or that someone had already taken a step that made his current experiment redundant. No problem in the first article, no need to change any of his procedures. He turned to the second.

Goddamn.

In all his years at Michigan, he had been investigating a bird virus that he suspected caused tumors to grow in mice. Other biologists had also been looking at viruses' effects on mouse DNA. If anyone could show a mechanism at work in the mouse model, the next step would be seeing if it caused human cancer. Now, before his eyes, some guys on the West Coast were speculating that bird viruses do not "infect" mice in the sense that they do not introduce any foreign DNA that makes a mouse cell cancerous. Viral DNA, the authors theorized, does not enable a genetic reaction that directly subverts the normal mouse cell; instead, the virus prompts the mouse DNA *itself* to turn rogue. Something that the virus does turns on the mouse cell's *natural* ability to grow and multiply unchecked.

Paul's mind spun.

He had been searching for bits of DNA that promoted tumor growth and trying to fit them to the bird virus's fingerprint. But if the engine of tumor growth lay within the host DNA, his search was wrongheaded. Agitation spread from his chest through his torso. He could sense the structure of his experiment imploding, like a building collapsing from within when you knocked out the beams. He willed himself to clear the rubble and start fresh. His ability to keep clear, to put reason ahead of dogma, was a point of pride. It would take years for the cancer biology community to test the West Coast team's theory, but he had no doubts. His gut told him they were right. He would have to reimagine his hypotheses and rewrite his procedures. Something inside him shifted gears; in a rush, he understood the next steps to take.

He pulled out a yellow pad. He couldn't write fast enough to capture the cascade of ideas flowing through him.

The office meeting that afternoon went late, until almost four. The lab director maintained a formal agenda, calling on staff in order of seniority. When it was Paul's turn to speak, he mentioned the startling article. He didn't want to share his thinking—point out the article, for sure, but not lay out the implications—until he could claim the turf. The boss passed to the next person without comment. Paul sat with head down, fiddling with his pen, hoping no one would question him. He paid scant attention to the rest of the meeting. He couldn't wait to get back to his desk. When the others invited him to join them for the customary postmeeting beer, he begged off, saying his baby was sick. He charged back to his cubicle.

The phone rang. Annoyed, he picked up the receiver.

"She's down below a hundred." Maggie's voice trembled.

"She's on the mend, Mag. That's great."

"She's still sick."

"You can't expect an instant cure. Don't believe what you see in the movies."

Maggie's voice grew lower. "When will you be home?"

Her tone set his teeth on edge. He didn't need to go home; the baby was healing.

"In a couple of hours. You have everything under control."

A year earlier, when Maggie had told him about the pregnancy, he had been angry about the timing. She had promised to be the primary caregiver, to manage the household without a ripple. He had known that he wouldn't be off the hook; nor had he wanted to be. But now he detected an accusatory note in her voice. It was unfair—he did his share. From the minute he walked in the door in the evening, he cared for the baby, except on the rare nights when an experiment kept him late.

Maggie continued, "She doesn't want to nurse. I'm worried about dehydration."

"Try a little water in a bottle. And don't fuss. She needs rest. I'll be home as soon as I can."

He hung up.

Why did he feel like a heel? Maggie was perfectly capable of handling Jennifer, fever and all. He needed to stay there, to capture the thoughts barreling through his head. Lately, Maggie had seemed so mercurial. He contemplated confronting her about her mood and its effect on his. Once again, he backed down, expecting this crabby chapter in their marriage to pass when Maggie's hormones stabilized. Theoretically. He sympathized with her—he remembered the six months or so before he had finished his thesis, when dragging himself to the library at all hours had caused a constant headache that aspirin couldn't relieve—but he was tired of her begging off sex, of her locking herself in an emotional cocoon with the baby. He had his own needs. He loved Maggie, but he was no longer in love with her.

He picked up the yellow pad he had left on his desk. Ideas lay scrawled on pages in no particular order; some were in the margins, linked to others by loopy arrows. This was his style—generating a mess of loosely associated ideas and then going back to reorder, prune, fill in gaps. He usually liked to talk the logic through with someone, because good stuff came out of his head when he was able to speak his thoughts aloud. Maggie often served as a sounding board—she asked good questions that spurred him on—but he didn't want to open the Pandora's box of her worry about fever and feeding or anything else.

His own father had been the lousiest of husbands: pushy, selfish, never earning or saving enough. Paul was convinced that his mother might have survived had her disease gotten the attention it deserved. But the old man hadn't stopped drinking and spending his own damn way. And, after the money dried up, the old man turned mean.

Back then, Paul had sworn he'd be a better husband, if he were ever a husband. He meant to keep his word. But being a superior husband did not require going home this instant when his research needed to take a new direction. If he could get ahead of the pack now, there'd be plenty of opportunity in the future. More prestige, more money. Anything Maggie and Jennifer might need. He could out-think the rest of the staff on a normal day; with luck and a little more work, he might parlay the new approach he was about to take into securing a lab of his own. Maggie would understand. He'd tell her she had to understand. She wanted his success as much as he. She knew cancer would not yield its secrets without a fight.

He focused on the loopy diagrams on his pad. It would take hours to parse them, and the excess adrenalin rippling through him spoiled his concentration. He tried to re-create the sequence of his thoughts before the phone call, without success. He ripped the top two sheets from the pad and folded them so they fit into his jacket pocket. Maybe the others hadn't left yet. He could use a beer. A quick one. Lovely Jennifer awaited.

TEN

Jennifer's first birthday dawned damp and chill, threatening Maggie's plans for a picnic party. She had borrowed the manicured garden of one of Paul's thesis advisors and prepared lunch herself to save money. She needed the party as a marker, a potentially happy ending to a torturous postpartum year. All those dreary months, she'd hidden the worst moments from Paul, moments when for a split second she'd wanted to smash the bawling baby against a wall and then hated herself for the thought. So much love, so much pain bundled together. Paul couldn't have known how hard it had been.

She'd invited Paul's colleagues, the neighbors, her parents, and her boss. Sarah, who had abandoned politics after college and moved to New York to become a banker, was unable to attend. Maggie missed her desperately. It was she who had counseled Maggie—after Paul had said no to a baby year after year, even after his thesis was finished—to reach for her heart's desire. Maggie worked those seven years as a bookkeeper and managed their minimal household. But she wanted joy, so when Sarah advised poking a hole in her diaphragm, she went for it. She was thrilled when Paul warmed to the baby, as she'd known he would. But she flushed hot with shame at the knowledge that she'd tricked him. He'd been so pissed off at the timing that she'd vowed never to confess. The secret bored a hole in her heart.

Maggie stepped into the middle of the garden to survey the arrangements. The picnic was spread on a table covered with paper imprinted with flowers the size of pizzas; a cooler with wine, water, and soda stood beneath. Toys and games for the older kids lay spread on a blanket on the floor of the gazebo at the far end of the lawn. The drizzle had stopped, but the gray sky threatened. She prayed rain would hold off for Jenny's big day, her redemptive day. With nothing left to do, she entered the house to wait for her guests. She found Jennifer squirming in the arms of her grandmother, who sat talking with the wife of Paul's advisor. Maggie sat next to her mother, reaching for her child, who smiled brightly and stretched toward her.

"Thank you, Mrs. Penrod," she said, gathering the baby into her arms. "We really appreciate your opening your home."

"You're most welcome. My husband thinks highly of Paul. We want to encourage the next generation of scientists." Claire Penrod was lithe, well coiffed, and wore slacks and a sweater that would blow Maggie's clothing budget for a year. "I'm going to join my husband in the sunroom. Do let us know if you need anything." She disappeared down the hallway.

"I thought you said her husband was one of Paul's professors," Maggie's mother, Claudia, said. "I didn't know teachers made that much money."

"Her husband consults for pharmaceutical companies. He discovered something a while back. She's very generous to students. Where's Paul?"

"He took your father to the lab. I don't know why. He said to tell you that he'd be back in time. Hope he makes it." Claudia folded her hands in her lap.

Maggie looked at her mother, ten years younger than Claire Penrod, dry and coarse in comparison. She wore a turquoise pantsuit; dyed, permed hair stood out from her head in a cloud, each individual strand twisting away from its neighbors in chemical agony. Claudia treated her hair herself, avoiding beauty salons with their "annoying young women in ridiculous clothing who want to tell you what to like." Years before, Maggie had learned not to comment on her mother's appearance, although her own was fair game. She took a breath and nuzzled the child playing with her earring. "Paul knows what he's doing. He's a wonderful dad." And, she wanted to say, you are in no position to judge. But she held her tongue.

She'd been surprised and intimidated when her parents had agreed to come to the party. Inviting them had seemed like the right thing to do, although she dreaded the critique that would invariably ensue. Her father rarely traveled. He'd seen his granddaughter only once before, when Maggie had visited at Christmas. Maggie's mother had made the trip to Michigan twice, once when Jenny was born and again after her fever, ostensibly to help care for the baby. Claudia had spent the week reorganizing the room that tripled as nursery, office, and occasional guest bedroom for the student babysitters they could afford.

Claudia and Roger Gilford made an odd couple, he silent and remote, she verbose and opinionated. Roger had

had a munitions job during World War II, being too old and too flat-footed to serve. He met Claudia, twelve years his junior, through a friend just after the war. Claudia latched on to him; Roger had the money to show her a good time. A quiet good time, but more luxurious than she had known. After a few months of dating, Roger thought he might as well propose; Claudia acquiesced, envisioning a maid and a position of respect in her church and family. The maid never materialized, but Claudia acted as if one had. She took on airs, altering her vocabulary and writing elaborate thank-you notes on cheap stationery. She had resented the absence of a maid throughout Maggie's childhood.

Maggie knew that her mother had miscarried twice before she was born, and then there were no more children. Claudia busied herself with church activities and bridge, which she played well, and later the PTA. She paid just enough attention to Maggie to appear a competent mother. She bought her a back-to-school outfit every September, but she didn't mend it when it tore; she enrolled Maggie in Sunday school and Brownies, but she didn't participate in the events. She lectured her daughter on being ladylike, but she smoked and drank like a sailor when she played bridge.

Claudia had rarely indulged her daughter. Maggie could remember only one perfect day: one spring, when mother and daughter sat on the floor together in sunshine playing with her dolls, a cool breeze coming through the open window. Most days, Claudia's attentions took the form of instruction in proper behavior, how a homemaker should care for her family, how a lady dressed for church on Sunday. Maggie tried to be good enough and nice enough to make her mother proud. When Claudia carped at her, the child Maggie thought she had displeased her mother.

The adult Maggie knew she was impossible to please, but still she tried.

The doorbell chimed. Claudia edged closer. "Let me take her. You have enough to do."

Maggie hesitated. She wanted to run her hand through Jennifer's silky curls and along the curve of her fat little neck, to lose herself in the softness.

"Maggie, you need to learn to share." Claudia shifted her bottom deeper into the couch and opened her arms.

It occurred to Maggie that her mother might be joking, but her body stiffened. Too many years of tension lay between them. She handed Jennifer over. "See if you can help her walk. She needs to explore."

The doorbell chimed again. Maggie's boss, Mr. Greenberg, stepped across the threshold and thrust a bouquet of daisies at her. Paul and her father entered close on Greenberg's heels.

"I can't stay," Greenberg said, putting hands in the pockets of the old brown cardigan he wore all winter. "I came to say congratulations to the mother and the baby, and . . . " turning to Paul, "to the cancer doctor. You are a lucky man. Such a lovely wife. And smart!" He pulled a ring box from a pocket and held it toward Maggie. "For Jennifer. When she's old enough, if I'm still alive, I'll tell her what it means."

Paul clapped Greenberg on the shoulder. "Here you go again, threatening to depart prematurely. This is Maggie's father, Roger. Come in and meet her mother." He gestured toward the living room, where Claudia sat staring at the group at the door.

"No, no. I have to go. Have a wonderful party. I'll see you Monday, my dear." He waved awkwardly as he left.

Maggie called after him, "Thanks for the flowers." She turned to Paul. "He's so unpredictable. I once told him I liked daisies, in a different context." She paused. "It was nice of him to come."

"And even nicer to go." Paul grinned.

"I'm going to put these in water. Check on Jennifer? She's with my mom."

In the kitchen, which felt as large as their entire apartment, Maggie opened cabinets looking for a vessel. She took a tall water glass to the sink. As she stripped leaves from the daisies, she thought about how kind Greenberg had been to her this past year. He never pressed her to come in when she was dragging; he covered for her when the baby was sick. He would say "the child comes first" and pretend he didn't notice the circles under her eyes or the stains on the pants she hadn't had time to change. The thought of his unexpected, uncomplicated tenderness made her want to weep.

She returned to the living room, glass of daisies in hand, to find her mother and husband sitting on the couch, Paul bouncing the baby on his knee. Her father sat a bit apart as always. Claudia switched gears midsentence: "Paul says that man is your employer. Did he give Jennifer a ring? I couldn't see."

She knew her mother wouldn't let the subject go, so she retrieved the box from her pocket, pulling out the contents—an old-fashioned, wooden top decorated with faded writing.

Claudia huffed. "Well, that's a disappointment. What kind of present is that for a one-year-old?"

"Tops are fun," Paul said. "Greenberg probably found the box in the back of a drawer. He doesn't pay attention to wrapping. He's a bottom-line guy."

"He's certainly watching his bottom line," Claudia said.

Maggie couldn't help but rise to his defense. "He said it's for the future, when Jennifer's old enough to understand what it means." Her heart heaved. "Isn't that enough? You've always said it's the thought that counts." She put the top back in the box and snapped it closed.

Without stirring in his chair, Roger said, "Respect your mother. You're a mother but you're still a daughter."

"I do respect her. But she's wrong about my boss." Tears welled in the corners of her eyes. "I'm going to turn on the coffee." She escaped to the kitchen.

Greenberg had been the closest thing to a confidante she'd had in the past months. Sarah had offered to commiserate long distance, but she talked banking, and Maggie couldn't feel her vitality over the phone. Greenberg, on the other hand, had buoyed her up with tales of his nieces and nephews. He had a funny story for every little facet of babyhood, and he never judged. More than once, she'd confessed to doubts about being a good mother. She'd told him she wanted to give Jennifer everything, if only she could figure out what she needed. Each time he'd assured her that she was good enough, which was all any baby should expect. His old-fashioned words calmed her when nothing else did.

Maggie lifted the chrome handle at one of the sinks and stared at the frothy stream. She remembered Sarah's remark about how brave she was to invite her parents to the party. She hadn't thought herself brave, just doing the right thing. Too bad insight came so late.

With a start, she realized that Paul was standing behind her. Lanky and relaxed, he leaned on the countertop next to the sink.

"Your dad sent me after you, believe it or not."

"To scold me some more?" She kept staring into the sink.

"Maggie, cool it. He's confused. You ask them to come and then you put up a wall."

"She shouldn't have criticized Greenberg."

"Come on, you make fun of him yourself."

'I'm not a bigot." She turned to face him. "And I respect him. He's been so good to Jennifer . . . and to me."

"That's not the point." His voice hardened a notch. "You wanted this party. Pull yourself together and enjoy it. I'm gonna take Jennifer to the gazebo to play."

He was right, of course. Nothing her parents had said or done would spoil the party. They weren't the problem. In truth, she was pleased they'd come. Claudia had been so angry when they had married in a courthouse—Paul didn't want to spend money on a big church wedding—that she had refused to visit for years. Maggie suspected that her mother had been less concerned about the sanctity of their union than about skipping an "appropriate" party. She'd tried to explain that a civil ceremony suited her skeptical, scientist bridegroom's temperament. But Claudia wouldn't be mollified. Jennifer's birth, thank goodness, had made things a little better between them. No, her parents weren't the problem. Paul wasn't the problem. He'd been so kind, helping her organize the tables and toys. But that tightness in his voice meant he was tired of her moping, of her inability to get it together. Whenever they talked about her funk, he said he didn't blame her; he blamed biology. She couldn't tell how much he actually resented her disarray.

The doorbell chimed its four tones. A neighbor arrived with her baby girl and five-year-old boy. The two moms had met pushing strollers around the block and they visited often, depositing their babies on the floor to play in parallel while they talked and sipped tea. Maggie introduced Laurie to her parents, and after a polite minute, she ushered Laurie's family out onto the lawn. The little boy made a beeline for the gazebo. He let out a squeal and grabbed a toy hammer from Jennifer's hand. She looked up, her face beginning to crinkle into a cry. With one hand, Paul gave her a doll; with his other arm, he corralled the boy around the waist. Maggie could see him talking to Jason but couldn't hear him. Laurie said that Paul was a natural dad and that they should have oodles more kids.

More children! How dare she think about another baby when her hold on mothering was so tenuous? But she had missed so much of the pleasure of Jennifer's infancy that she longed to try again. Paul didn't want to risk it. He understood her yearlong distemper to be hormone driven and thought it would recur. She knew what lurked behind her struggle—the hole in her diaphragm. She would love to be able to enjoy another baby the way a mother should, a baby conceived honestly.

She watched Laurie enter the gazebo and set her baby girl down next to Jennifer. Jason raised both hands to show his mother a toy wrench and screwdriver from the plastic carpenter bench that Paul had bought for the occasion. Laurie and Paul chatted and laughed as the children played. Seeing Paul maintain the peace among the kids made Maggie want to cry. He adored his daughter, even if she'd been born too soon. She couldn't thank him enough for making Jennifer happy. She promised herself to make things right for both of them, at whatever cost. Paul and Jennifer deserved all she could give.

ELEVEN

Hope Caldwell propped elbows on the lab bench and leaned forward to watch Alicia prepare a blood sample. The tops of her firm-looking breasts emerged from the scoop-necked T-shirt she wore beneath her open lab coat. Paul watched from the lab's threshold; he wondered if she was signaling to him. If so, she had balls as well as breasts. He listened as Alicia mechanically described the procedure Hope was to follow. He had bargained with Stamford, trading an advance on the grant funds for the hire. This was Friday of week one and she seemed competent enough, although she took no notes. He would have to monitor her closely; this stuff was too important to leave to a grad student. He turned on his heel.

Sandi brought the mail and another mug of black coffee to his desk. He started, not having seen her sky-blue smock in his peripheral vision; her nurse's shoes were inaudible.

"How's the princess doing?" Sandi said, placing the mug on a coaster.

"Why do you say that?"

"Because she lords it over everyone. Not you. Not yet."

He thought Sandi must have gotten her toes trod. He made it a policy to ignore staff squabbles. They sorted themselves out eventually, as long as he didn't take sides and the researchers continued to cooperate. But mutual respect was essential; Hope had better fit in.

"Do me a favor and make sure they all get bench space. Make 'em take turns if necessary. I need all their results to push this thing ahead." As he talked, he booted his computer and cleared a space on his desk.

"When are we getting a bigger lab?" It was a joke between them, her droning like a kid in a car: "Are we there yet?" She paused in the doorway. "What else do you need?"

"I need a chunk of luck. I know that result's there. I've seen it. Let's hope I've picked the quickest way to finally prove it." He was more nervous than he let on. The grant would cover eighteen months' work at the rate he wanted to spend it, and if he came up empty, he'd have a hell of a time getting more money. He had bent himself out of shape these last few years hustling funding. He was so close to achieving significance in a field where most people took tiny, incremental steps that amounted to nothing. In odd moments when his concentration waned, he fantasized standing at the speaker's podium to give the keynote address to a sea of biologists, telling them that what they were about to hear would change their lives. He would relish the surprise in their faces when he detailed a new disease process. He would spurn requests to collaborate from the multitude who would want to use his findings. Twenty-five years hence, he wouldn't have to share the Nobel Prize. "Ask Hope to come in here, would you?" He wanted to impress upon her the need for precision and professionalism. He wanted her to know his experiments were the real deal.

Sandi shook her head no ever so slightly and turned away. She left the door open. After a few moments, Hope sauntered in and stood with hands clasped behind her back, lab coat gaping. He came around to the front of the desk to look her in the eye. She was almost as tall as he in her fuck-me heels. Her jaw was too big and eyes too close together, which made her look horsey, like the Upper East Sider she was, except for the tight red pants showing off very good legs. He cleared his throat.

"Do you mind if I call you Hope? We're informal around here."

"Certainly. Shall I call you Paul?" Her face formed a question.

Okay, he thought, pretty forward for a technician. But maybe she'd taken him literally. "I noticed you didn't take any notes. You know you've got to be accurate. I'm giving you the base experiments for a giant leap forward." He folded arms across his chest.

"I've had a lot of practice handling blood samples. More than I wanted." She lowered arms to her sides. "If you like, I'll document every step I take. I read the grant proposal last night. It's an honor to work with you." She smiled into his eyes.

Damn straight, he thought, but did she really understand? He tried to read her face—nothing showed beneath her smooth, tight skin. He knew himself to be susceptible to flattery but also to have a nose for manipulation. This dame came with complications. He felt mildly aroused. "That's not necessary. But I expect you to stick to the protocol."

"Of course. I promise you'll be satisfied." She smiled

again. He could swear she was about to bat her eyelashes. "Is there anything else?"

He shook his head no. She nodded and stepped quickly through the doorway. Watching her calves ball up beneath the red Lycra with each step, he made a mental note: push her hard, wring every penny's worth of Stamford's money out of the deal. He had no time for dilettantes, good legs or no.

⤶⤷

He let himself in through the mudroom door shortly after six, as promised, to the smell of garlic sautéing in oil. The pang in his gut reminded him that he'd missed lunch—too excited about the work. The new money set him up perfectly.

Maggie stood at the kitchen sink, her back to him. He'd expected her to fuss because it was Arun's last meal with them. Going to see his folks, Jenn had said, and some other stuff that hadn't registered in Paul's consciousness. He thought Arun got around a lot for someone who lived off the charity of others. He suspected there was a hidden source of money somewhere in Arun's doings, but he didn't want to bother finding out. Jenn would drop him soon enough, if he knew his girl.

His girl. In a flash he remembered the excruciating moments when she had wormed deeper into his heart—when baby Jenny had crawled out onto the roof of their apartment building and he had to coax her back in; when the house had filled with smoke because she'd put her doll to bed in the oven; when the police had called at 3:00 a.m. to say there had been an auto accident. Her dating, on the other hand, had caused little pain. The pimply, creepy guys she brought home hadn't hung around. She'd had too much sense to fall for a lout.

In years past, when he'd imagined Jenn's future, he'd seen her in a smart suit behind a desk in Midtown, making money. Or teaching her beloved philosophy in a classy girls' school. He had brimmed with confidence for her. But her hooking up with Arun? A man with no prospects to speak of, a beggar, a poseur? She would wise up and do better.

Maggie turned to him, wiping her hands on the dish towel slung over her shoulder. "I need another few minutes in the kitchen. Please go make drinks and conversation."

"He's Indian. He doesn't drink."

"Jenn enjoys wine, at least she used to."

He grunted. Maggie's mouth pursed. He said okay and pushed through the swinging door, thinking this would be the one and only time he'd wait on Arun. The naturalized American fakir should be out of Jenn's life by Christmas, if he had to kick him out.

It was still dusky outdoors, but in the living room, lamps glowed and candles floated in bowls on the coffee table. Arun and Jenn sat on the couch, Arun in a polo shirt and khakis as if going to a barbecue, Jenn wrapped in a filmy, orange cloth that looked left over from the eighties. Paul barged in and asked if they wanted drinks. Arun declined. Paul asked if alcohol was against his religion. Arun replied no, it didn't suit his constitution. Jenn laughed and reached for his pudgy hand.

"I'll have a glass of rosé, Daddy. Mom wouldn't let us into the kitchen, so I don't know what's coming. Besides vegetables." She looked at Arun. He winked at her.

Paul poured wine for Jenn and bourbon for himself, thinking, How could she go gaga over such a mediocre specimen of manhood? Thirty-five years old and begging for a living. Flaccid limbs and a shit-eating grin. Couldn't be a good lay. Maybe Jenn couldn't tell the difference. Paul thought his daughter deserved more and better sexual experience. Then again, sex could wait. He handed her the wineglass and seated himself in the leather recliner where he used to read at night in better times.

"Jenn has told me about your project, Dr. Adler. How wonderful to make progress against cancer. I would like to hear more about it." Arun pulled Jenn's hand in his closer to his thigh.

"It's not your kind of thing. It's hard science. I deal with facts."

"I like to think that Jenn and I do too. Facts of a different kind."

"There's only one kind. Facts verified through observation and experiment."

"Yes, that's what Jenn and I rely on as well. Perhaps you remember the story of Descartes and the pope? It seems they came to an agreement. Descartes wanted permission to dissect the human body. He had to promise to say nothing about the human soul, which the pope maintained as his territory, if you will. So body and soul have been artificially separated in Western thinking ever since. In our work, in our modest way, we try to unite them." Arun returned Paul's gaze—round, brown arms protruding from his sleeves—without moving a muscle.

"Dad, we're not talking randomized clinical trials. Arun has a philosophy that we apply and then we watch what happens. You'd be amazed at the results." Jenn fixed eyes on him too.

Christ, Paul thought, that slimy guy's got her bamboozled. What else could Arun make her do, hit him up for cash for their schemes? Well, he wouldn't be conned.

Maggie appeared carrying a tray of hors d'oeuvres, her spinach and goat cheese special. Arun stood to take the tray from her while she moved candles to make space on the coffee table. Arun lowered the tray, and Jenn took two of the pastry squares and popped one in her mouth. Maggie looked pleased. "Don't let me interrupt," she said, sitting on the rug opposite her daughter, her legs in slacks folded beneath her.

"Arun was asking about Dad's work, but we got sidetracked into scientific method."

"You could get lost on that track. How about telling us about Arun's trip? I've got ten minutes until the buzzer calls me back to the kitchen." She turned to Arun with an expectant face.

Paul thought she looked like the dog in that ancient RCA commercial, sitting at the Victrola and listening for "his master's voice." He didn't want her to play lady of the manor when she should be poisoning Arun's food. The graciousness that he had found so appealing in the beginning now grated on him. He took a sip of bourbon. If Lenny were around, he'd see through Arun in a nanosecond. Maybe he should give Lenny a call.

Jenn said, "Since you're both here, we have something to ask." She folded her hands in her lap and leaned forward. "We would like you to host a wedding for us in the backyard in May, on my birthday. And in July we'll marry in Bangalore, Hindu style. We'd be honored if you came to the second wedding too." She looked at Maggie and then Paul. The floating candles lit her face from below, exaggerating the baby-fat curve of her cheeks and the hollows of her soft, hazel eyes. She waited.

Maggie spoke slowly, "I don't know what to think. It seems so sudden."

"I know what to think," Paul said.

Maggie interrupted him. "We hardly know Arun, and we don't know how to react to your plans."

"Just give us your blessing. The rest will come."

"Why the backyard? Why not All Saints'?"

"We're nondenominational," Jenn said, "and we'd like to be outdoors."

Paul drained his glass. The burn in his esophagus felt good. "I think you should do an experiment. Join the military and see what you're made of. Then come talk to me about a wedding." He couldn't sit still and listen to this nonsense. He got up to refill his glass.

Maggie said, "In a way, your father is right. You could try out your relationship before making a commitment that might be too hard to keep."

Paul stared at her from across the room. First time in a long time that she had stood up for him, albeit in a mealy-mouthed way. When they argued, what he called "mealy-mouthed" she called "diplomatic." He distrusted diplomacy, an excuse for lies.

Jenn leaned back into the cushions and said, "I know what I'm made of. You two gave me the opportunity to learn." No one spoke. Jenn rose. "Let's not spoil Mom's dinner. It smells so good. We can talk later."

Queasiness crept from the pit of Paul's stomach to his gorge. He swallowed, trying not to think about how limited his capacity for booze had become with age. His intolerance to alcohol, his aching arches, gray hair at the temples—all signs he didn't want to see. He'd eat Maggie's dinner, indigestion be damned. No one else should sit at the head of his table. He felt ambushed and more than a little pissed off.

During the meal, Arun told stories about his childhood. Maggie asked polite little questions here and there, and Jenn egged him on. She acted like a kid fascinated with a new toy. Arun caught the softballs she lobbed him and ran the bases. What a show! Impatient to be set free, Paul poured drink after drink.

cⵐ Ꮐⵜ

He flicked on the light switch in his office at the lab, and the fluorescent glare made him cringe. Too much bourbon last night, and not enough sleep—his roiling gut had waked him every hour. As usual, Maggie had slept through his tossing and farting. At six, he had given up and gotten dressed to drive into the city. The lab would be quiet on a Saturday, and he wouldn't have to see Jenn fawn over the fakir. He'd busy himself with work until Arun left. Then he'd go home and fix it with his girl.

He booted the computer and went looking for a clean cup. Alicia had left a magazine open on her desk. His eye caught on a picture of a bulbous green cloud enveloping a spiny yellow blob at the end of a red string of knobs floating in a turquoise surround. The caption read "Image from animated visualization of human mitochondria," produced at a Harvard laboratory. He doubted that seeing molecular-level simulations helped the Harvard biologists discover anything. What he could do with a fraction of the money they spent on toys!

On the cabinet behind Sandi's desk, he found a tray of coffee-making things. He filled one of the cups at the watercooler and drank. The last time booze had made him feel this sick was when the hospital threw a party to celebrate the opening of the new wing. They'd told him he could keep lab space in the old building on a permanent basis, and he had celebrated hard with the research team, most of them at least ten years his junior. It had been great fun; he danced the samba with all of them, male and female, and poured them shots of his best bourbon, toasting all around. Irene had taken him in that night, bless her. He told Maggie he'd spent the night on Tim's couch, and she bought it. Now she might not.

Still too fuzzy to tackle numbers, he sat at his desk and opened email. As he deleted his way through the chaff, a noise came from the lab. Getting up to investigate, he found Hope Caldwell, in skintight jeans, riffling through a drawer. He said hello; she startled and faced him, looking flustered.

"I didn't expect anyone to be here," she said. "I forgot some notes I made after we talked, and I wanted to study up over the weekend."

"Go right ahead." He stood in the doorway and watched her, amused by the change in demeanor. She closed the drawer and opened the one below.

"Someone could have tossed them," she said, still burrowing. "I think Alicia doesn't like me. But I haven't done anything."

"You're breathing."

She looked up, puzzled. He leaned against the doorjamb. "Women with no confidence can't stand the sight of women who look strong. It has nothing to do with you. It's kinda like an allergic reaction. I bet you've provoked it before."

She stood up. "I think I have." She appeared to brood for a moment. "You know, I thought those irritated women were worried about their men. But you're right. They were worried about themselves. Thanks for the tip."

"I expect you to cooperate with Alicia." He wanted peace among the staff. She needed to know his expectations. She could live up to them or she could leave.

"Yes, of course. Despite her allergy." Hope closed the drawer and took a few steps toward him. "I'm so glad to be working with you." She folded arms across her chest, pushing up the juicy breasts beneath her ratty purple sweater. A sexy, young woman unmistakably coming on to him. He felt tempted, and he enjoyed it.

"See you Monday, Hope." He returned to his desk and busied himself shuffling paper while she gathered her belongings and made her way out. He felt invigorated: it was clear that she'd welcome his advances—in the right setting of course. And where would that be? Did she live alone or with a roommate? He remembered her saying something about her parents—working for them, not living with them. Pushing thirty, old enough to know her own mind about men.

Pressure built inside his chest; he released it with a long, low belch, tasting Maggie's lentils from the night before. What a sodden evening it had been. Jenn and Arun went round and round on philosophical tangents. They tried to convince him that quantum mechanics—particles blinking in and out of existence—expressed the same view of the universe as the Vedic sages. As if life could be lived at the quantum level! He disliked pseudoscience even more than politics. He had retreated to the Lair as soon as the meal ended. Jenn might have been disappointed in his reaction, but she deserved to be, acting like a dummy, attaching herself to that pitiful guy. With a jolt, he realized that only a couple of years separated Jenn and Hope Caldwell. But Hope seemed much more sophisticated, and she had better taste.

He clicked out of email and into yesterday's results, but he couldn't focus. Frustrated, he rummaged in the center drawer for his brother's latest number and punched it into the phone. Saturday morning, Lenny might be home.

Lenny boomed, "Hey there, bro. How are the test tubes treating you?"

"Tubes are good. Better than my progeny. Got a minute?"

"Sure. I'm doing well, thank you. And you?"

"Lenny, I'm serious."

"Something wrong with the lovely Jennifer?"

"She brought a guy home from India you would despise. He's not man enough for her. I can't stand to look at him."

"So she's tasting the curry, eh?"

"He spouts mumbo jumbo and she thinks he's some kind of genius."

"Too brown for you?"

"Indians are Caucasians. She wants to marry him. In our backyard, on her birthday in May. This is not like her. He's got some hold over her I need to break."

Lenny's voice lowered a notch. "Calm down. May is six months away. One thing I know about girls, they change their minds."

"Jenn's not like that."

"Sure she is. Tell her how you feel and then back off. She'll come around."

Paul's gut eased. "How do you know? When's the last time you talked to her?"

"Listen, I know girls. You've got to give her a chance to do her thing."

"Her thing is short and oily and wants to preach to poor children in India. And take her with him."

Lenny's voice lowered again. "Is he mistreating her?"

"Besides wanting to take her to India?"

"Is he slapping her around?"

"Of course not. Do you think I'd allow that?"

"Well then, you have no case. You got to let girls be girls. She's a good kid. She'll come around."

"No thanks for the advice." But he felt better. Lenny had the common touch. He could always see straight when things got rough. Even long distance.

Lenny said, "What does Maggie say? She's pretty levelheaded."

"She doesn't like him either."

"So he's a creep. Time is on your side. Jenn will come around."

"At least I won't have to look at him. He's going back to India for a while."

"And Jenny's staying home? You've got it made."

Paul grunted.

Lenny said, "Why don't I invite her to visit her uncle? I can get her cousins to show her a good time. You come too. Since I'm single again, there are things growing in my refrigerator you wouldn't believe. You might find the next penicillin."

Paul could see him grinning over the phone. You had to hand it to Lenny, master maker of lemonade.

"Can't. I'm doing the final experiments that prove my hypothesis. You'll be able to read all about it in a couple of months."

"Okay, but the offer stands. Say good-bye to Maggie for me."

Paul hung up. Lenny had soothed him. He looked at the double page on his screen, with its intricate calculations and elegant assertions. Time for some incisive work.

TWELVE

Maggie lay in bed, about to rouse herself. Next to her, Paul snuffled. During the night, the snuffle had turned into a roaring snore that had wakened her, as so often before. In the early years of the marriage, she had tried to ignore his snoring. She would roll away from him and bury one ear in her pillow. After Jenn was born and she had to fight for sleep, she stopped respecting his rest. She discovered that if she nudged his shoulder, he'd roll over and the snoring would stop. Most of the time, he didn't remember in the morning. She'd had to nudge him three times last night. She slept better the nights he didn't come home. Ironic, all those years she pined for him, and now she preferred that he stay away.

The house was quiet. Jenn and Arun lay together in Jenn's old room, filled with college memorabilia. Maggie resented the impropriety; they shouldn't have made a show of their lovemaking. He should have spent the night in the guest room. She had prepared it for him, piling her sewing machine and paraphernalia into the garage so he would have plenty of space for whatever rites he practiced. And she'd washed the curtains, put lavender under the pillows. When he'd deposited his backpack on Saturday, Arun had noticed the scent and thanked her. He seemed okay in the guest room, but last night Jenn had taken his hand and drawn him into her room. Paul hadn't notice the indiscretion. Paul complained about Arun's being pompous, not promiscuous. Paul was usually either completely right about people or dead wrong. She thought he was wrong about Arun, but she wasn't sure.

Yesterday at dinner, Arun had talked about the books his mother had made him read when he was a kid and how boring they had seemed. But he said that later they became his treasures. It would be nice to have had a mom who cared about what you read. Her own self-absorbed mother had preferred women's magazines she didn't share. Maggie, on the other hand, had taken baby Jenn to the library's reading program for years. She sighed, refusing to follow that mental thread.

What had Arun said he liked best about the old books? The language: *a thousand suns rising in the noon sky.* He'd said it made him wonder about all of creation. She wanted to know more. She was trying so hard to be objective, to learn what Arun was all about for Jenn's sake. For her own sake, really, so as not to build another barrier between herself and Jenn. The thought of Jenn's embracing Arun's religion, being swallowed up by his family, frightened her. She wanted to live in the same world as Jenn; Arun might spirit Jenn out of reach.

She pulled back the covers gently and swung her feet onto the chilly, wood floor. Paul didn't stir. The thermostat switched on the furnace at six thirty, too late for the floors to warm before her rising. She hurried into the bathroom, even colder tile under her bare feet. Slippers, she always said, were a waste of time and money. There was something life affirming about warm feet on cold tile. The dog must have thought so too. She used to sit patiently on the tile, watching Maggie's morning routine.

She hustled downstairs, picking up the newspaper at the front door, planning her Friday, the last day Arun would spend with them. She was going to make a send-off dinner. She'd look online for a vegetarian recipe that everyone could enjoy. At least the food would be good. In the kitchen, making coffee, she heard the plumbing groan overhead. Someone would descend shortly. She hoped it would be Paul. She didn't want to have to greet the others with "Did you sleep well?" or other conventional words that would ring insincere in her ears. Their hot physicality disturbed her, and her own discomfort embarrassed her. Moving toward the refrigerator, she spotted her reflection in the window. She looked angry. But she wasn't angry— she was thinking. Ellen always said that she could tell when Maggie was thinking because she scowled, even at Zumba. When she opened the door to reach for the milk, last night's dream popped into her head.

In her dream, she needs to go somewhere and orders a taxi. Two red cabs pull up outside. She goes upstairs to collect her stuff, and when she comes back down the cabs are gone. She sees another cab, also bright red, and hails it. The driver is unkempt; he pulls out his phone and starts thumbing it, shaking it, leers and says *it* doesn't work so *he* can't work and drives away. She sees a bus coming down the boulevard and jumps on. She finds a seat and the bus turns off onto a different street in a dangerous-looking slum: dark, sullen men sit on stoops; women in gaudy shirts lean out of tenement windows, showing off their bosoms and glaring at her. She gets off the bus, heads back to the boulevard, tries to call Ellen to come get her. Ellen's line is busy. The rest is fuzzy.

Maggie scrutinized the dream: bright bloodred taxis, an impossible color. Where was she going? Why couldn't she get there? Most of the time, she welcomed dreams and the coded messages they contained. This one stumped her, and she didn't have time to noodle it. They'd be coming down soon; she needed to organize breakfast. She had planned vegetarian, but last night Jenn said Arun would appreciate vegan. Paul wouldn't eat with them; he'd hurry off to work. She admired his productivity. Too bad more of it wasn't directed toward her. Since Jenn left home, she thought, we have existed in parallel. We are two steel rails without wooden ties to bind us. Now there was a third rail.

She heard fast footsteps on the stairs. Paul came into the kitchen dressed for the lab. He scanned for coffee, looking disappointed that it wasn't ready. He said he was late for the train and had to run. When she reminded him to come home early for the farewell dinner, he grunted, which she interpreted as a concession that he would. Paul took a jacket from the hall closet and closed the front door behind him.

Arun's pending departure promised to bring relief. She felt crowded out of her own house, compressed by his presence. He was terribly polite, which made him so hard to decipher. Jenn was uncharacteristically quiet around him, sitting back and letting him occupy the limelight. He deferred to Jenn often enough though. Perhaps Jenn wanted him to strut his stuff. Who was he, beneath all that philosophy and polish? She pulled the *Moosewood Cookbook* off the shelf and looked for "brunch" in the table of contents. Steps on the stairs drew her attention.

"Morning, Mom." Wearing a sweatshirt over a long, flared skirt, Jenn opened the fridge and poured orange juice into a tall glass. Her hair hung in dark, wet ringlets that had moistened the back of her top.

"You're up early."

"Mmmm. Jet lag, still." She drank half the juice and made a sour face. "You should taste the fruit in Bangalore. We buy it every day from street vendors in from the countryside. I don't haggle even though people expect you to. It's cheap enough." Jenn angled herself into the breakfast nook and sat. She ran a hand along the yellow tile wall. "I love these cracks. I used to play mind games with them when I was a kid. Can I help?"

Maggie imagined her daughter at an Indian market, holding a baby in one arm and a bag brimming with mangoes in the other, chatting with vendors who patronized the odd American woman. How could a girl with spunk and brains want to be buried alive in ancient customs? She handed Jenn the cookbook. "I'll put out some inferior fruit and bread. See if you can find a casserole for dinner that Arun would eat and your father would tolerate. I'll go shopping lunchtime when I pick up my car."

"Already fixed? That didn't take long." Jenn leafed through the cookbook.

The dealership had called two days earlier, but Maggie had waited, deciding whether or not to take up Brian Sayler's offer of help. He had called three times since the accident. She'd ignored the first two, but yesterday she decided to speak to him. He repeated his offer to check out her car repair. She accepted. She wanted someone neutral, and younger, to talk to about Jenn. Robert and his Indian doctor friend had been no help.

⤾ ⤿

They sat in a diner not far from the Toyota dealer. Brian munched potato chips left over from lunch, and Maggie watched his strong-looking hands move. The grimy hands of a man who worked with his hands. There was paint on his jeans and the tips of his work boots, but he seemed un-selfconscious about the stains. He had an ordinary, clean-shaven face with ordinary brown hair. His body was lean and tight; he appeared to have all the time in the world, munching and waiting for her to speak.

He'd met her at the dealership as agreed and inspected her Prius. He'd okayed the repair job and suggested they go for a sandwich before he had to get back to work. Reno-vating a porch, he'd said, no big deal. She'd turned in the rental and driven to the diner he'd selected, parked next to his van. They ordered, and while they ate their sandwiches, she asked about his work. He answered her questions with a minimum of words. He said the job wasn't important; he had other interests. Then he asked why had she really called. It took her a moment to reply.

"I want to know how your generation thinks about things. My daughter is dating a thirtysomething-year-old Indian guru, and it's giving me the creeps. He's from India, but he went to school here. He wants her to follow him around India while he ministers to people, and she wants to do it. As if all the progress women have made since the 1960s never happened."

Brian picked up another potato chip." How old is your daughter?"

"Twenty-five."

"Are you paying her rent?"

"She's been independent since college."

"Forget about it. She's on her own."

Maggie would not be dismissed. "Tell me what's going on. Is there some kind of nostalgia movement? Or do they all want to go to China or India because Europe is old hat?"

"Beats me. Never did travel." He paused. "I don't think there's a 'they' anymore. People are different. There are a lot of options."

"My daughter's in danger of taking the wrong one."

"Nope. You're the one in danger." He picked up the last chip between his first two fingers, like a cigarette, and held it in front of his mouth.

"What do you mean?" She felt her chest tense.

"You're in danger of blowing the hour. We could be getting to know each other in the way that really counts." He offered her the chip, holding it near her lips.

Here it was, the invitation she'd thought would come. Could she imagine herself in bed with this man with dirty hands? A lean, hard, younger man whose only interest was sex. Straightforward. Potent. So different from Robert, who stirred no desire. She remembered the best times with Paul, when they longed for each other, before Jenny changed her. If she slept with this guy, would she feel the way she used to? For years she had brushed aside thoughts of an affair out of respect for Paul and in hopes that their intimacy would return. But Paul had not held their marriage sacred. Why not break an obsolete vow?

She pulled back, embarrassed at sending mixed messages

to this man who wanted her. She took the potato chip from his fingers and set it on her empty plate. "Thank you, but another time. I have a vegetarian banquet to cook." She put a ten-dollar bill on the table and rose to leave. "That should cover my meal. Thanks for helping me with the car."

"Call me next time you want to talk," he said, fishing his wallet out of his jeans. Evidently her retreat hadn't ruffled him.

She drove the Prius to the supermarket mechanically. Brown rice, onion, garlic, tomato; enough to make a pilaf for dinner and tomorrow's lunch, anything else that looked good. She couldn't really plan. Her mind felt wobbly, bouncing from her pantry to Brian to Jenn to conversation with Arun. Last night Arun had said something that resonated; he'd said that the goal of his work was to help children become the fullest versions of themselves rather than some ideal version of a child. Could the fullest version of herself include accepting a man like Brian Sayler? Or would yielding to him betray everything she had struggled to accomplish for her family? She could not banish her unwelcome desire to see him again.

∽◉ ◉∾

She stood at the sink, sleeves pushed up and hands in soapy water washing wineglasses while Jenn and Arun finished clearing the table. After Jenn had asked for a wedding, the dinner conversation had been polite enough; Jenn and Arun described some of the work they had done and the places they had visited during the year, and Maggie did her part, of course, asking questions about the sights they had seen. Paul glowered silently throughout the meal.

After dessert, still sulking, he took a glass of bourbon to the basement.

"Mom, please sit with us. I'll finish the dishes later."

She turned to find Jenn and Arun standing at the breakfast nook. Wiping her hands on the dish towel, she joined them, and they sat.

"Mrs. Adler, Jenn has suggested that I prevail upon you," Arun said. "I hope that I may speak frankly."

She nodded.

"It appears that I have offended your husband. Naturally, he is concerned about Jenn's welfare. I would like to discuss our plans in detail so he can see that Jenn will be well cared for and that I have the deepest regard for your family. But he does not permit me."

Maggie looked down at her hands. She rubbed the hard, dry stretch of skin on her right index finger that no amount of lotion could restore. "My husband has always had to work hard. He's never taken time to travel. He gets impatient with privileged people. Perhaps some of that's going on." She refused to look at Jenn. She didn't want to represent Paul or defend him.

Jenn said, "He's not being fair. We're not exploiting privilege, we're fighting it."

"I think you should take it up with your father." She rose and moved toward the hallway. "You can use my car tomorrow. It should take about an hour to get to the airport."

"Thank you, Mrs. Adler," Arun said. "I appreciate the advice. I will endeavor to be more careful when I speak with your husband in the future."

As Maggie climbed the stairs, she heard voices murmur over the clang of pots and the slosh of water as Arun and Jenn finished the cleanup. She did not attempt to eavesdrop. In her bedroom, she sat in the old rocking chair at the bay window without turning on the light. How many hours had she spent in this chair nurturing her child or examining her feelings with Paul away somewhere? She would push with one foot, rocking slowly, watching the flickering shadows of leaves on the trees outside. Ellen called it meditation; she called it woolgathering because it didn't make her serene. Like tonight.

She felt defeated. She had been so patient with her daughter, encouraging her to follow her interests and explore life. Music lessons. A string of volunteer jobs. That summer in California with Sarah. Sophomore year abroad. Now Jenn had made up her mind to follow a bizarre man to the third world. Good-bye freedom, good-bye opportunity. Young women could do anything these days, not like when she was an adolescent and feminism felt new. She pushed herself up out of the chair and stepped to the bathroom. She turned on the faucets. Waiting for the water to warm, she told herself that she had best make her peace with the coming wedding. Jenn went her own way.

THIRTEEN

P aul opened the "current" file and clicked over to Alicia's notes. He liked to check her progress when no one was around. Tim didn't write up his experiments regularly, and C. K. couldn't string together five clear English sentences, so he monitored them verbally. Alicia's reporting, on the other hand, was methodical and consistent. He opened the entry, made the day before, summarizing her week's work. She had laid out the logic of the experiments as directed but shied away from the conclusions. Always too cautious. He'd fix it Monday. He needed her answers in order to take the next step, the one for which Hope's tasks would lay the baseline.

Hope. Her appearance at the lab that morning had tickled him. She'd said she was looking for notes. Probably out to impress him. He was impressed, all right—by her strong legs in skintight jeans. He wondered if she wanted to fuck him. The others wouldn't notice a liaison, and if they did, they wouldn't care. Least of all Alicia, nicknamed Alice in Autoland by the guys because they thought she worked like a machine. They didn't see how malleable she actually was, and how valuable. He counted on her doggedness to push the principal line of inquiry ahead and on her submissiveness to make it come out the way it should.

His cell phone rang and he clicked out of the file. It was Jenn, calling from the airport after dropping Arun off. She asked to meet for lunch since she was practically in the city. He suggested Zabar's, thinking a greasy corn muffin would settle his gut. He wanted to take the subway to Columbus Circle and walk the rest of the way. It was a fine day, and half an hour's walk would clear the hangover. Jenn needed talking to sooner rather than later.

⁂

In deference to Jenn's sore ankle, they sat on a bench in Central Park, sipping coffee from Zabar's take-out cups. It was unseasonably warm and the park was crawling with people, jackets slung over their shoulders or hanging from one crooked finger. Dogs off leash flashed past them. Joggers with plugged-up ears trotted by. He nibbled a crumb left over from his muffin; he felt better.

"I do love New York," Jenn said. "You can't sit in a park in Delhi without drama. Someone solicits you, someone harangues someone next to you, or a scooter whizzes past your feet. It's like here but concentrated. Like frozen orange juice before you dilute it."

"This is supposed to make me feel better about India?"

Jenn laughed. "Yes. Look there!" She nodded toward a couple walking by, speaking a voluble Spanish, followed by a string of eight children in size order with successively lighter complexions. "Is that genetics in action or socialization? Or is it just New York, where people from anywhere get a new life?"

"No speculating without evidence." He used to answer her little girl's questions with that line whenever they reached the imponderable. He used to be so proud of her ability to follow the logic of any argument. Even at age eight, she could categorize the differences between mushrooms and green plants. When she decided to study philosophy in college, he had approved. Maybe he should have steered her toward something less theoretical.

Jenn turned and looked him in the eye. "Arun will be gone for a while. He's meeting with microfinance people who want us to work with them. Then he's going to see his parents. He'll be back in the spring, for the wedding." She set her jaw and pursed her lips, an awful gesture she had learned from her mother.

"What's microfinance?"

"Lending poor people a tiny bit of money so they can start a business and get a leg up. Mostly women, which is why I like it. They pay it back."

"Where will you get the money?"

"The microfinance organization will take care of the money. We'll take care of the soul."

"This is getting more and more preposterous."

"Microfinance isn't preposterous. It's all over the world, and the Bangladeshi who started it got the Nobel Prize in 2006."

"What does that have to do with you?"

"Everything. I see that you can make change at the grass roots. In fact, you have to. The politicians accomplish nothing except hold onto power and hold people back. Arun and I can do better."

He couldn't contain his disgust. "I'm not going to tell you how to live your life, but I am going to tell you you're making a mistake. This is not the guy for you. Any thirty-five-year-old man worth his salt would have a career by now. You can't live on pipe dreams."

"Dad," she said coldly, "we spent the last year testing Arun's vision. You haven't given him a chance to explain. And he's thirty-one."

"He's explained enough. I get it. He wants other people to pay for his lifestyle. He wants you to pay too."

"Other people pay for your research."

"I work my ass off to get peer-reviewed grants. Apples and oranges, kiddo. The point is, why should you start out with a burden? Life's tough enough."

"Yes, it is, which is why I want to share it with Arun. He's the most compassionate, intelligent person I know." She stared at him, as if daring him to contradict her. "You have no idea."

"So tell me."

She sighed. "The guys I dated in college were childish. The guys I dated in Brooklyn had more going on, but it was all about them. Arun is different. He's ambitious, but it's for something bigger than himself. He's smart and humble."

"And humorless. You want to live with that?"

"He makes me laugh all the time! He's trying to impress you and Mom that he's serious about our future together."

"How did he sell you on becoming Mother Teresa?"

"He didn't sell me on anything. He didn't chase me at all." The tone of her voice changed, as if explaining to a child. "One day I watched him talking with this woman in her house. It had a dirt floor and walls made out of black plastic stretched between poles. They were talking seriously, and he saluted her. When he came out of the hovel, his eyes were flashing. He said he had just learned that the woman's brother was in jail and had somehow heard a rumor that someone was going to rob the microfinance group she was part of. The brother managed to make a phone call to the telephone lady in the village, telling her to warn his sister, who warned Arun, who alerted the group leader. Do you see how important that phone call was? Arun says there's no better measure of how much the group and our work meant to the woman and her community."

Paul harrumphed.

"Once I saw how good Arun was with people, I went after *him*. It took him a while to turn on to me. Indian men are a lot more emotional than Americans, but Arun kept his distance. He was concentrating on the work."

"It's an act, kiddo, to get into your pants and my wallet."

"I can't believe you said that. You must think I'm an idiot."

"No, inexperienced. Maybe you should look around some more."

"For what? Someone with a job you approve of who'll cheat on me at the first opportunity?"

Paul felt slapped. "What are you getting at?"

"Come on, Dad. You know you're not qualified to give relationship advice."

"What has your mother been saying?"

"Mom doesn't talk about personal things. But I know. There's been plenty of evidence over the years."

He wanted to challenge her facts, but he didn't trust himself to stay cool.

"Your mother and I have an understanding."

"Maybe so. Look, you know I admire you and love

you, but I won't let you lecture me about something where you haven't a clue." She stood. "I have to take Mom's car back. Should I tell her to expect you for dinner?"

"I'll call. Depends on what I find back at the lab."

Jenn pecked him on the forehead. "Thanks for the coffee." She headed toward Central Park West, stepping gingerly.

He raised the rim of the cup to his lips, tasting the cardboard as well as the brew. He was angry; Jenn had played offense as her defense. He wasn't going to let her get away with it. She needed to hear the truth about lover boy, and it was up to him to tell it. That evening. Tossing the cup into the trash bin, he rose and took out his phone. Irene just might be home on a Saturday afternoon, and her place was on the way back to the lab. No romantic, she would agree with him. Her machine answered; he left no message.

✦

He pushed through the mudroom door, a basket of fruit under his arm, expecting to see Maggie in the kitchen. He'd picked up the fruit on the way home to show her that he appreciated the fancy farewell dinner she'd made the night before, despite his behavior. As the last of the day's light played across the dim yellow walls of the empty room, he deposited the basket on the counter next to the sink and went to look for her. He found her upstairs, sitting at her desk in the dusk, bent over some paperwork.

"Want to go out for dinner tonight? You could use a break." He leaned against the wall beside the desk.

"Jenn's cooking. My spice cabinet may never recover." Maggie looked up, pen in hand. "She went to the supermarket to pick up fish. I think she's thanking me for a week of vegetarian meals."

"Want me to switch on a lamp?"

"No. It's time to stop." She put down the pen. "Jenn said she met you in the city and you'd probably be home for dinner. She's clairvoyant." She swiveled her chair to face him. "What's going on with you two?"

He bristled, resenting the implication that he and Jenn could converse as equals. Jenn was his daughter, dammit, and he could school her if he wanted to. He'd always refused to pussyfoot around other people's sensibilities—he knew his mind and didn't care what anyone else thought.

"She wanted to talk about the wedding she thinks she's having. What have you been telling her about our marriage?"

Maggie looked surprised. "I haven't said anything. We haven't had a chance to talk yet."

He felt a little calmer; Jenn was just fishing, clever girl. "I'm trying to show her what a loser he is. She's resisting me."

"What does our marriage have to do with it?"

"She's our daughter. We need to stop her now, before she gets the wedding bit between her teeth."

Maggie spoke slowly. "You're taking the wrong tack. He's not a loser. Not to her. Maybe not at all. But she shouldn't marry him."

Jesus, Mary, and Joseph, he thought, count on Maggie to split hairs. In their early years together, he'd been grateful for the way she'd analyze situations and help him understand the angles he was too busy or too hurried to see. She'd been his secret weapon at the university, talking him through his frustrations and charming his competition. But he'd learned the angles and had outgrown her help. Except when it came to Jenn. Maggie had been able to predict her behavior better than he could, so he listened. "Tell me what tack you think I should take."

Maggie got up and walked to the window. She lowered the blinds and switched on the overhead light. It cast unflattering shadows on her tired-looking face. She said, "I've been thinking. There's nothing to do about her affection for Arun."

"I don't get it."

"We need to find her an alternative. A person or a cause or both—on this continent. She needs to know she can lead the kind of life she wants without turning her back on her culture. I'm going to talk to Reverend Stevens."

He groaned. "You're not going to find anyone attractive in that shop."

"No, but he might have some ideas." She crossed arms over her chest. She had that righteous look. He willed himself silent.

"We have a couple of months until Arun comes back to the U.S. Will you go along with me?" Now her face was pleading. She looked prettier, vulnerable.

"Don't you see what a loser he is?"

"He's not your kind of guy. Jenn knows that. She'll discount whatever you say."

His gorge rose; everything about that inferior man angered him. But Maggie understood Jenn in some underground, female way. "What do you want me to do?"

"Back off. Let her get situated, make new friends. Her apartment's sublet, so she'll stay with us."

"Should I try to get her a temp job at the hospital?"

"She won't want to commute. I'll help her find something local."

He weighed his alternatives. "Okay. I'll shut up. For a little while."

Maggie rose and laid her hand on his arm. "Thank you. Let's go down. She'll be home momentarily."

He followed Maggie down the stairs, recalling the times in past decades when they'd taken on a life project together and gotten results. She'd coached him through his thesis, found the cheapest house in one of the best neighborhoods, helped him set up the lab—she had patience for personnel issues—and had taken care of hospital politics. Together they got Jenn through school when she threatened to drop out. Maybe they could be a team again. This one time.

It wouldn't hurt to throw her a bone, let her handle Jenn and talk about weddings. He'd be free to focus on work now that everything was about to boil.

It was full dark in the living room. He switched on the lamps while Maggie fussed in the kitchen. As he contemplated a bourbon, Jenn bustled through the front door, shopping bags in hands. The yellow scarf bunched around her neck made her eyes glow like a cat at night. She smiled broadly at her father, as if she had been anticipating meeting him at that very spot. She thrust one of the bags at him and limped to the kitchen. He followed, swallowing the comment he wanted to make. This was now Maggie's show.

Unpacking a bag made of recycled pop bottles, Jenn waved a paper-wrapped package in front of her mother, saying what a lovely piece of fish she had found and how much they were going to enjoy the curry. Maggie offered to help cook, and the two women began to spread ingredients on the countertop. He bowed out, retreating to the living room. He decided to spare his gut the bourbon and headed downstairs.

He sat at the old table he used as a desk and switched on the lamp and the computer. Glancing down, he noticed the scars in the surface of the wood that Jenn's soldering had left a decade ago: concave, dark brown spots and fine cracks filled with residual dirt. He had helped her make jewelry from discarded silicon chips and then sell it. She never turned a profit, but she learned how to handle money. It was fun. They'd spent so many hours together in the Lair, she working on projects, he on his science. And Maggie had cheered them on. Maggie, who had been sweet and supple and sexy back then. In those happier days, it was easy to be the father he wanted to be, and Jenn adored him for it. Then Jenn rebelled, and Maggie sulked and wrinkled, and his research grew more demanding. Somehow he'd taken his eye off the ball. He was proud of the fact that Jenn had grown up with everything it takes to lead an exemplary life: smarts, chutzpah, education, opportunity—more than he'd had. Yet here she was, preyed on by a leech of a man. He wanted to excise the leech, like cutting out a malignancy. He wanted every cell gone with no damage to the host. He wanted Maggie to get his girl back for him; she was good at getting things done.

He clicked on Outlook and waited for email to open, consciously switching focus to the problem he'd found that morning at the lab in Alicia's notes. Breast cancer was Alicia's specialty; he'd asked her to quantify the prevalence in breast cancer tissue of the variant biochemical he'd identified in brain tumors. Her findings thus far were not significant, and the evidence of the chemical's activity was ambiguous. If she could show unequivocally that his discovery applied equally to another tumor type, he'd be able to confirm—and announce—the intellectual leap he'd been preparing these past years. If their work under the new grant didn't produce though, his window of opportunity would slam shut. Waiting for email to populate, he decided to intervene in Alicia's experiments. He'd use every bit of his experience to restructure them, and he knew he'd get the results needed. Plus, in Hope he had an extra pair of hands.

He logged out of email and closed the laptop. Nothing to do until Monday. Rising and stretching, careful not to hit the overhead light fixture, he felt a twinge of hunger in his empty gut. Time to replenish. A bourbon now would taste good. Just one, since he might get lucky later. Maggie had looked so grateful a little while ago. Switching off the lamp, he took the stairs two at a time.

FOURTEEN

The event that rocked the Adlers' marriage happened the spring when Jenn turned seventeen. Maggie had sensed something wrong with her daughter a few weeks before her birthday. She began to withdraw to her room after school and stopped seeing friends. When Maggie had asked her to explain, she'd clammed up and stayed clammed up. Then, Jenn's favorite English teacher called to say that she had failed to turn in a major assignment. Maggie grew impatient and pressed; Jenn burst into tears and confessed that she'd been raped while on a date, but she refused to say by whom or how it came about. At first Maggie panicked and grounded Jenn. When Paul came home after work and Maggie told him, he turned ashen. He stormed out of the house in search of the morning-after pill. When later they determined she wasn't pregnant and didn't have a sexually transmitted disease, he hugged Jenn and said life could return to normal.

But it didn't.

For a week after the confession, Jenn didn't come to the table, descending to the kitchen for peanut butter and crackers only when she thought her mother would be absent. But Maggie waited, offering to make her beloved grilled cheese sandwiches, begging her to talk. When Maggie told Paul how worried she was, he told her to leave Jenn alone; she'd eat when her biology told her to. So they began to fight, Maggie insisting they do something, Paul saying let nature take its course.

Maggie couldn't wait. She called the school counselor and, without mentioning specifics, asked for a referral to a shrink. The woman advised her to take Jenn to a Park Avenue specialist for a psychiatric evaluation. Paul rejected the idea, saying, "Why attach a stigma to the natural healing process?" Maggie replied that she didn't want to find herself six months later wondering if she could have done something to head off disaster. Paul said, "Why imagine the worst?" Maggie replied that many teenagers committed suicide for less. Paul said that maybe she wouldn't talk because she had egged the kid on; Maggie was appalled at the suggestion. They took the fight to bed with them every night for a week, arguing for hours until one or the other wanted sleep and called a truce. Then she unilaterally made an appointment with the specialist. She drove Jenn into the city to see her after school.

Driving home on the Cross Bronx Expressway, a deep scar across a poor part of the borough made more desolate by the highway itself, Maggie watched Jenn from the corner of her eye. Jenn sat slouched and sulky, toying with Chinese worry beads in her lap. She'd been silent for the past half hour.

"So what did she say?" Jenn asked without looking up.

"She said it would be good for you to find someone to talk to closer to home, and she gave me a few names."

"Useless."

"She said you've suffered a trauma and you need to get it out."

"Jargon."

"She also said you'll be fine because you're smart and sensible, but it takes time and it would happen more quickly with support from someone other than just Dad and me."

"Right on that score." Jenn turned her face away, as if interested in the dirty brick wall that bounded the highway.

Maggie took the exit for the Hutchinson River Parkway, and they wound their way beneath overhanging branches tipped in chartreuse, alongside purple-flowering hedges, in silence. Jenn's seventeenth birthday would come in a week, but there would be no party because Jenn said she didn't want to talk to anyone. Maggie would leave the lilacs on their bushes this year.

She parked the car in the driveway and unlocked the mudroom door. Jenn went straight upstairs. In the kitchen, Maggie opened the fridge to look for something to cook that might tempt her daughter. Nothing called out to her. She shut the fridge door. The shrink had diagnosed post-traumatic stress and recommended six months of therapy. Maggie felt vindicated but unhappy.

The phone rang: her mother, wanting to know what to send Jenny for her birthday. Claudia insisted on saying "Jenny," although she'd been asked innumerable times to use the grown-up nickname her granddaughter preferred. Claudia always responded with "Yes, fine" and kept saying "Jenny," as if she didn't hear or, more likely, didn't care to hear. Maggie told her mother to send a gift card for books and hung up as soon as she decently could. Maggie had not told her mother about Jenn's rape. Such things didn't happen on Claudia's watch. Claudia had held a tight rein as a parent and objected to the supposed indulgence with which Jenn had been raised. She would have held Maggie responsible for the sordid mess, a thought Maggie couldn't bear.

Posttraumatic stress—same as the soldiers in the Middle East? Maggie descended to the Lair to Google, hoping to find a clue to restoring Jenn's appetite and curing her melancholy. The search confused her: PTSD, posttraumatic stress, acute stress syndrome. Wikipedia said people in acute stress don't always proceed to trauma, which is diagnosed after thirty days of decreased functioning. Had it been thirty days since the rape? Could she trust Wikipedia? Could the shrink be overreaching? Wikipedia recommended therapy for both posttraumatic stress and acute stress syndrome. She decided to phone the therapists whose names she'd been given, to take the next helping step first thing in the morning.

She kept searching, following the embedded links: date rape, trauma, genetic factors in predisposition to violence, cognitive behavioral therapy. She thought about all the pasty kids Jenn had brought home over the years. Had she been wrong to assume high school held little danger for a girl as feisty and capable as her daughter? Should she have gone back to working only mornings, like when Jenn was little, and monitored Jenn's social life? Jenn would have hated being scrutinized, and they would have fought. Would it have been better to piss her off? Maggie had given Jenn breathing room to encourage communication between them. Fat lot of good it had done. Jenn still refused to discuss the details.

She heard commotion overhead and climbed the stairs. Paul stood in the fading light from the mudroom windows, briefcase in hand.

Maggie blurted, "We went into the city to see that shrink the school recommended. She said Jenn has posttraumatic stress and she needs counseling because you and I are too close to her and we'd muck it up."

"When you ask a surgeon, he's gonna say cut."

She grew testy. "Just listen. I want to find a therapist, in Pelham if possible. Don't pooh-pooh it, and if you can't be encouraging because it's against your laissez-faire principles, don't get in the way."

She rose and entered the kitchen.

He followed.

"Not fair, Maggie. I said I don't want Jenn to feel like a freak. I don't want her to feel guilty for whatever happened with that boy." He thought for a moment. "What did Jenn say about that shrink?"

"Have you talked to her lately? Does she acknowledge you? If so, you're a better man than I am, Gunga Din." She turned away to hide unbidden tears of frustration. "How is she supposed to know what's right in her state?"

He growled, "How do you know what's right in yours? Will you get off the therapy kick? Waste of time and money."

"Since when are you an expert at emotions? You haven't been good at understanding mine."

The dog bounded into the room; Jenn stood on the kitchen threshold, leash in hand. "Stop it. Stop talking about me."

"How much have you overheard?" Maggie said.

"You don't know anything."

Paul said, "That's the problem."

"It's my life. I'd rather talk to a shrink than either of you." She grabbed a banana from the basket on the counter and fled.

Maggie glared at Paul.

He called the dog to follow him down into the Lair.

Maggie searched her purse for the paper on which the specialist had written therapists' names and addresses. She found the map of Westchester County and sat at the table to pinpoint their locations. Lips pursed in concentration, she determined to find the best therapist within an hour's drive for her sad little girl.

❧ ❧

Three weeks into therapy—twice a week for forty-five minutes, with Maggie sitting in the tiny waiting room trying to read—Jenn announced that she wanted to go away for the summer. She wanted to go where she didn't have to answer questions. She wanted to go to California and relax on the beach. She said her therapist thought it was a good idea and offered to hold sessions by phone, and Aunt Sarah said she could come. Maggie was incensed.

"Why didn't you tell me you called Sarah?"

Jenn sat on the banquette in the kitchen, passing bits of cheese to the Labrador at her feet. She was eating now, selectively. "Because it was my idea, and you would have said no."

"I can still say no."

"Please, Mom, let me go. Aunt Sarah said I could work at the bank, and we'll go snorkeling on Catalina when she has time off."

"She's a workaholic. I don't think she knows how to watch over you."

"I don't need watching over! That's why I want to go!" Jenn appeared on the verge of tears.

Maggie softened. Then anger suffused her. "What about summer school?"

"I can do extra-credit assignments. I promise I'll pass."

"I'm going to call Sarah." She picked up her purse and hurried into the living room, feeling petulant, and foolish for being petulant, angry at Jenn and Sarah for conspiring against her. She sat on the couch and poked her cell phone. Sarah came on the line with her banker-lady voice, asked Maggie to wait a minute while she cleared out her office and shut the door. She came back on, saying that Maggie had her full attention.

The words burst out. "Why are you making plans with my daughter without talking to me first? This is a delicate time for this family, and you don't know what's going on."

"You mean about the date rape and the therapy? Jenn gave me a pretty thorough account."

So Jenn had confided in Sarah when she wouldn't talk to her own mother. She could feel her cheeks start to burn. "You should have called. I'm her mother. I need to make the decisions."

"Jenn said her therapist approved of the visit. I assumed you did too."

So Sarah hadn't betrayed her; shame welled up and flushed some of the anger. "What makes you think you can care for her? You're so wrapped up in your bank. She can't tool around LA all day waiting for you to come home with a take-out meal." Sarah had never nursed anyone—no child, no parent, no lover, no one. How could she succor Jenn?

"I'll overlook that statement. I wouldn't have invited her if I didn't think I could do right by her. You need to take a deep breath."

Right. Sarah's not the enemy. Who was? The kid who stuck his adolescent dick into Jenn? "Oh Sarah, I'm so worried I could scream . . . "

"Go ahead. I can take it."

Maggie felt the tears coming. "I could quit work and come to LA. She's the most important thing in my life. I can't turn my back on her," she sobbed, "even if she's angry at me." Claudia had always been angry. Claudia had spurned her little girl. When Maggie came home with a high fever to an empty house, Claudia stayed at her bridge game until the session ended.

Sarah spoke softly. "You're not turning your back. Jenn wants to take a positive step for herself. You raised her to be independent. Let her follow your lead."

She felt herself clinging to Sarah's confidence, a buoy in a sea of doubt. She stopped sobbing.

"Maggie, are you there?"

"I'm sorry, I can't think straight. Let me talk to Paul tonight. I'll call you tomorrow." She ended the call, suddenly aware that Jenn waited in the kitchen. She wiped her cheeks with her hands. She would promise Jenn an answer about California tomorrow, for sure.

⋐⊚ ⊚⋑

She sat in semidarkness at the dining room table waiting for Paul. He'd missed dinner, said something got screwed up at the lab. She stared at the plate with the now cold chicken leg sitting atop a mound of pilaf. Jenn had eaten most of the meal at the table with her, and everything would have been normal, almost, if Paul had come home. She rehearsed what she wanted to say yet another time.

A car crunched gravel in the driveway, door slammed, footsteps in the mudroom and through the kitchen. She rose and turned on the dining room light. Paul approached, looking disheveled.

"Sorry. Couldn't be helped. Looks good." He sat at the place she had set for him and picked up knife and fork. He never washed the lab off his hands before a meal, although he knew it made her feel squeamish.

"You should have come home. Jenn ate a real meal." This was not how she had planned to start the conversation, but his indifference annoyed her. She took a deep breath.

"Jenn has been talking to Sarah. She wants to spend the summer in California, and Sarah said yes."

"Good for Jenn. Change of scenery will do her more good than sitting on a couch complaining." He loaded the fork; it went zing as his teeth scraped off the food. He chewed hard and prepared another mouthful.

"How can you be so arrogant? Haven't you noticed therapy's making her better?"

"Maybe she's getting better on her own. Healing is built into the system. Maggie, I'm tired, I don't want to argue."

"And I don't want a biology lesson." She got up and walked into the dark living room. She leaned against the mantelpiece and absently fingered the soapstone talisman Sarah had sent from a business trip to the Pacific Northwest. She would tell Jenn yes; she could go to California if she passed all her classes and continued therapy. Not because her father approved of the trip but because her mother honored her desires. Because her mother paid attention to her heart as well as her mind and body.

That night, in the hours she was able to sleep, with Paul oblivious beside her, she dreamed again about finals week at college. She had forgotten to study and misplaced her books, and no one would answer her questions about where to take the test, and a lake appeared between the buildings and so on and so on, one obstacle after another. Waking, she recognized the state of mind her dream reflected: guilty, afraid of not meeting her obligations. She would beat back the dream. Above all else, she would keep Jenn safe.

Paul snorted and rolled toward her. She suppressed the urge to shake him. Why was he being such a damn know-it-all about therapy? He had no precious data from which to extrapolate, and no expertise. He acted as if no opinion mattered but his. In this arena, he was inadequate. He deeply disappointed her. She felt a coolness toward him spread from her head to her heart. She turned away from him and closed her eyes.

⤷⊙ ⊙⤶

Jenn came home from California slightly tanned and calm. She resumed her schoolwork without a hiccup. After another couple of months, she began bringing friends home for grilled cheese sandwiches and music in her room. In January, the shrink told her "Good-bye and you can always call me if you need me." It turned out that Jenn didn't need the shrink anymore; nor did she talk about her recovery with her parents. Maggie stopped inquiring, reluctantly. Paul treated Jenn "business as usual."

But everyone had changed; each had moved one degree away from the others. Maggie tried to restore harmony to the household. Until Jenn left for college, she cooked lovely dinners for the three of them, on the nights Paul came home, so they could communicate. But she could not bridge the gap that had emerged between herself and Paul, to which his increased absences contributed. Goodness knows she had tried.

FIFTEEN

The summer Jenn spent in California, Paul reacted badly. At first, he wanted to kill the kid who had raped his daughter. Then, since no permanent damage had been done, he insisted that she be left alone to heal. He said that he didn't want a shrink filling her head with doubts. In truth, he felt powerless to help, clumsy in the face of her silence, afraid his anger would alienate her. And Maggie's constant carping pissed him off.

All summer he phoned Jenn once a week—from the office, because he didn't want Maggie to see how unsatisfactory the conversations were. Each time he'd ask a question, he could practically see Jenn roll her eyes. She'd say she was fine, but her voice was flat: data-entry work was okay; the beach was okay the couple of times Sarah took her; Sarah was okay because she left Jenn alone. Her voice brightened when she mentioned her shrink; they were talking twice a week. No, she did not want her parents to visit; yes, she'd be home before Labor Day to get ready for school.

Bye, Dad. He supposed this was par for the course, but he would've preferred to hear more words, friendlier words.

He phoned at eleven in New York, eight in Los Angeles, to catch them before they left for the bank—crazy Sarah had actually come through with a summer job. He wondered if Jenn could see how nutty Aunt Sarah was. Usually Jenn could read people like a pro, but maybe not now. He told himself to be grateful that Sarah had taken Jenn in and that, so far, they were getting along. But he missed Jenn's sparkle, and he resented Maggie's gloom.

One day after the eleven o'clock call, he decided he had time enough before lunch to read an article on prostate cancer imaging in the latest *Science*. Might have nothing to do with his work; might connect somehow later on. There were too many journals to read, so he'd divided them among the junior researchers in his lab, asking them to report on anything connected to their various projects. He wanted to scoop up any bit of information that might advance the research, and he wanted to know if anyone, anywhere, was closing in on the idea he'd been pursuing for the past decade. Of course he had to keep up with discoveries in genetics and immunology as well as his own field, but it made him antsy. He wanted to turn over all the stones necessary to stay ahead of the cancer biology curve.

The journals those days talked about developing vaccines against cancer and HIV, hyperactivating the body's immune system against the pathogen so that the disease couldn't progress. He thought vaccine research would go nowhere fast because the AIDS virus and cancers mutated too fast to get caught in a T-cell web. Hell, even the relatively simple flu vaccine had to be updated year to year. No, his approach— stopping cancer cells by attacking the mechanisms they use to suck life from host tissue—would pay off far sooner. The detour he had taken when Jenn was a baby had proved wise; within a few years, everyone else had followed, looking at the cancer itself, rather than at foreign genes, for clues to malignancy. His work had moved further: he no longer examined genes but rather the proteins they create that interact with the cancer's environment. Plenty of other researchers shared his approach, taking their own angles, but he was convinced he'd get results first. He was so close he could taste it. Even fusty Robert Stamford believed in him—hence the invitation a few years back to start a lab of his own.

Nothing in this issue of *Science* either threatened or illuminated. Satisfied, he tossed the magazine onto the pile of journals in a cardboard box on the floor next to his desk. Sandi would file them. Sandi, hovering in the background, always on cue, worth her weight in gold, and he told her so at every fitting juncture. He couldn't pay her well, but she didn't complain. She got a kick out of fussing at him and bossing the kids, with whom she had a sure touch despite the vast differences in education. He inspired the team; she tended to them. The team hummed along, and he loved it.

"Going to lunch!" he called to Sandi in the next room. He walked down to the elevator.

Expecting to beat the lunchtime crowd in the hospital's second-floor cafeteria, he stepped out of the elevator and into a short line at the sandwich counter. As he waited his turn, the woman in front of him, a big-boned nurse he had noticed before, ordered a Reuben. Wanting to save time, he stepped beside her and told the cook to make two. The woman turned to him.

"I don't think I can eat two of those," she said with a straight face.

"Neither can I. But we could polish them off together. I'm Paul Adler."

"Irene Barnes."

He carried the tray holding two Reubens and a bag of chips to a table against the wall while Irene got drinks at the pop machine. They sat and exchanged coordinates as they ate. She told him she was a practical nurse who had recently come to the hospital after the death of a long-term private patient. He told her he ran a cancer research lab on the ninth floor. She said she was glad he wasn't a medical man—they never listened. He liked the way she held the leaky, squishy sandwich in both hands and talked boisterously with her mouth full. He liked her ample chest and brassy red hair—obviously dyed, but so what?—and her flat midwestern accent. She reminded him of his brother's first wife, a big, exuberant dame who could fuck a horse, as Lenny used to boast. Irene appeared a little shopworn, but so would Lenny's ex-wife by now. On impulse he asked her if she'd like to go for a drink after her shift. She looked him straight in the eye and said not tonight, because she had to work a ten-hour shift, but she'd take a rain check. Done, he said, and he meant it.

ᴄ⁄❍ ❍⁄⁓

"I see you wear a ring. How come you didn't go home to your family tonight?" Irene wriggled a maraschino cherry at him. They sat beside each other at a bar down the street from her apartment building, she sipping a Manhattan, he taking bourbon straight. It was after eleven o'clock—she worked late on Thursdays—and he had offered to walk her home after their cheap pasta meal, a meal Maggie would have shunned but that Irene enjoyed as much as he.

"Because it's no fun and you are."

"Come on, Paul. I have a right to know."

He wanted to bed her—that night. "My seventeen-year-old daughter is in California in long-distance therapy for a date rape, and my wife obsesses about it."

Irene lowered the cherry. Her voice softened. "What happened to your daughter?"

"She won't say. We used to be close. Now she only talks to her shrink. I suspect she did something she doesn't want me to know about."

Irene swiveled on her stool to face him. "I've seen so many kids in trouble. They're wracked with guilt, even when they're innocent. If your daughter is talking to any-body at all, that's good."

He saw something in her face: eyes narrowed as if watch-ing those sorrowing kids, mouth like Mona Lisa's. She must be good at her job, a dirty, gutsy job he could respect. "Why did you come out tonight with a married man?"

She laughed, leaned against the bar. "I like sex. Mar-ried men are less trouble. They don't want you to keep house for them; they leave you alone when you want." She clapped him on the shoulder, as a man would. "You seem like a stand-up guy. Want to come upstairs?"

"You bet." Unusual broad. There had to be a story there. He would find out later.

They fell into a pattern of Thursday-night sex. He'd work late, or go to an evening seminar, or use his perks at the hospital's gym while she finished her shift. He'd wait for her in the bar and they'd grab a bite and go to bed. He'd stay over, telling Maggie he was sleeping on the couch at Tim's place to save himself a long, late commute. She didn't question it.

Except for Irene's one peculiarity—she insisted he wash his parts before sex, not his body, not even after a sweaty handball game, just his parts—she was a terrific lay. Instantly hot, playful, accommodating, and, eventually, deeply satisfied. No work on his part, all pleasure. So much more exciting than relations with his wife or the other women he had nibbled in the last little while. Irene was lusty; Maggie was willing. Irene was coarse; Maggie subtle. Irene threw polyester leopard skins over her chairs; Maggie favored pillows with needlepoint roses. Irene celebrated the masculine; Maggie personified the feminine.

He would never have married Irene.

And at first it seemed Irene made few emotional demands. She told him she'd been married once, to a guy who turned alcoholic and left her with a pile of debt it had taken years to clear. Hubby brought her to New York, and when they split, she didn't have enough money to go back to Chicago. Now she had a good job and a rent-controlled apartment, so in New York she stayed. She said she didn't want to marry again, and she didn't need an exclusive relationship. She made the perfect mistress. Except that, sex aside, he was a little bored. For one thing, Irene loved her doggie and assumed he would too. She liked to chat about the characters in her favorite television shows or celebrities in the news. She lived in the concrete and the local; he got no traction when he brought up science or politics. On the other hand, he could rely on her opinion about personalities—she did a great Pompous Robert imitation—and, for some unknown reason, she was interested in Jenn. When he vented frustration about Jenn's noncommunication, she counseled patience. She advised him to reach out to the shrink together with Jenn's mom—Irene's sympathy extended that far. When he asked her why she cared about his daughter, she laughed and said she'd fallen for him because he talked about Jenn on their first date. Jenn was part of the package, and she liked what she saw. With Irene, he could relax completely. He felt so comfortable at her place that little bouts of boredom didn't interfere.

Nor did little bouts of guilt. Maggie became crabby and distant after Jenn went away. She no longer went to bed when he did in the evening, staying up to read or sew. It was easy to rationalize looking elsewhere for warmth. Soon his qualms faded away.

ᘓᕲ ᕱᘔ

Later that summer, another woman assumed significance in Paul's life. One day at the lab, reading a memo, he decided to give Alicia, his new hire, an important role. The memo contained a notice for yet another convocation on the promise of personalized medicine. The usual suspects would meet in another stuffy room to make the usual promises that, the world didn't realize, couldn't be kept.

His peers wanted people to think that because cancer susceptibility has a genetic component, your doctor would soon be able to sequence the tumor genome and concoct a drug specifically targeted to your particular cancer's vulnerabilities. Totally irresponsible, he thought. So much more goes into a tumor's genesis and defense than can be read in a chart of A-T-C-Gs. The truly important discoveries would leap over an individual's genetics and address the central fact that all *successful* cancer cells, unlike normal cells, never die. People develop mutations in their genetic code every day, and those cells die or get wiped out by the immune system. But every so often one cell manages to evade extinction and succeeds in colonizing normal tissue, like an embryo implanting in the womb. How does the resulting tumor turn off the immune system around itself? How does it convince blood vessels to supply it? How does it develop the ability to break away and colonize altogether different tissue types? Why do some external toxins help and others hurt? For years, his work had focused on a particular set of conditions in the biochemistry of the microenvironment that, his gut told him, served as the gatekeeper to cellular immortality. He was gambling, striking out alone on a path with few signposts. It had better pay off.

A knock on the open door: Alicia stood pale on the threshold, notebook in hand. He had taken her on a few weeks back as a favor to a former professor who now sat on the NIH panel that funded research like his. Although well qualified for the research assistant job, she moved slowly and took constant notes, as if afraid to forget a word. She wore her hair in a severe ponytail and hid her figure in a dingy lab coat. Even her makeup looked tentative, a pale pink smudge on her lips. He couldn't look at her any length of time without wanting to shake her, to propel her into higher gear. Maybe she reminded him of his mother, powerless to protect her children from the drunkard she had married and powerless to leave him.

"Dr. Adler, Sandi said you wanted to see me?"

"Have a seat. I have an idea for your thesis."

She sat on the chair next to his desk, slow as molasses, her moon face registering what he took for puzzlement. She murmured, "I have a topic. I already did the lit review and the first experiment with Professor Blumer."

"Yes, and he sent you to me for a reason. You're doing good, basic work on breast-tumor tissue, but you can do something innovative using my analysis of the microenvironment. It would give you a leg up. And it would be good for the rest of the team." He paused to let the implication sink in.

Her brow wrinkled. "I don't think I can start all over again."

He leaned back in his chair. "Who said start over? Build on what you've got, just adjust the parameters."

"But the data don't warrant it."

"Alicia, everything is subject to interpretation. I'll help you set up."

She frowned. "I don't understand."

"I'll revise your protocol and send it back to you to look over. Then we can talk. You'll understand and you'll be glad. Okay?"

"Okay." She looked dubious. She clutched the notebook to her chest.

"You can go now. I'll come find you in a couple of hours."

She rose with the speed of a three-toed sloth and walked out.

With Alicia churning away in parallel, he'd confirm his hypothesis all the sooner. This was one female he could control, and she'd love him for it. He reminded himself to send a note to Blumer, thanking him for recommending her and letting him know how far along the lab had come. His prospects looked good. So good that he could forget about his daughter's troubles and ignore his crabby wife.

❧ ❦

That fall, after Jenn returned from California, the routine in Pelham almost returned to normal. Maggie calmed down and tried to make it up to him, but he saw no need to give up his hot Thursday nights. Jenn seemed content to prepare for college, but she rejected his help. Meanwhile, at the office, Alicia became more involved in the work and more valuable. If he'd thought about it, he would have realized that the office had defaulted to home. And when he thought about sex, it was Irene's person, not Maggie's, that stirred him. The marital bed had irreversibly chilled.

SIXTEEN

Paul stood directly behind Hope, leaning forward to watch her hands adjust the microscope slide, smelling the lemony scent of her hair. Not perfume, perhaps shampoo or a gel of some kind—something clean, as befitting the horsewoman he imagined she was. He supposed she had bought it at a Madison Avenue boutique with a foreign name. Or maybe she'd picked it up last summer in the Hamptons. Graduate students never had that kind of money. Hope proved the rule in so many ways. It was only week three, yet she had been amazingly productive, mastering the protocols and running more trials successively than any other technician the lab had employed. He knew he could stop double-checking her, but he liked watching her work. Competence pleased him.

Sandi walked in and he straightened. She said, "It's Friday. You have the administrative meeting at four." He nodded. "Don't be late again." She left the room.

Hope replaced the slide in its holder with all due care.

Making a note in her computer, she said, "Will your meeting last long? I'd like to invite you to an opening at my parents' gallery tonight. Cocktails start at five thirty. The artist is one of my favorites."

"I'm not a connoisseur. And I don't have a tie." He was intrigued. Where was she going with this? She'd been flirting with him since day one.

"You'd like Arturo. He does performance pieces with a social angle. I told him that my boss is going to cure cancer, and he exploded with pleasure. If you come, you might find yourself part of the piece." She folded her hands like a supplicant. Her eyes didn't beg.

He hesitated. He didn't need complications at work; he needed results. Besides, he had Irene. And Maggie. Plenty of women already rattled around in his head, taking up space that could otherwise be devoted to science. But Hope was different from other women, like an alien creature. And he admired those fabulous legs. "The meeting shouldn't take long. Where's the gallery? I could meet you there."

"Madison and Seventy-Second. It says Caldwell above the window. Arturo will be delighted. Me too." She turned back to the microscope.

He returned to his desk, wondering if the scene at the art gallery would be hard to stomach. He'd had no time for art galleries on his path to becoming lab director, but curiosity pricked him. He left a message on Maggie's cell saying that he'd be late.

⚬⚬⚬

He walked along Madison Avenue, a chilly corridor between tall buildings, in the twilight. Wrapped around scrawny sidewalk trees, strings of white Christmas lights twinkled; it was only November, yet shop windows sported glittering ornaments and plastic greenery. No inflated Santas or wire-frame deer nodded their electrified heads in this tony neighborhood though. He passed people standing in front of the displays, catching glimpses of their faces reflected in the glass. They looked happy, pointing and chatting, as if they cared about each other. Easy to get the Christmas spirit when you have lots of bucks. He remembered why he didn't frequent the East Side—so predictable, so snobbish, so boring. He crossed Seventy-Second Street, dodging a couple of taxis. New Yorkers hung casual about traffic. New York, apart from the Upper East Side, suited him so much better than the Indianapolis of his childhood. In New York, you smelled opportunity; it was a sharp, hard smell that he relished.

The gray lettering on the brown wooden facade at Caldwell's was barely legible. The old, polished wood must have darkened with exposure to weather and grime. Understated, a signal to the cognoscenti. As he reached to ring the bell set into a bronze plaque, the door opened and Hope smiled him in. She looked demure in a soft, clingy black dress. She took his jacket and invited him to look around while she tended to something. Arturo was anxious to meet him, she said, and Arturo would be easy to spot.

The gallery consisted of a succession of doorless rooms with crisp white walls and a gleaming wooden floor. A guitarist played classical music in a corner. In the first two rooms, paintings hung on walls and a few dozen people stood sipping cocktails and chatting. White-haired men in dark suits stood beside painfully thin women with dowager humps in brightly colored knits, diamonds glittering as they gestured with knobby hands. A mustachioed young man in black passed hors d'oeuvres.

A tired-looking young woman holding an infant in a carrier slung against her chest walked in behind Paul, followed by a nerdy guy hoisting a three-year-old on his shoulders. Paul followed the young family, past a stanchion that read "Performance at 6:15," into the third room. No paintings. A tiny man in a red silk shirt sat on a chair next to a man-sized cage in the middle of the floor. A ring of gray hair descended to his shoulders from his otherwise bald head. The young mom approached him and pecked his cheek. He fondled the baby while they talked in Italian.

A camouflaged door in the rear wall opened, and Hope entered, followed by an older woman with the same horsey face and long legs, obviously her mother. Mrs. Caldwell fussed over Arturo, and Hope beckoned Paul to join them. She introduced him as the brilliant scientist with whom she was fortunate to work. Arturo rose and embraced him. Paul looked down at the top of Arturo's inadvertent tonsure. From this angle he could see a snake coiled in the bottom of the cage. Arturo released him, saying, "Will you stay after the performance? I want to know how you will conquer the devil."

Hope said, "We'll be here. Tend to your grandchildren." She drew Paul away from the group. Looking at her watch she said, "It's almost time."

"What have you signed me up for?"

"Arturo will take the python out of the cage and wrap it around himself and sit on the chair for half an hour or so. People can talk to him or not, as they wish. He will focus all his energy on staying alive while addressing the emotions that snakes bring up in the viewers."

"Sounds like something out of *Harry Potter*."

"It's actually deeply moving. You'll see. And afterwards he'll chat you up about cancer, and then I'll take you to dinner. It's the least I can do."

"Anything for art's sake."

"No," she said, "anything for a friend helping out another friend. Excuse me a minute." She walked past the stanchion to greet a cluster of newcomers.

Paul withdrew to a corner of the room and phoned home, asking Jenn to tell her mother not to wait dinner. He expected Hope to take him to a snotty restaurant that her set frequented. He hoped to hell the food would be tasty, not just pretty. He walked to the bar to get a bourbon before Arturo's show.

∽⊙ ⊙∾

She had her own apartment, a studio high over Second Avenue, painted white and almost bare of furnishings except for the bed in the middle of the room and two six-foot canvases leaning against walls without windows. Paul sat on the lone stool at the countertop in the kitchenette, surveying the place while Hope hung his jacket and her coat in the closet. There were no clothes or books lying around, no dirt on the kitchen counter or appliances. It looked like she only camped out there. Where, he wondered, did she really live?

She rummaged in an overhead cabinet in the kitchenette and removed a pair of china cups, setting them on the counter. She opened the bottle of Fernet-Branca that had been foisted upon her after the Italian dinner Arturo had cajoled them into sharing with him and his family, and poured a shot in each cup. Paul hadn't wanted to eat with Arturo, but she had pleaded with him. The meal turned out to be big and good, and he'd enjoyed Arturo's riff on the vanity of performance art, including his own. When Paul and Hope refused tiramisu, Arturo told them that sipping a digestif was the best way to end such an occasion and presented the bottle. They had gone to Hope's place, "just around the corner," for a taste.

They each raised a cup.

"Smells foul," he said.

"Arturo says they make it with herbs that grow on the hillsides above the vineyards. It's eighty proof, you know."

"You drink this stuff?"

"My family has represented Arturo for thirty years. He used to make sculpture. I remember climbing on pieces in his studio as a little girl. My mother was aghast, but Arturo indulged me. I grew up with his family."

"He knows a lot about cancer. His questions were pretty astute."

"He read up for you. He wanted to make the most of your acquaintance."

"What if I hadn't come?"

"Then both of us would have been sorely disappointed." She gestured toward the bed. "Can we sit down? I've ordered a couch, but it won't arrive for another few weeks, so we have to make do." She perched on the edge of the bed, knees together, cup in lap. He sat a foot away, a respectful distance.

"Tell me about those canvases. Are you a painter?"

She shifted, crossing her legs. "No. A friend left them here. There're supposed to be metaphors of me. I don't see any likeness."

"I'm no judge, but all that red and black. What kind of a friend was he?"

She looked directly at him. "Not good enough. We broke up a while ago. I should dump the paintings, but they'll be worth something in a few years. Does that make me venal?"

That's her story, he thought, on the rebound. "No, it means you're practical. Scientists don't make money." Women on the rebound wanted a hug, he'd found, not a lover. Being needy made her less attractive. He stood and meandered over to look at one of the canvases. He traced the thickest brushstrokes with his hand as he contemplated leaving.

"Before you go," she said behind him, "let's have dessert."

He turned around. She stood naked next to the bed. Gorgeous, muscled legs; sleek torso; real, full breasts that stood up prettily—he was aroused. First time a seductress had beaten him to the punch, and the novelty appealed to him. As he undressed, she lay on her side, languid, like an odalisque, watching him, opening her arms when he reached her. Her flesh was warm and smooth. She wrapped her legs around him. He went for it.

ᥰᥰ ᥰᥰ

She stirred when he got up, but he shushed her and she fell back into sleep. Leaving a note, claiming to have forgotten an early golf game, he dressed silently and made his way out. She couldn't have known that he didn't play golf. He wanted a hot shower, and he didn't want another screw lest he disappoint her. It had been a while since he'd spent all night having sex.

It was still dark outside. He hailed a cab on Second Avenue to go to 125th Street to catch the next train to Westchester. In the taxi, on the platform, in the train, he drowsed and thought about her. He'd been wrong about her being needy. She was a voluptuary, alternately rousing him and being roused, savoring each caress, the press of their bodies, the hot height of their coitus. In between screws, she exuded contentment. Her lust disarmed him. He wanted to possess her; he wondered if he could. She was far more skilled at lovemaking than any thirty-year-old should be.

He let himself in the mudroom door and descended into the Lair. It was too late for a shower—Maggie rose early and might hear. He removed his shoes and belt and lay down on the couch, pulling up a throw. He tasted Hope again. He smelled sex on his body, warming beneath the coverlet. Tired, he closed his eyes.

Muffled sound overhead. Something was happening in the kitchen. He squinted at the television against the rear wall: eleven thirty. He'd slept five hours. Saturday. Someone should check the new batch of cultures.

Turning on the basement shower spigot, he let the water run for a minute; in December, the basement water never really got hot. He stepped into the stall and soaped. Hope came to mind, and the guy who jilted her. She'd mentioned in passing that he was an artist her parents had been promoting, older than she by quite a lot. She'd traveled with him for a year, showing his portfolio to galleries all over the world. She said he was divorced, not that it mattered, because he was unavailable in other ways. He wondered if she thought him available. Did he want to be? He didn't need a young woman, an employee for God's sake, nosing around him. He was perfectly comfortable with Irene, who kept it casual. And there was always Maggie.

He found a bottle of shampoo on the floor of the stall and poured some in his hand. In the quiet moments last night, Hope had asked about his work. She'd asked deep questions. She'd said he was probably the only person she knew, including her friend Arturo, doing something truly important. He believed her. She knew enough science to appreciate the significance of what he wanted to do. She'd told him that she was sure he'd make a breakthrough. Yes, he would.

He stepped out of the stall and used the slightly damp towel that hung on the rack—nothing completely dried in the basement—to wipe himself. Clean clothes lay upstairs, past whatever was going on in the kitchen. As he climbed the stairs, Hope's face and figure came to him. He could almost feel her legs wrapped around him, smell her perfume and sweat. Such a spicy young lady, so strong, so challenging. It would be hard to refuse her. Should he try?

Jenn nodded to him as he emerged from the basement. "We didn't wait breakfast for you. I can make you scrambled eggs if you like. Mom's at her friend Ellen's house."

"Yeah, eggs sound good. I'll go change my clothes and be right down. The train was late last night."

She went to the fridge. "Two eggs or three?"

"Three. My cholesterol's better." Stepping to the stairs, he avoided looking at her. If she thought anything amiss, she was too smart to say. He was relieved that Maggie wasn't home. There was no need to belabor his excuse.

SEVENTEEN

It had been warm for the entire month before Thanksgiving, and some of the neighborhood trees had remained green, which Maggie found disconcerting in December. The whole world seemed out of alignment, maybe only a little, but enough to destabilize her mood. She walked home head down, idly kicking fallen leaves, half hearing the rustle as her conversation with Ellen meandered through her head. On the sidewalk in front of their driveway, her toe caught on a crack hidden under a mound of leaves and she pitched forward. She reached for a tree to catch her balance; the tree that saved her, she realized, was also the cause of her stumble, its roots having forced a section of concrete upward. You never perceive underground forces until it's too late. Like the disappointment that had festered between her and Paul, gradually reordering their lives.

She kicked a pile of leaves at the base of the tree and entered the backyard. Kicking leaves was a habit formed in childhood. She used to pile leaves up and jump on the piles to release the powdery, spicy smell. Her mother hated the game because it brought dust and dirt into the house. In her mother's orbit, there were few games. By fourth grade, she longed to play at friends' homes, because each visit revealed a new treasure: Chutes and Ladders, Monopoly, canasta, a hamster. And in those homes, she usually looked on while the other girls played, because she feared appearing ignorant or breaking something. Her best friend's mother offered snacks; the woman also turned her into a reader, thank goodness, lending her books after the friend had finished them, teaching her to use the library. Of course, Maggie had given Jenn games and books, the accoutrements of childhood that Claudia disdained, at the appropriate age and in the proper measure.

Earlier that morning, she and Ellen had put their heads together about a job for Jenn and had drawn up a list of people to call. Ellen had taken half the names, promising to get on the horn in the afternoon. She said her lawyer husband might have something to offer when he came back from the gym. Maggie had put the other names in her pocket; she would start calling when she got home, although it might be hard to reach people on a Saturday so close to Christmas. A short while ago Jenn would have objected to her butting in. Today Jenn was grateful for the help. To what should Maggie attribute the change: Arun's influence or an empty bank account? She kicked one last mound of leaves, which scattered in all directions.

Entering the house through the mudroom, she found Paul eating in the breakfast nook while Jenn washed dishes at the sink. The odor of frying greeted her. She removed the red fleece vest that Paul used to mock as frumpy but no longer seemed to notice and sat with him.

"Can you hang the Christmas lights today?" she asked.

He shook his head no and swallowed. "I've got a new batch of cultures to check."

"Can't you get someone else to do it? Alicia lives close by the lab, doesn't she?"

"She went home for Christmas week. But you're right. I'll call the new technician. Your daughter can scramble an egg." He tucked the last morsel of egg onto a bit of toast, added a bite of sausage, and maneuvered the stack into his mouth. Chewing, he picked up his mug and headed for the Lair.

A few years before, she would have asked him what time he got home last night and why he hadn't come to bed upstairs. Today she would wait for him to get off the landline and his computer so she could use it to troll for a job for Jenn. And bug him about the lights. She hoped to spend the weekend as a threesome, enjoying the decorating rituals they had started when Jenny was small. Lights on the garage and front portico; the un-tree, a wire frame hung with ornaments and tinsel, in the living room; the handmade crèche on the lawn. She wanted to re-create the sense of comfort they had enjoyed in the early years before Jenn burst loose. Paul used to enjoy the family side of Christmas; he might come through.

"More tea, Mom? What did Ellen say?" Jenn said from the sink.

"You know her husband, John? She thinks he can help. We have a plan."

Jenn laughed. "You two always have a plan. Remember Women Leaders of America? I thought it was ridiculous to call a bunch of high school girls women, let alone leaders."

"They're still meeting," Maggie said, "but they changed from newspapers to something with media. Ellen and I aren't involved anymore, but our names are still on the masthead."

"Are you disappointed that you didn't produce the next generation of Pulitzer Prize winners?"

"No. It was good fun."

Jenn wiped her hands. "Well, you were right. I was being a brat at the time."

Maggie kept a straight face despite the urge to grab Jenn and hug. Back then, she had tolerated Jenn's hostility to the club she and Ellen had dreamed up. Jenn had insisted that girls should be left alone to flower organically, and she'd criticized for months. Paul had wanted to ground her for it, but Maggie had defended Jenn's right to her opinion. Although Jenn never acknowledged that the club helped girls with fewer resources than she had, she stopped griping about it after her sophomore year in college. Today's conciliatory words lifted Maggie's spirits: Jenn had outgrown her adolescent intransigence. But had Arun fostered intransigence of another kind?

"No more tea, thanks."

She pulled her computer closer and powered it on to search for a recipe for walnut stuffing. Women Leaders of America. Perhaps Teenage Sleuths of Pelham would have been more apt. She and Ellen had created the club to get girls from both ends of town to work together despite the snobbery that caused so much ill will. They had asked the girls to work in teams to identify problems in town and taught them how to research issues and survey attitudes. The girls published their work in the local shopper's weekly and developed a reputation as investigative reporters, which became a matter of pride. It was so satisfying to see the look on a girl's face when she showed off her byline, especially a girl from a compromised family situation. One of Maggie's favorites, an unkempt sixteen-year-old named Steffi, handed in assignments torn from a notebook, grease stained, without much punctuation, but gutsy and on point. Steffi watched over her siblings while her single mother worked. She came to club meetings as often as she could until her mother, annoyed by the attention the girls attracted, forced her to quit. Maggie tried to talk to the woman, but she wouldn't listen. Maggie's own judgmental mother would never have understood the club either. So wonderful that Jenn, at last, appreciated it.

The cell phone in her vest pocket chimed. It was Ellen calling for Jenn. One of John's partners had a new trust case that needed research. Would Jenn like to interview for a temporary project clerk position? And did she know the landline was off the hook?

Maggie passed the phone to Jenn to follow through. She felt one of her bundle of cares slip away and evaporate. Jenn could spend her days with thoughtful people in a socially relevant context. Step one toward bringing her home.

Paul emerged from the basement. "Got my cultures taken care of. The new technician's going to cover it. She's new but she's good." He called to his daughter across the room, "Hey Jenn, wanna help me with the lights?"

"Shush. Jenn's talking to Ellen's husband about a job in his law office," Maggie said.

"That was fast. Your usual efficiency."

"It's not settled yet, but I think she'll make it work." Rehearing "You were right," she smiled deep inside. "I'm going to make a classic holiday dinner. Your reward for hanging the lights."

Paul grinned and poured coffee into his mug. They heard a loud "Yes" upstairs. In a moment, Jenn flounced toward them.

"I meet John's partner Monday morning. Someone died without a hard-copy will but with all sorts of things in email and online. They need a young brain to figure out what happened so they can prove the man's intention in court. Sounds interesting enough, and we could use the money. I need to go Christmas shopping."

"Not until you help me hang the lights," Paul said, pulling her toward him for a hug. He turned to Maggie. "With the house all snazzy, maybe I should invite the lab over? Nothing elaborate. Drinks and snacks on New Year's Day. We have a lot to celebrate."

Maggie stared at him without comment. For years, he had refused her offer to throw a party for the lab. Why now?

"I'll go get the ladder. Jenn, you need to put on better shoes." He placed his mug in the sink and left the kitchen.

Jenn looked at her mother. "Do you know what that's all about?"

"I'm guessing your father wants to encourage solidarity. He has new staff."

Jenn lowered her voice, "The new researcher is female. Sandi told me the other day when I called Dad. Sandi doesn't like her."

"Sandi's pretty possessive."

"What about you?"

"Not anymore." She focused on the computer screen, signaling the end of conversation.

Jenn laid her hand on Maggie's shoulder. "I'm going to change my shoes."

It's true, she thought. It's finally true. After so many disappointments, so much time spent hoping for better, her love for Paul had become a remnant, like a moraine, ground down by years of worry and jealousy and defeat.

She no longer cared if he dallied with his new technician, or his old flame. She had grown immune to the pain of his deceptions. She would continue to keep her own counsel; she would continue to withhold her trust. But she required him to be reliable and paternal, and she wanted him to be discreet, for Jenn's sake. Poor girl, watching her father fall off his pedestal. A sigh rose from the bottom of her belly, half sad, half relieved.

The landline rang. Maggie reached the kitchen extension at the same time that Jenn picked up the call upstairs. Arun, calling from Bangalore, telling her how much he missed her at night. Maggie hung up the phone. She didn't eavesdrop. She hadn't eavesdropped on Paul's cheating when she could have. She hadn't wanted to hear about his intimacies then, and she didn't want to hear about Jenn's now. Poor girl. Stars in her eyes for a crazy love.

Ellen had raised the issue again that morning, asking in her jovial way why Maggie couldn't let time resolve things, as of course it would. Ellen had pressed her to articulate precisely what troubled her about Jenn's romance. Each time Maggie gave a reason, like the incompatibility of their cultures or the flimsiness of their finances, Ellen said, "Trust Jenn to handle it." Ellen thought Jenn a responsible young woman, far more mature than her own two sons, and insisted there was more to Maggie's objection, an arrière-pensée she wouldn't share. Maggie replied no, she had come clean. They'd pecked each other's cheeks, and Maggie had left for home, list of names in pocket.

Alone in the kitchen, she cross-examined herself. She had not come totally clean. She had not told Ellen about meeting Brian Sayler or her urge to toy with him, which was, after all, under control. She had not wanted to confess because, as she realized in the shower that morning, the root of it all was wanting to be like Jenn, to exploit her body's capacity for pleasure. How foolish to be jealous of a twenty-five-year-old! Yet understandable, Ellen would have said, and then discounted the rest of Maggie's words. Her emotions spun: she distrusted her ability to stay objective, to keep her own needs out of the picture. The most important thing: preserve her child from danger. Paul objected to Arun out of ego. She objected because Arun, wrongheaded, would lead Jenn to harm.

She heard noise in the mudroom. Paul poked his head around the door frame. "This ladder is heavier than I remember. Where's the Christmas elf?"

"On the phone with Arun. It may be a while."

"Oh, boy." He stepped into the kitchen. "Do you want to help me with the lights?"

"No, wait for Jenn. She'll enjoy it." She pretended to busy herself with the computer.

He eased his large body onto the banquette in the nook. "If she doesn't get off the line soon, I'm gonna take a nap. Too many tissue cultures last night."

Why, she thought, does he bother to lie? Doesn't he know he has no secrets? For a brilliant man, he's so stupid. So stupid that he squandered her trust, and her love. Yes, she had fallen out of love with him without feeling the fall. With a little spurt of pleasure, she realized that she could stop trying to restore their marriage. She could admit defeat and reap liberation. She felt another one of her bundle of cares fall from her shoulders and, crashing to the ground, disintegrate into dust.

Jenn appeared in jeans holding her sneakers. "Arun called," she said, sitting on the banquette opposite her fa-

ther and bending over to put on the shoes. "He's very encouraged by a meeting with the microfinance group. He's
sending a link to their material. Oh, and his parents have
sent you guys a Christmas present. He said it *should* come
in time, but you never know with the Indian post office."
Her face flushed, clearly not from the effort of tying laces.

"Do his parents celebrate Christmas?" Maggie asked.

"No, it's a gesture of respect to you."

Paul said, "Or a gesture of hypocrisy."

"Dad . . ."

"Okay, okay. But there are other possibilities. Maybe
they're angling for a big dowry. Ouch . . ." Jenn slapped his
shin with a sneaker beneath the table. He pretended to rub
his shin, obviously in good humor despite too many tissue
cultures, Maggie thought.

"Is that an offer?" Jenn said. "Watch out, we'll take you
up on it." She finished tying laces and stood. "I'm ready."

They left through the mudroom. After a moment, Maggie put on the maligned fleece vest and stepped outside to
watch. Paul had propped the ladder against the garage and
mounted halfway. Jenn handed a string of icicle lights up
to him, untangling it carefully as she lifted each successive
piece. Maggie's eye flitted past Paul, who no longer had the
power to hold her. She focused on her grown-up girl, heart
swelling with pride, and beneath the pride, fear of the alien
forces threatening. Maggie pressed her lips together; she
would make this a memorable Christmas, come what may.

SPRING

EIGHTEEN

In April in Westchester County you expected spring to come at any moment and rescue you from cold and wet, but instead winter dragged on and you waited. Maggie stood at the lilac bush beside the patio fingering the firm, green buds, wondering if they would burst open in time for Jenn's birthday next month. The bush she had planted when they first moved to Pelham now stood head high, green most of the year, promising a few short weeks of exquisite bloom in May.

Twenty-six years earlier in Michigan, when they'd brought newborn Jenn back from the hospital, a vase of purple lilac blossoms had greeted her at bedside, their perfume so delicate and sweet that it made her cry. That was the first sudden bout of tears in her sad postpartum year. When Paul refused to have another child and she couldn't persuade him, she accepted his decision, without rancor, as a judgment she deserved. But she had longed for a second child, so that Jenn wouldn't have to face the adult world alone, as she had had to. Would the woman she was now have made a different choice?

Daylight was fading. She climbed the three steps to the mudroom door, looking at the corner window, where it would be so easy to build a shelf and add two glass panels to make a little greenhouse. Last fall she had thought about starting an herb garden that she and Jenn could tend together. Then everyone got so busy—Jenn with her lucky job downtown, Paul redoubled at work, and she with her new adventure, a community college course on Indian civilization that, she had thought, would help her understand Jenn's attraction to Arun. It felt like months since she'd looked up a recipe, and her basket of mending had overflowed.

The course wasn't supposed to take up much time, but it had. Three hours a week in seminar and then the reading: it seemed that every Indian scholar wrote in a style as convoluted as India itself. She could have audited the course, but being thorough, she'd joined a study group. The others insisted on submitting video instead of papers; they were busier and more scattered than she, so she wound up organizing them, to Jenn's amusement, and struggling with video at her computer. It was worth the trouble; she and Jenn had had hours of good conversation about the mythology and centuries of invasions that had shaped Indian society. Whenever arcane terms confused her, Jenn refocused her thinking on the reality in the streets. She'd grown in respect for her daughter's acumen and compassion, if not her taste in men.

India had proved to be more layered than expected, both fascinating and exasperating. She admired India's respect for the wisdom of elders; she hated the superstition that tyrannized the uneducated. She applauded democracy in a country where banknotes had to be printed in seventeen languages. She suffered for families aborting female fetuses because girls require impossible dowries. She wanted to see the terrain and the temples, taste the spices, feel the relief brought by the first monsoon. She wanted to apologize for the mess the British had left behind.

And the course had yielded a bonus: she discovered she liked hanging out with the other students, the sorrowful twenty-year-olds trying to undo their mistakes and the mature people pursuing a hobby or a different slant on life. She'd forgotten how much fun it is to learn something new. She could imagine returning to campus again in the fall, and perhaps making a new circle of friends.

She hung her jacket on a peg in the mudroom and entered the kitchen. As she put on the kettle, Jenn walked in wearing the blazer-over-long-skirt costume she had adopted for work. Tossing her bag onto the breakfast table, Jenn flounced down on the banquette.

"This stuff gets more interesting the more I do. I'm going to miss seeing how the case turns out. They'll post it, of course, but I'd like to see everyone's face when the verdict gets handed down." She unraveled the endless scarf around her neck. "What's for dinner? Dad coming?"

"Salmon. No, your father's having dinner with people from the lab."

"He's missed a lot of good meals lately."

"You know that conference he goes to every year? This year it's in June. He's preparing to make an announcement. It's a big deal, evidently."

Jenn removed the filigree earrings Arun's mother had sent. "Do you need any help?"

"No, go make yourself comfortable." She waited a beat.

"Brian's coming over later to help me finish the final video."

The course final was due the next day. For her segment, she'd interviewed Robert's Indian doctor friend, who'd turned out to be a gentle soul. She'd asked him to explain, on camera, how the newly prosperous justified their middle-class consumption amid such poverty and human drama. His face had strained into a tight smile as he told her the story of his first clinic in Calcutta. He had bought cheap land near a dump but couldn't start construction for almost a year because snakes kept creeping out of the garbage. While he waited, he went around the neighborhood, taking a census of people's problems. He realized that he could focus only on two or three at best, or be overwhelmed. So he did wonderful work on a few disease conditions for thirty years, laboring at the height of his powers to lift up others less fortunate. Eventually, fatigue had forced him to the United States. Maggie had admired his candor, his bravery, and the grace with which he responded to her request.

"Would you like to see my segment now? I can show you everything after Brian finishes putting the pieces together."

"You know, Mom, if it was anyone but you, I'd say you were having an affair with that guy. Tit for tat with Dad."

Maggie flushed. "Careful with your accusations."

"Sorry. I didn't mean to hurt your feelings. But Dad can be such a jerk. I used to be so angry at him for what he did to you."

"Are you still angry?"

"No. But I imagine you are."

Maggie said nothing. How could she possibly explain that the wound had healed over and her loyalty had dissolved? Especially when Jenn herself was about to marry?

Jenn opened her bag. "Here's a present. One of the

partners came back from Seattle with goodies." She handed her mother a jar of preserves.

Maggie held the jar in both hands, glad for a reason to look down. What might Jenn think if she could see her mother's face?

Jenn stood. "I never heard of marionberries, but they're supposed to be good in sauce. Maybe you could use them on the salmon." She pecked her mother's cheek. "I'm going upstairs to change." She gathered her belongings and left the kitchen, scent of cloves lingering behind.

Brian had answered Maggie's phone call in January. She'd told him she needed tech support for her course. Was he willing? Silly question. At first they met at Starbucks, tablets in hand. Then she went to his place. Then he came over one afternoon when he was on break and Jenn was at work. Then he came for lunch and lingered. She'd told Jenn that a friend with media savvy was helping her post. She'd mentioned Brian's name but nothing about his person. Tonight, although she didn't want Brian in the house with Jenn, she needed him to merge the files her group had sent in multiple formats. Paul staying away made it easy.

That first afternoon at his place, it had felt so good to be wanted. He was a solicitous lover, admiring her body with his words and hands, and she'd responded. Their lovemaking felt voluptuous; afterward, her passion faded fast. She didn't really care about him, a hard, self-sufficient man. But she liked his leanness, his quiet, his animal grace. And she was grateful that that seemed to be enough. She called him every so often, when she wanted to leave the cooking and the All Saints' accounts behind. It grew easier to pick up the phone each time. They made love in the afternoon. He kept the blinds open because he liked to look at her. She liked the way he looked at her body, appreciative, cool. She didn't rush to shower after sex because she liked sensing the residue on her and in her. They didn't talk much between visits, which suited her mood.

Of course she told no one, not even Ellen, who wouldn't have judged her. Ellen would have pressed her, though, asking why now, after all these years of neglect? And Ellen would have come up with some theory about a secret motivation that Maggie would deny. No one at church, or the shelter, or the gym, or her book club would discover the liaison; she was safe from recrimination, except from her own conscience. Her bifurcated conscience. Getting to know Jenn as an adult these past few months, she'd seen how unlike herself her daughter was—Jenn so expansive and daring, she so careful and subdued. She had thought she'd transcended her own mother's conventional formality, but no, not in comparison to Jenn. The failure hurt more than her shame over screwing Brian just to feel juicy again. She forced herself to think about dinner; didn't they serve salmon with huckleberry sauce in Seattle? She opened her computer to search for a recipe. She closed it; she'd wing it.

The kettle whistled. Deciding against tea, she turned off the gas and picked up the teapot to return it to its place on the shelf in the dining room. The faux-celadon pot was one of her favorites, a modern version of an ancient Japanese design with even sleeker lines. In past years, pots had been her one indulgence; pots of different kinds sat on the display shelves she'd had a carpenter build years earlier, and tall vessels stood in the corners of the rooms. She didn't fill them with plants or umbrellas or anything else; their solid roundness, their very capacity to contain, satisfied her. But it had been quite a while since she'd added to the collection. She'd lost her fervor for enriching their home.

A vehicle crunched pebbles in the driveway. The bell rang. Brian stood in the open doorway in a clean T-shirt and jeans, no jacket, laptop under his arm. He slouched with the lean, sinewy look that had attracted her from the start.

"I got off early. We'll finish the video and you can cook me dinner." He walked into the living room and set up his computer on the coffee table, looking around for an outlet for the power supply. "Not enough wiring in these old houses. Got an extension?"

"You were supposed to come over later."

"I'm here now, at your service."

"Jenn's home."

"Great. We can make friends."

"That's presumptuous."

"No it's not. I'm a nice guy. Where can I find an extension?"

"I'll bring one."

She rummaged in the junk bin in the pantry, collecting her thoughts. Brian liked to provoke her, push her closer to lines she didn't want to cross. In sex, it made for tension that excited her. But at dinner with Jenn? Finding a coil of brown, plasticized cord, she told herself the ship had launched. She had to trust Jenn to make the best of the situation. She returned to the dining room, extension in her outstretched hand, tension mounting in her veins. What would Jenn think of her, supposedly better than Paul, if she knew?

Brian said, "I'll have this open in a minute. Show me what you want to do."

She fetched her computer from the kitchen counter and

showed him the list of files to merge. "I can't get them all in the same piece."

"No problem. You can check the product when I'm done."

Leaving him to fiddle with the computers, she focused on the meal. There was plenty of salmon; she'd double the rice and open a jar of olives and a container of hummus to stretch the veggies. She'd serve in forty-five minutes.

They ate in the dining room. Brian had finished the editing job shortly before dinner, and Maggie had forwarded the report to her study group, barely glancing at it, straining to hear the conversation between Brian and Jenn as they set the dining room table. Over dinner, Brian, bless him, didn't ask questions and willingly answered Jenn's. He talked about the pleasure of working with his hands. The conversation segued to making music with one's hands, and then to Brian's opinions about music. Safe enough. Jenn talked about working as a legal clerk and the clients' shenanigans. She appeared to enjoy herself, bless her.

They moved to the living room for coffee. As Maggie went to get the lemon pound cake she kept in the freezer for surprise visitors, a moan reverberated through the house. When she returned, Jenn was showing Brian the CD she had brought home from India, pointing out the harmonium in the cover photo as the music jangled.

Brian said, "I wouldn't want to hear that at my wedding."

Jenn raised her eyebrows. "Are you getting married?"

Brian laughed. "You are. Your mom told me."

Jenn's tone lowered. "What did Mom say?"

"Something about a Hindu shindig."

"Not exactly. My fiancé and I are writing our own ceremony." Jenn looked quizzically at her mother.

"That's cool. Do you need a band? I know a good one."

Not safe. "Isn't it time for you to go, Brian?" Maggie stod, retrieved his laptop, and walked to the front door. She could hear him behind her saying "nice-to-meet-you" things and Jenn mumbling in reply. Why on earth had she let him into the house with Jenn home? Shame flooded through her.

He caught up in a moment. "You're off base, Maggie."

"You made friends."

"I was hoping to stay a while, maybe have some fun."

"Go home before you get me in trouble." She pushed the laptop into his hands and shoved him back out the doorway. "Thanks for the help." She shut the door; she'd deal with him later.

Jenn stood at the sink, scraping plates into the disposal. Maggie gathered the glassware and brought it to her.

"That was pretty abrupt, Mom."

"Brian likes to tease. I wanted to respect your privacy."

"What have you been telling your friends?"

"Hardly anything. That you're thinking of marrying an Indian."

"I'm not thinking of marrying an Indian. I'm marrying Arun next month! We've been planning the wedding for weeks!" Jenn placed the last plate into the dishwasher. "I thought I had your blessing."

"You always have my blessing." This was not the opening Maggie had hoped for, but she felt compelled to proceed. "You seem to have settled into life here so well. Do you really want to give it up?"

"A nothing job clerking for a lawyer? That's not a life. Life is commitment to the best in humanity. Life is sharing with a partner who you admire and trust."

"Are you sure you've found that partner?"

"I have no doubts."

In for an inch, in for a mile. "I have to tell you that I do. Arun's values are so strange. They come from a different culture, and I don't think you appreciate how hard it would be to live with him year after year in the world he understands but you don't. You could save yourself all that pain."

"You don't get it. I'm not you. And Arun is his own man. He's not a stereotype. He's not like Dad. How can you judge him, you hardly know him?" Jenn wiped her hands on the dish towel. "Excuse me. I have a telephone date. It's morning in Bangalore." She turned on her heel.

Cheeks burning, Maggie finished loading the dishwasher. She'd blown it. Months of careful conversation down the drain. The dishwasher drain glinted at her, mocking. She closed the machine.

Jenn was right. She didn't really know Arun, hadn't gotten close to him when he had visited in the fall. When he arrived next week, she'd better embrace him. Open her mind, if not her heart. The point was to regain Jenn's confidence.

Should she apologize? Wait for the phone call to end and catch Jenn in the hall? Apologize for what . . . being clumsy? Maggie mounted the stairs slowly, hoping to hear Jenn's step behind her, hoping for a chance to say a loving good-night.

ॐ ॐ

At eleven she heard the front door open, then noise in the hallway. Climbing out of bed, she wrapped a shawl around her shoulders and went looking for Paul. The lights were off downstairs, but in the faint LED glow from the entertainment console, she saw him sitting in the living room, drink in hand. She sat opposite him.

"Why are you in the dark?"

"Long day. The last round of figures came in. Alicia didn't come through."

"Surely you can help her?"

Paul took a sip. "I'll fix it." He put down the drink. "Why are *you* in the dark?"

"It's Jenn. I challenged her about Arun and now she's pissed."

"Great." He raised both hands and rubbed his eyes. "What do you want from me?"

"Be careful. Don't make it worse. He arrives next week. I have a plan."

"So far you're striking out."

"Paul, support me in this."

"Okay, okay." He rose. "We'll talk tomorrow. I'm going to bed."

She sat in the dark while he climbed the stairs to the bedroom. He'd be asleep in a matter of minutes. Unlike hers, his conscience didn't seem to demand nighttime attention. She replayed the evening, cringing at Jenn's rebuke, seeing Brian's pissed-off face as she pushed him out the door. Then she realized it could have been worse; Brian could have trumpeted their affair. The realization calmed her. She stood and walked to the stairs. Now to conjure a plan.

NINETEEN

Paul sat at the bar nursing a bourbon. He hadn't wanted a drink but felt conspicuous without one because, dammit, Hope was making him wait. Again. Although dinner had been her idea. She had picked this restaurant, far from the hospital as he preferred, but raucous, voices and clatter reflecting from the tin ceiling, the way she liked it. Sometimes he wished Hope weren't so obstinate.

The bartender—is there such a word as bartenderess?—reached for something on the top shelf, and Paul saw her face in the mirror behind the chorus of bottles. She didn't look old enough to serve booze. Some of her customers, who were leaning into each other to shout over the noise, skinny and casual in black, didn't look old enough to drink. Paul felt the weight of his gut canted over the barstool. He could use a new pair of jeans.

A hand pressed his shoulder. Hope stood behind him, towering over him in those fuck-me heels. She chirped,

"Shall we eat? I'm hungry," and turned to lead him away from the bar. He followed, watching her calves bunch up and relax in sequence, her tight ass swivel inside the skirt that looked black and soft in the mood lighting.

They settled down at a four-top, and Hope studied the menu. She waved the waiter over to ask about the specials. Paul watched her face as she listened, asking questions like a lawyer before making her choice. As usual, he was impressed by the amount of food she ordered. He knew he should avoid cholesterol, but he matched her order, rich dish for rich dish, to show her he could keep up with anyone half his age. He selected an expensive wine; he wanted Hope in an expansive frame of mind.

"I'm glad you called," he said, twirling the water in his glass after the black-clad waiter departed. She buttered a chunk of bread, didn't look at him. "I wanted to tell you that we've dodged a bullet."

She raised eyebrows, munching the bread.

"Alicia finally finished the series. She's writing it up, and the figures look good. The data are giving us a green light." He expected her to share his pleasure. She nodded, continued eating.

"You know how important this is."

"Yes. Can we not talk about the lab?"

He was surprised. She usually demanded to hear lab news. "Okay. Then let's talk about Jenn."

"That's a switch."

He reached for her left hand, uncurled on the tablecloth. "Hey. Always full of surprises." When he cupped her fingers, they didn't respond. "Something wrong?"

She withdrew her hand. "I'm hungry. So what's the deal?"

"Her boyfriend's coming back from India, and she says

she's really going to marry him next month. I can't get her to see what a liability he is."

"Maybe he makes her happy."

The waiter returned to pour the wine.

"Don't you always say happiness is not enough?"

"Not enough for me. But I'm odd." She sniffed her wine, tasted it slowly. "This is good."

"Glad you like it." He pictured Jenn's face framed by a sari, a bindi between her brows. If she married the guru, her sweetness and smarts would be wasted, submerged in chores and cares. He wanted to see her married to a stand-up guy with prospects, making the trinkets she loved to make, producing adorable kids whom he could spoil. A boy he could teach to hit.

The runner brought salad, and Hope dug in.

"I'm serious, Hope. He's older and hasn't held a steady job since college. And he fancies himself a guru." He paused. "Maybe you could talk to her."

Hope's eyes opened wide. "I don't know her. And I don't think she likes me."

"You two should give each other a chance. You could be friends."

With a nub of bread, Hope loaded lettuce and blue cheese and nuts on her fork. "Uh-uh. She's not my type. I like jocks." She swallowed. "The one time we met at your New Year's party we had nothing to say to each other. You're dreaming."

He winced. She had been doing this lately, stabbing him verbally, almost offhandedly. She used to hang on his words and laugh loudly at his jokes. He pressed onward. "Maybe Jenn's a little jealous."

"Of what? I have nothing to do with her." Hope pushed the few remaining lettuce leaves onto her fork.

The waiter came to clear the salad plates and set steak knives; the runner brought their entrées. Paul carved a chunk from his steak and chewed slowly, temporizing. Hope took a dainty slice of hers and then another, holding the fork European style. Perfect etiquette from boarding school. Mouth from the gutter.

They ate without speaking. The sound of indistinct voices and silverware on china filled the space between them. Hope ate with eyes lowered. He watched her strong, almost masculine jaw. Everything about her was so familiar, yet she seemed remote. And obtuse, Lord knows why. Last week—wasn't it last week?—after their lovemaking, she had lingered in bed, chatting about their work, questioning his statements and reflecting them back in her cool, precise way. She used to be so easy to talk to, far easier than Maggie. Or Irene.

The busboy came to clear their plates. He decided to try again. "I'd like you to talk to Jenn. I suspect she's angry at me."

Hope didn't look at him.

"Because of us." He hadn't planned to point the finger, but she needed prodding.

"If she's angry, why should I get involved?" Hope laid down her utensils. "Excuse me a sec." She took her phone out of her purse to send a text. Replacing the phone, she folded her hands in her lap.

"Is it my turn?" she asked.

Puzzled, he lowered his fork. "It's always your turn." She blushed. He had never seen her blush before. Out of character but oddly appealing.

"I'm leaving."

"We haven't had dessert."

"I mean I'm leaving the lab. I put in my six months for the credits. I only have one exam left, which I can do online."

"But you have a job . . ." and, he thought, you have me. This is crazy.

"I'm going to work for another lab starting in May. Doing epigenetics research. Thanks for everything you taught me. I'll put it to good use." She leaned back from the table.

His chest tightened. "I don't get it."

She looked into his eyes, voice straining. "I mean it, Paul. Thanks for everything. I learned a lot from you, and not just biology. I *am* grateful."

"What are you talking about? You can't just leave. We're a team." He glared at her.

"No we're not. You're a married man."

"You never mentioned my marriage before." Blood pulsed in his ears; his jaw clenched of its own accord. "Don't talk nonsense."

The waiter appeared with the dessert menu. Hope brushed it aside with a wave of the wrist. He clutched it with both hands, didn't look at it.

"You made a commitment to me. To the hospital. To your buddy Stamford."

"Robert knows about it. He helped me get the job. Please don't be difficult."

Hope pushed her chair away, scraping it on the hardwood floor, and stood. As she turned away, she said something he didn't make out. He wanted to grab her snake of an arm and twist hard, force her back to the table, make her explain. He couldn't understand why she wanted to leave. Stamford must be behind it. He would find out, ASAP.

He waited in Stamford's office, supine on the leather couch. Aimlessly he scanned the framed photos, the diplomas hung on the mauve wall where everyone could see them. He had walked past the secretary without a word, and the skinny little Brit hadn't lifted a finger. Must have been in the know. At first he had paced, tasting bile. As the minutes passed, he calmed. His object, after all, was not to knock Stamford out cold but to get Hope back. He wanted her to finish her experiments, to say the least.

Stamford opened the office door with a smile. He removed his tweed cap, hanging it in the closet. Silly, pretentious cap—no need to protect your balding head from the April sun. Paul swung his legs to the floor, and Stamford sat in the leather chair opposite him.

"I suppose you wish to discuss staffing." Stamford crossed his legs.

"I want to keep my current staff."

"If you mean Ms. Caldwell, she's no longer on staff. I can recommend another candidate."

His arms and legs grew tense. He forced himself to stay seated. "Cut the crap, Robert. Hope said you found her a job. What are you up to?"

Stamford brushed some lint from his slacks, taking his time. "It's a very good situation, and it's advantageous to the hospital as well as to Ms. Caldwell."

"That's absurd. Hope needs to finish her work with me. She needs my credibility with the cancer community." Anger edged out his cool.

"Isn't it evident that she doesn't? She qualified for a

place in Martin Miller's lab. He's doing excellent work in epigenetics."

"Ridiculous. Hope knows nothing about epigenetics. My work is more important."

"I beg to differ. Epigenetics research may be the wave of the future. If we can learn how the embryo's genome interacts with its environment, we'll be closer to understanding how nature produces a unique individual."

Paul rose and stepped to the window, looking without seeing. "How did you do it?" He turned to face Stamford.

"The tumor microenvironment assay Ms. Caldwell has been using will work in other contexts. Martin's lab is a good fit."

He wanted to smash his fist in Robert's face. He didn't dare move. "You know that's my technique. You know I've spent the last five years perfecting it. You know it's my ticket out of here."

Stamford uncrossed his legs, placing his hands on the arms of his chair. "Well, you've published several articles, so the information is in circulation. Anyone can use it for his or her own purposes. Isn't that how science progresses?" His eyebrows arched as he smiled.

Paul fought to keep his voice down. "I will find a way to stop you from stealing my stuff. You condescending shit."

Stamford eased himself up from his chair and walked around behind his desk, as if to use it as a barricade. "Paul, no one is stealing. Hope came to see me saying she wanted to leave, and I knew Martin was staffing up. It's in the hospital's interest to cooperate with another important scientist." He sat and opened a file drawer, keeping his eyes on Paul.

"This isn't the end of it."

Paul strode through the door, startling the skinny little

Brit, and down the hushed hallway and the jangling corridor to his lab. Alone in his office, he punched Martin Miller's number into the phone. As the connection processed, he calculated. He didn't particularly like Miller, but they had always respected each other's work. That would probably be enough. Miller's assistant put him through.

"Let me get right to business," Paul said after they exchanged greetings. "You're interested in my microenvironment analysis. All you have to do is ask, and I'll drill your team in my techniques."

There was a pause. Miller was silent.

"I want Hope Caldwell to finish running my experiments. You don't have to hire her to use my stuff."

"Ms. Caldwell has several reasons for joining my lab. I intend to honor them."

Paul lost patience. "Let's stop being polite. I don't know what Robert promised you, but you and I have been colleagues for a long time, and you owe me the courtesy of keeping your hands off my staff."

"It's the other way around. You're the one who needs to keep your hands off your staff. I'm not going to repeat what Ms. Caldwell has said, not to anyone. But you should be more careful, Paul."

He slapped down the phone. So Hope had lied about their relationship, and they believed her. And what else had she lied about? What else had she said? Doubt poured through his veins, drowning the anger. With a start, he recalled the day she had first reported to work in skintight slacks and high-heeled boots, arms covered in brassy bangles. She had interviewed the week before, demure in cashmere and pearls. He had been amused by the bait and switch. Now he saw it as her modus operandi. She had played him for a fool.

A shiver of fear sliced through him. Had she damaged the project? Could he trust anything she'd done or said in the lab? Mentally he cataloged the problem definition he'd given her, the number of cytokines she'd worked with, the number of trials she'd seen. Could she have misunderstood anything crucial? Probably not. She wasn't really a cancer biologist; she was a sharp grad student out to kill the competition. He barged into Sandi's office.

"Get me all the weekly reports for the new grant."

Sandi shrugged her shoulders and opened a file drawer at her desk. "Paper or electronic?"

"I don't care. Just make sure you get all of them."

He sat at his desk, furious, staring into the past, reviewing everything Hope had said over the previous six months. He could not remember a single word of protest. She had been the aggressor, showing off her tits and her tight ass, working extra hours just to impress. It was she who had first wanted to fuck, luring him to her apartment, stripping naked before he could leave. He hadn't misinterpreted; he had been deliberately misled. But why? His pulse raced. It had to be a setup—Robert trying to knock him down before his breakthrough. No dice, Robert, my work stands alone.

Sandi walked in and laid a pile of papers in front of him. "These are from November and December. I forwarded the rest." She hesitated at his door. "I'll be in early tomorrow in case you need anything else."

"No. Thanks." He didn't want company, not even Sandi's.

Yeah, his breakthrough would be spectacular. But others were sniffing around the edges of his discovery; he needed to solidify his place at the front of the pack. He would have to push Alicia to publish immediately so they could get cited. A spasm gripped his chest: What if Hope had thrown in a monkey wrench? What had she said to Alicia, from whom he needed absolute loyalty? As he dug into the files, his palms began to sweat. Zap! He was fourteen years old and his drunken father had kicked him out of the house. Big brother Lenny hadn't been there to protect him, and he'd had to fight his way back in. He punched Lenny's number in his cell phone. No one home.

TWENTY

Maggie dropped Jenn off at international arrivals and drove to the terminal where Sarah's flight would land. She parked close and found a Starbucks, where she sat at a table to wait. Everyone at the other tables faced a screen; no one looked anxious or expectant, as she no doubt looked. She checked her watch. Fifteen minutes more if the flight was on time. It had been a couple of years—how many, exactly?—since she'd seen Sarah, since Sarah had quit the bank and hung up her consultant shingle. She wondered how Sarah would present her consulting self, extravagantly no doubt. When she'd asked Sarah to come east a couple of weeks before the wedding, she'd envisioned Sarah and Jenn going off together to a spa or some such, where Sarah could counsel Jenn to value independence more than romance, something Sarah had standing to do, more so than Maggie herself. Sarah had grumbled a bit, knocking Maggie for trying to put words in her mouth, but she'd agreed, for Jenn's sake. Then Arun emailed his itinerary: Arun and Sarah were scheduled to arrive within ninety minutes of each other, necessitating a change in plan.

The arrivals monitor blinked notice that Sarah's flight was on the ground. Maggie walked over to the security barrier, car keys still clutched in hand. She scanned the disheveled travelers lumbering through, holding jackets among their burdens, clearly not from the Los Angeles flight. As if watching would make Sarah appear faster. As she gazed down the corridor, their last phone call replayed in her head. Sarah had said that she never suspected Maggie could be so deceitful, organizing a backyard wedding while planning to subvert it. Maggie had replied that she would try every means of persuasion at her command. Sarah had responded, "Fair enough," but she would make up her own mind about the groom's suitability. Maggie had assumed that Sarah would agree with her. Now it occurred to her that there was a slim chance Sarah might not.

A cluster of travelers bunched in the exit way. Sarah stepped from behind them, a transformed Sarah, silvery-gray hair, ever-so-light makeup, navy blue outfit and matching flats, a tiny gold cross on a chain around her neck. Maggie embraced her, trying not to gape. Sarah took Maggie's arm and swept her along the passage to baggage claim, saying she wasn't tired and couldn't wait to see Jenn. It had been too long. As they made their way, Maggie explained that Jenn was waiting for Arun at international arrivals in another terminal, and if Sarah didn't mind, the four of them would drive to Pelham together. Sarah murmured assent.

Standing at the baggage carousel, Maggie had to ask, "What's new? You look wonderful. Different."

"The world moved on, and I reinvented myself, yet

again." She inclined her head in what Maggie took to be a gesture of noblesse oblige. "I was raking in money as a banking consultant, but I felt flat. I realized I didn't really care about the banks who were my clients, but I cared about the people in them. I found myself helping them reconnect to their passions, to why they went to work in the first place. Most people want to do good as much as they want to do well." The carousel lurched into motion, and Sarah began scanning it.

"And so?"

"It seems I have a talent for inspiring people to make the changes they need to make." She grinned. "I've had enough practice myself. So I rewrote my business plan and became a coach. I love it. And I'm still making money, enough to cover the pro bono work I want to do. There's my bag, the blue one with the red tag!" She hustled along the conveyer, excusing herself as she stepped in front of others, and retrieved her oversized roll-aboard. Turning back to Maggie, she said, "Let's go meet those kids."

They threaded their way through crowded corridors to the parking lot and deposited Sarah's bag in the trunk. Sarah settled into the passenger seat. Maggie started the engine, wondering what Sarah's change of heart would mean for her plan. Chagrined at her own selfishness, she said, "Tell me more about your new work."

"I am so much happier," Sarah said, clasping hands in front of her heart. "People let me see into their souls now, and I've come to realize how important the spirit is. It's the only continuity. Everything else is flotsam and jetsam. I've rededicated myself to spirit." She lowered hands into her lap, relaxed.

"What does that mean?" Maggie peered through the windshield, looking for directions to the next terminal.

"You know all that Sunday school stuff they fed us as

kids? At the time I hated the hypocrisy, fat burghers saying live like Jesus. I rejected the message because I rejected
the messenger. But I understand now. Jesus is spirit. So is
the Buddha, and the Greek philosophers." Sarah looked
out the side window, then back at Maggie. "I realized I'd
always been looking for something, and I finally found it in
my backyard. Pretty ironic." She paused. "I want to share
the love of spirit with you. And Jenn too."

"What do we have to do?"

"Oh, just listen with an open heart. You two are far
more evolved than my clients. It won't take long." Sarah
turned to face her. "Too heavy for the airport, huh?"

"You read my mind." Maggie concentrated on the traffic, bewildered by Sarah's words but glad for her presence.
She wondered what spiritual Sarah would make of Jenn's
intended and his metaphysical bent. She focused on meeting the next arrival.

☙ ❧

Yet another Starbucks, outside customs at international arrivals, twenty minutes to go. Jenn had looked so happy to
see Sarah. The two women had hugged tightly. Sarah insisted on buying three tall green teas and led them to a table in
a quiet corner. They sat, exchanging "it's-so-good-to-see-
yous" and asking about each other's happenings. Over the
years they had stayed in contact electronically, but visits
had been few. Maggie watched them resume the friendship
that had proved so healing for Jenn a long time before, and
for which she remained grateful.

Sipping her tea, Sarah pointed to Jenn's blazer and long
skirt. "Is this what the fashionable people in India wear?"

"This is what I wear to work in a suburban lawyer's office. The earrings are Indian. Arun's mother sent them to me for Christmas. They're an heirloom." She reached out to touch Sarah's navy blue-clad arm. "I'm so glad you're here early. You'll have time to get to know Arun. You'll like him, Aunt Sarah."

Maggie felt a little twinge of what, envy? Jenn no longer confided in Maggie about Arun and her hopes for the marriage. When they discussed wedding logistics, Jenn remained polite and appreciative, but she stopped there. Maggie wanted to be the one Jenn turned to for happy things as well as practical. Perhaps inviting Sarah to speak for her had been a mistake. She hated feeling so volatile and messy.

Jenn said, "I haven't seen Arun since the fall. You'll forgive me if I fall all over him."

"Lucky man," Sarah said, riffling in her navy blue handbag. She withdrew a little turquoise gift box and placed it in front of Jenn. "I can't wait. For the bride, something old and blue. From my former life."

Inside the box: a ring, a sapphire surrounded by diamonds, a jewel Maggie remembered having seen on banker Sarah's right hand opposite the wedding ring she wore for the three years of her marriage. With the divorce, both rings disappeared; Sarah said she liked symmetry.

"Thank you, Aunt Sarah. But it's way too much. I might not get to wear it. Arun and I will lead humble lives in India."

"Ah, you never know. Think of it as an heirloom, from me."

Jenn leaned forward to peck Sarah's cheek. Maggie's gut twisted: one more thing to undo if there were to be no wedding. Then, realizing Jenn could keep Sarah's ring whatever happened, she drew taller in her chair. She decided to join the party.

"Now you have three heirlooms. Remember Mr. Greenberg's dreidel?"

Jenn said to Sarah, "Mom's old boss in Michigan. He used to play with me. Mom has terrific friends."

Sarah said, "Thanks, kiddo. Tell me, will you live full time in India? What will you do?"

"Right now our work is there, but we could work here too, after we get established. I plan to come back regularly once we have children. To see family and maybe for school. Our kids will go to college here for sure."

Sarah put her hand on Jenn's. "Honey, I meant next year. I try not to predict more than eighteen months ahead. Life is full of surprises. Things change."

Jenn withdrew her hand. "I'm dedicated to Arun. That won't change."

"Of course not. But when you eat ice cream, sometimes you like chocolate and sometimes you like vanilla."

Maggie said, "Nuts." They stared at her. "Pistachio, maple walnut, and butter pecan."

Jenn laughed. "You always get blackberry, Mom."

"Only on vacation near a body of water. It's nuts for me otherwise."

Sarah gave her the high sign; Maggie took heart.

The arrivals monitor flashed its changes: Arun's flight had landed and passengers were in the terminal collecting baggage. They rose, dumped their cups in the recycle bin, and moved closer to the customs exit doors. Jenn paced back and forth. Sarah mugged surprise at Maggie; she leaned toward her, whispering that she'd never seen Jenn so physically agitated before. Maggie whispered back that a lot was new. They composed themselves for the wait.

People began straggling through the doors. More travelers emerged, scanning for familiar faces or their names on placards, blinking fatigue from their eyes. "There he is!" Jenn said. She ran to him. Arun lowered his bag to the floor and hugged her. He took her hands in his and kissed her cheek. He looked shorter than Maggie remembered, and tired: stooped shoulders, deep shadows beneath his eyes, almost black in his complexion, and the beginning of a beard. He put Jenn's arm in the crook of his left elbow and they approached. He offered a handshake.

"It's a pleasure to see you, Mrs. Adler. I must apologize for my appearance; it's been a long journey." He turned to Sarah. "You must be Aunt Sarah. Jenn has told me how much you mean to her. I look forward to our acquaintance."

Switching into efficiency mode, Maggie herded them toward the parking garage. As they wound their way, Arun chatted with Sarah about her journey and his. Jenn appeared content to hang on his arm without a word, causing Maggie's gut to tighten and head to ache. She hoped they'd reach Pelham before the headache worsened.

⚜ ⚜

Maggie stood beside the lilac bush, fingering the tightly curled blossoms. In the last little while she had taken solace in the garden, planting and pruning and preparing for the ceremony. This noon it looked lovely, phlox in full bloom, the beds tidy and bushes trimmed. She bent to examine the newest flowers; April's weather had held, and they were budding just in time. Nature appeared to be favoring a wedding.

She straightened, wrapping her sweater closer. Still not warm enough to spend the whole afternoon outdoors, but there was a good chance it would be by May 20. All the trappings for the wedding were in place; she feared it was inevitable.

In the cool, green quiet, her thoughts reverberated around the events of the morning. Arun had looked hearty after a night's rest, so solicitous of Jenn going off to work, and of herself too. Paul, dammit, barely greeted him; why the huge hurry to go to the lab? Couldn't it have waited an hour? And Sarah had turned her nose up at Paul's escape—more of their old animosity, like two alpha dogs growling at each other and pissing on top. The new, spiritual Sarah, the latest new Sarah, was still Sarah underneath. When Sarah had been an environmentalist, then a radical capitalist, and then a corporate wife, Maggie hadn't identified with her preoccupations. It was the force of her commitment that had won Maggie's respect. Maggie loved her powerful, vital Sarah in spite of ideology, not because of it.

Expecting Sarah and Arun back for lunch—they had left the house together to walk off their jet lag—Maggie reentered the warm, yellow kitchen. She planned to serve eggs, a hearty salad, and that good rye bread from De-Cicco's market, a feminine meal, but it would have to do. Jenn had said not to fuss about food, but Maggie felt she should accommodate the vegetarian. God knows she didn't want him as a son-in-law, but as a houseguest he had privileges. And Jenn would approve of her consideration. As she removed her sweater, she heard voices in the front hall. Sarah glided into the kitchen and sat on the banquette in the breakfast nook. She looked peeved.

"Do you have any green tea? I meant to bring some, but I ran out of time."

Maggie stepped into the pantry and returned with a basket containing an odd assortment of accumulated teas. Sarah examined the boxes as Maggie put the kettle on.

"How was the walk?"

"We got to a crossroads past the railroad and then we turned back. He went upstairs for something. He said he's still a little tired. I feel fine, *physically*." Sarah opened a packet and sniffed it.

"How are you mentally?"

Sarah lowered the tea bag. "I'm distressed. I don't want to make snap judgments, but I don't like what I see."

"What happened?" Maggie brought a mug to the table. She sat, listening intently.

"I couldn't get him to engage, and I'm very good at getting people to engage, unless they're putting up barriers. I asked him about Hindu religion. He said he doesn't belong to a church and he doesn't believe in clerics. Okay. But he didn't say what he does believe in. He turned my questions aside like a pro. Why do such a thing if you truly love Jennifer? Wouldn't you engage with her family?"

"Maybe it's jet lag."

Sarah shook her head no. "He's shifty. I can't connect with his spirit."

"What did he say?"

"I'll give you an example. I asked him if Jenn had been comfortable in India last year, and he said she had been learning his philosophy. That is not an answer."

"But it's accurate, according to Jenn."

"Not acceptable. He should have showed more heart."

Maggie had judged Arun to be relatively forthright, if inappropriate for her daughter. In a flash, she remembered Sarah's initial, suspicious reaction to Paul. Did Arun somehow remind her of Paul or was she wary of all male interlopers? "Give it time. He comes from a culture where formalities count."

"Of course. But I am issuing an alert. You did well to bring me in." She leaned back, sentence pronounced.

The kettle began to burble at the same time Maggie's phone chirped receipt of a text. She picked up the phone: Brian wanted to see her. She texted, "not now I've got company" and turned off the gas under the now shrieking kettle. Brian would not be placated by a text message; she owed him an explanation for staying away since that unfortunate dinner. She would arrange a meeting. Send Sarah and Arun off together again on the pretext that they needed to get to know one another. She took the kettle to the table and poured water for Sarah's tea.

Sarah said. "He's changed her. She used to chatter, peppered with 'likes.' Now she's quiet and uses proper English."

"I asked her about 'like.' She said she realized it wasn't necessary."

"Or he told her so."

Maggie shook her head and returned the kettle to the stove.

"Why so silent? I'm your ally now that I see what's going on."

"Sarah, what can you really see in such a short time? If you leap to conclusions, you'll alienate Jenn."

"You are wound tight." She took a sip. "I know I don't have the whole picture, but when I tune in to spirit, I am truly guided."

Maggie thought about the times prior Sarahs had claimed to have found true north. Each time she'd begun a new life, she'd followed it with gumption. Gut, or spirit, or whatever Sarah chose to call it, had worked for her, hadn't it? "Well, I'll follow your lead."

"No you won't. You'll go your own way. You always do." She looked straight into Maggie's eyes. "Be warned, I'm going to make you listen because I've found the source, and someone as spiritual as you should tap in." She took another sip. "Got any honey?"

Maggie retrieved a plastic container shaped like a bear from the pantry. Passing the honey bear to Sarah, she said, "I don't think Arun's shifty. He's complicated." Why was she defending him? She wasn't defending him; she was defending Jenn. "I don't mean to defend him. I just don't want to cross Jenn."

"Understood. I know what I'm doing. My clients say 'It's complicated' whenever they want an excuse not to change things. We get there, by the grace of God and my persistence. Trust me." Sarah rose, sweetened tea in hand. "Do I have time to do email before lunch?"

"Is half an hour enough?"

Sarah nodded yes and slipped out of the kitchen.

Maggie opened the fridge to start the salad. *Trust me.* That might be a problem. She didn't question Sarah's affection, but she worried about her judgment. Had something transformed Sarah, or was she herself different, still loyal and grateful for the friendship yet more hardheaded, more demanding? It pained Maggie to consider Sarah in a new light, not as the energetic enthusiast she sometimes envied but as the obnoxious dilettante Paul had long disliked. How many decades had she and Sarah known and loved each other? That wouldn't change. But this visit might not go as planned.

⁓⃝ ⃝⁓

Maggie carried two fresh bath towels into the guest room for Sarah, already in the shower. As she raised her hand to knock on the bathroom door to hand them in, her eye caught on a note in Sarah's loopy hand atop a ratty spiral notebook on the bureau. She hesitated, then paused to read. Sarah had written, "I found this on a shelf in the garage, from a very long time ago. Love, S." Her heart contracted as she opened the book: there, in Jenn's adolescent handwriting, lay jottings from that awful summer. She read the first entry:

Dr. K. wants me to write every night so I don't keep going round and round. Aunt Sarah drives us to work and she doesn't question me. She leaves me alone at night. I could borrow her car but the freeways are too confusing, and where would I go? I'm bad company, which is why she wants me to write. I am trying to believe that the whole thing wasn't my fault. I don't. Why didn't I see it coming? How stupid. He said you are the only one who ever believed in me, and I fell for it. Joan of Arc. Kidnapped by a nasty drunk. No, not kidnapped, I walked in with my delusions. Dr. K says my anger is misplaced. Ha—how do you pick up your anger and put it in another place? Whoever figures out how to carry anger in a baggie will rule the world.

Maggie flipped pages, past doodles of dogs and what looked like waves at the beach, and sideways writing, and splotches that might have been caused by a fluid, to the last entry:

Tomorrow I get on a plane to go home and start my senior year. Mom and Dad will meet me at the airport, and she will have that slightly terrified look on her face and he will be all noise. They'll ask me what my summer was like. How can I explain/ I don't need to. They will worry but it's not a question of whether or not they can trust me around boys or at school. It's a question of whether I can trust me. I'm still not sure, but Dr. K says she does, and I think I can. At any rate, I'm going to find out. You gain nothing sitting on the sidelines. And we know complaining is not my style.

What a brave girl, Maggie thought, braver than she herself might have been if life had betrayed her at seventeen. She replaced the notebook on the bureau, glad she had snooped. She knocked on the bathroom door and slid the towels inside. Sarah trilled "Thanks," and Maggie shut the door behind her. It had taken Jenn quite a while to rebuild her self-confidence after the rape, most of college actually. And now she wanted to put herself to an extreme test. Maggie thought, my poor brave girl.

TWENTY-ONE

Paul used his hypotenuse technique to cut through the crowd in Grand Central Station. You looked down as you walked in a diagonal to your destination, forcing the other people to use peripheral vision unconsciously to avoid you. He emerged untouched on Forty-Second Street sensing spring—a layer of sweetness over the asphalt stink of traffic and the salty odor of pedestrians—and headed south in long strides. To clear his head, he wanted to walk to the hospital rather than take the rush-hour subway. Now that Sarah had turned sanctimonious, she annoyed him even more than before. He'd left home before breakfast, taking the early commuter train to avoid her, and the fakir.

As he reached Park Avenue South, his mind turned to the work he needed to complete before the conference in June. He had persuaded the tumor research society to give him a prominent place in the program. This was it. He'd announce his latest breakthrough, the capper to more than ten years' work, proving that his approach to the tumor microenvironment had been correct all along. He imagined the faces, some shocked, most of them impressed, as the presentation unfolded. They'd crowd around him when the lights came back on, clamoring to collaborate. But he'd reject their offers. No one would ride his coattails to glory. Let them find the courage to buck the trends and generate original hypotheses. He could almost taste his triumph now.

He crossed the street against the light, staring down an irate motorist, and his thoughts tumbled forward. As soon as he got to the lab, he would prepare the précis for his next grant proposal. He'd need to submit instantly once the news got out. A paragraph began to crystalize in his head. He considered finding the nearest subway station and taking the train the rest of the way. No, better to exercise—gut beginning to protrude over belt.

Subways were so damn efficient. He'd investigated them in all the cities where his various conferences had been held over the previous twenty years: Paris, London, Washington D.C., San Francisco, Barcelona. Compared to the others, New York's subway was smelly and loud— trains ricocheted along the tracks and the sound penetrated cars and tunnels—but it was also fast and logical. He was a fan. New York one; Midwest zero.

A woman in a sari carrying a baby and pulling a cart full of D'Agostino grocery bags crossed the sidewalk in front of him. As he strode past, he saw her enter a building using her hip to open the door. That could be Jenn a couple of years from now. What a waste of talent. He caught himself: maybe the woman was a medical doctor running errands before work. A swarm of Indian women brought curry in plastic containers to the hospital cafeteria, eating and chatting together, stethoscopes hanging around their necks. Maybe this one was delivering her child and supplies to the nanny. Maybe this one *was* the nanny. In New York, anything was possible.

What did he need to have in hand to write the précis? Some new tables and figures showing Alicia's latest results. He'd make them himself, in neon colors. Walking faster, he neared the deli next to the hospital. Should he stop for a quick breakfast? Nah, he'd ask Sandi to bring him a dry bagel. He needed to lose the gut—well, some of it—by June.

When he opened the anteroom door, Sandi said, "Alicia's waiting in your office. She was here when I came in. She looks like she's been crying." He walked to her desk and proffered a five-dollar bill. She grumbled as she rose, "This is the last time. In the future, you fetch your own coffee."

"Black, and a plain bagel, no schmear. Thanks."

She took the bill and stepped into the hallway, then turned back. "You're buying me a coffee. It'll give you two a minute."

"What's up?"

"No idea. She doesn't confide in me."

He entered his office and hung his windbreaker on the hook behind the door. Sitting on the folding chair beside the cluttered desk, Alicia looked paler than normal but otherwise composed.

"I'm surprised to see you so early."

"I have to tell you. I'm worried. It was so uncalled for."

Eyes on her face, he sat down behind the desk. Her hands, normally fussing with paper or computer, lay still in her lap. "Go on."

"Last night I was finishing up and Provost Stamford

came into the lab. He said he wanted to talk. He never said one word to me before this."

Paul felt his hackles rise. "And?"

"He wanted to know about the last two experiments. He said he read the weekly summary and thought they were complicated, so he wondered if they had gone smoothly. I told him yes and no—that I had to redo some parts. Then he wanted to know which ones and why, and if I did the work or if you did. I didn't know what to say."

"He's out of line. I'll deal with him."

Alicia looked down. "That's what I told him. I mean, that he should talk to you."

"Right. I need you to work, not gossip. I want to make new figures from last week's data. Set it up on your computer?"

She looked at him. "Will we be okay?"

"Of course. More than okay. You're going to be famous."

The corners of her mouth relaxed a millimeter. She rose. "I'll open the file."

He fussed with his computer as she left the room. He stared at the screen, mouse in hand. Whatever Stamford was up to had something to do with Hope. Maybe she'd said something about Alicia. No matter, he was safe. He had made sure himself that Hope's work had been properly entered. She didn't know enough science to be dangerous. He squinted at the screen.

A sour taste formed in his mouth. No other woman had ever rejected him. Ever since the army, he'd enjoyed every piece of flesh that had stirred him sufficiently, and the women had been grateful. But with Hope, the attraction went beyond lust. She understood his mind and it excited her. How could she abandon him, and for Martin Miller of all people?

In the two weeks since she walked out, he'd first doused his anger with thoughts of revenge. He fantasized about bursting into Miller's lab and calling her a liar, convincing Miller to dump her. After he'd cooled some, he reframed the ugly business. Bedding Hope, he decided, had been a sexual experiment. He'd wanted to screw an aristocrat, a young athlete with strong, long legs. He should have suspected her motives when she came on to him, but the sex had been good. He prided himself on mounting the thoroughbred so expertly. All in all, he gave the experiment a C. Irene got a B-plus because she treated him right, to the best of her ability. Maggie didn't count; she was like lab hardware, quietly functioning in the background.

This morning the sour taste lingered. Why did Stamford keep poking around? Son of a bitch needs to be the only hero in the hospital? He closed the computer and marched into the wet lab to work up Alicia's data once again, better this time.

When Metro North stopped at Pelham, it was full dark. He drove home from the station, weighing how much of that day's work he could preview to his colleagues without giving Stamford any leverage. He'd tell the team, of course—their work had made it all possible—and swear them to secrecy. He knew he had their respect and could count on their loyalty. Turning into his driveway, he could see into the lighted living room: the four of them appeared to be in conversation. He hesitated at the doorstep, anticipating a tiresome evening. Maggie came into the hallway to meet him.

"We waited half an hour; then we ate. Your meal is in the kitchen. I am appalled at your rudeness."

"Today's stuff was more important than manners."

"Manners? Don't you understand what's going on?"

"Cut me some slack. I'm hungry." He hung up his windbreaker and turned away from her. He heard her heels click angrily on the hardwood floor.

A plate wrapped in plastic lay on the top shelf in the refrigerator. He ate the cold meal standing at the counter, savoring the flavors. Maggie could cook. She always could cook, even back when they were too poor to buy a steak. He could count on her making a good meal, if nothing else. There was a time, he mused, when they enjoyed a healthy screw. He couldn't remember when they'd started avoiding each other or who was at fault. She'd blame him regardless. He placed the empty plate in the sink and, wiping his mouth and hands on the dish towel, went to face the company.

Jenn sat on the couch leaning into her lover, right hand planted on his thigh. Maggie and Sarah sat opposite them on the love seat. A depressing sight. He wanted to go down to the Lair and watch a baseball game, put his feet up, and sip bourbon. But Jenn would be hurt and Maggie ticked off, and then he'd hear about it. He sat in the wing chair near the fireplace, waiting for a break in the conversation to apologize for being late. Sarah glared at him. Maggie looked away.

Arun said, "I understand that you are on the verge of a discovery, Dr. Adler."

"Call me Paul. No, I'm on the verge of proving that my discoveries are correct. The standard of proof in science is sky high."

"As it should be," Arun said. "I look forward to hearing about your work."

"Not now, Paul," Sarah said. "We were discussing Arun's visit to India last month. He's made a fascinating discovery."

Arun demurred. "Not a discovery in the scientific sense. I have been telling the ladies about a technology that is having a great impact on the poor. In a village, one woman gets a cell phone that she rents to her neighbors for a few minutes at a time. The cost is low. Then everyone has access to information that they need."

Sarah said, "They can bank by phone. That's so important! People need a safe way to transfer money so they don't get robbed on the way to the market."

Arun said, "Yes, and farmers use the phone to find out crop prices so they know how to sell without being exploited by middlemen. The American government is sponsoring NGOs to send health information by telephone. It is social transformation without war, in the style of Gandhi. The blessings of the twenty-first century are coming to rural India."

Paul said, "What about the curses? Teenagers plotting terror attacks by cell?" He could feel his blood pressure rise as he watched Arun's pudgy face.

Arun said, "That too—more likely in Pakistan than in India. As you see, Jenn's and my work becomes all the more necessary."

Jenn said, "Arun thinks there may be a way for us to partner with one of the NGOs he met with. We won't know until we get there. I am so excited!"

Arun took her hand in his. "You have two weddings to think about first."

Maggie rose. "I'm going up. Knock on my door if you need anything. Good night."

As if waiting for the first person to make a move, the others stood. Jenn said good night and took Arun's hand as they climbed the stairs. Paul realized that Arun would be bunking with Jenn. Maggie must have given Sarah the guest room. She'd broken another one of her rules. Inviting Sarah had been a bad idea, and he wanted Maggie to know she'd made a mistake. He followed the others up the stairs.

Maggie stood in front of the narrow, old-fashioned closet in their bedroom, removing her clothes. He sat on the foot of the bed, watching the familiar contours of her limbs emerge as she pulled off shirt and stepped out of slacks. He wanted to prick her, like a balloon. Self-righteous about her precious Sarah. Time to deflate.

"Your old buddy seems to have taken to the fakir. She likes his idea of church by cell phone."

"She doesn't like him. She agrees with him that everyone needs a bank."

"Yeah, even people who live on a dollar a day."

"You can't stand it when other people have good ideas."

"Here we go again."

"If Arun were an untouchable instead of a Brahman, you'd cheer him on."

"That's ridiculous."

"You know you're a reverse snob."

"Irrelevant. I'm talking about my daughter. She is not going to marry that creep. I'm gonna put my foot down." He stood up, coiled to pounce.

"Where are you going to put it? On Jenn's neck? Don't be foolish. Jenn won't be bullied." She slipped the baggy T-shirt that served as a nightgown over her head.

He approached her. "She's naive. She doesn't know men lie. I will straighten her out."

"You're so busy strutting in front of Arun that you can't see who's lying and who's not."

"Watch your tongue." He would hit her if he stayed a minute longer. "I'm going downstairs."

"You can stay there."

He slammed the bedroom door behind him, shaking the old wooden framing, sending reverberations down the hall. He descended into the Lair and turned the television on loud. One shot of bourbon remained in the bottle in the cabinet. He found a passably clean glass and poured. Maggie had pushed his button. Years before, in a few weak moments, he'd let slip some comments that she'd interpreted to mean that he was prejudiced against the upper crust, even if he envied them. So what if he detested spineless little guys who pulled rank to get ahead? What mattered was Jenn sitting silently next to Arun, as if she meant to walk four steps behind him for the rest of her life. His plucky, chatty girl, full of adventure, transformed into a shadow. To hell with Maggie's cautions. He would get Jenn alone tomorrow and make her see straight.

He sat at his desk and sipped, confirmed in his resolve. The booze spread warmly in his mouth and slid down his throat, biting gently in his chest. He could feel the coil of gut beneath his ribs untwist. He sipped, a fine flavor on his palate, a tang mounting the back of his throat. Every sip a pleasure, every morsel of pleasure improving his mood. With a sigh, he booted the computer and connected to the lab. In a few moments the file opened. He inspected the graphs he had labored over at Alicia's machine. Two of the curves, in cherry red and acid green, arched solidly upward, showing a steady response to the treatment Alicia had applied to her breast cancer mice. He was comforted by the incontrovertible proof that the mechanism he had posited was, in fact, responsible for the mice's tumors and that the antagonist he had discovered could block it. It was only a matter of time before other scientists would translate his discoveries into clinical practice. Some drug company would make a fortune from his ideas. He didn't care. A lifetime of hard work would be recognized, and the world would be better off besides.

TWENTY-TWO

"How many for lunch?" Jenn said, preparing to set the dining room table.

"Four. Sarah said they'd be back before noon," Maggie called from the kitchen, hands coated with flour to punch down the spongy dough for christopsomo, Greek Christmas bread, rich and sweet. A yeasty smell emerged from the pantry, where the dough had been rising since early morning. With a whoosh, the sponge collapsed around Maggie's fist, and she kneaded the soft, stringy mass with pleasure. She used to make christopsomo on special occasions when Jenn was little. Jenn wanted to serve it instead of wedding cake, saying the family and friends she had invited would prefer it. Maggie couldn't find her old cookbook, but the Internet provided a recipe. She wanted to make sure this version would rise as forecast in her drafty pantry. So far, so good.

"I bet Aunt Sarah is giving Arun the third degree."

"You know our Sarah."

"He won't mind. She has good intentions. Last night she insisted I tell her the exact moment I fell in love with him. I said it was gradual, but she pushed me hard, and I actually found the moment."

Maggie kept her eyes on the dough atop the floured cutting board. "When was it?"

"About a year ago. We were in a slum outside Delhi, and we'd been meeting nasty people all day, and I was hot and tired and discouraged. We went to this restaurant, and they said they were closing. I was ready to cry, but Arun took the guy aside and talked to him. And then the guy walked us past the restaurant into his house and out onto a courtyard, and he brought fruit drinks and the most delicious food and left us there. It was so peaceful. Arun brings out the best in people."

Maggie could imagine being so stressed and tired in a foreign city that you mistook relief for love. She said nothing, glad to be let in on the story.

Jenn spoke in a faraway voice, "Arun makes people feel safe. He makes me feel safe."

Were those the words of a wounded teenager? Maggie wondered. Jenn never talked about being raped. Had she gravitated to Arun because he was so different from her aggressor? And if so, did it matter? The fact was, Jenn was in love.

Maggie broke off a small ball of dough and divided it in half. Then she called Jenn to finish the loaf. Jenn came to her side, smiling, and floured her hands. She formed the two balls of dough into long ropes and slit the ends. Maggie watched, swept by a wave of nostalgia, as Jenn crisscrossed the ropes on top of the mound of dough and curled the split ends into spirals.

"Walnuts or cherries?" Jenn asked.

"Walnuts, I think. Cherries would be pretty, but walnuts will go better with the meal." She passed a jar of mixed nuts to her daughter.

Jenn picked through the jar, removed four walnut halves, and stuck one in each of the four spirals. "You know, we could use three ropes and make six coils. It's not Christmas."

"Do you want to start again? It's not too late."

Jenn laughed, "No thanks. This loaf's practice, and you have enough to do."

How like Jenn, Maggie thought, to rewrite the instructions. Not because she was a contrarian but because she looked at situations, big and small, with unbiased eyes and created her own logic. Maggie herself was different. Since she could remember, her first impulse had been to figure out what was wanted in a situation and then to deliver it efficiently. She didn't wander from a path once undertaken, until it was done and done right. Not until recently, when she began to meander. That course on Indian civilization had turned out to be so invigorating, and it had led to the liaison with Brian, such as it was. It seemed to Maggie that Jenn had always been able to make her meanders meaningful. With a shudder, she realized that Jenn's ability to see possibilities might cement her to Arun. But would anything good materialize from their union? She herself had fallen in love with a vision of Paul—a noble vision of struggle against the pain of cancer—that was not fulfilled and that, she had come to realize, would never be fulfilled. She had so little to look forward to as Paul's companion. Fear for Jenn's future crept into her heart.

"May I say something? When you talk about Arun,

you remind me of me. I fell in love with your father because he was going to cure cancer. He didn't."

Jenn covered the dough with a dish towel. "Arun's very different from Dad, no offense. Arun doesn't have all the answers, but he's optimistic about change. I know he will make a difference. I never met anyone who turns philosophy into action as beautifully as he does."

"Sounds very abstract."

"Yeah, but he's a concrete guy. And he makes me happy. In every way." Jenn picked up the cutting board. "Where do you want me to leave the loaf?"

"Top shelf in the pantry. It seems to be warm enough." Maggie took little comfort in Jenn's words, although she was glad Jenn had chosen to share them. Yes, Arun and Paul couldn't be compared; was she off base comparing Jenn to herself at twenty-six? Her own history uncoiled in her head in a split second, and then Jenn's. The two histories looked similar in outline but so different in detail, the precious, impossibly fine-grained detail wherein God, or the devil, lay. She realized she could not predict the future trajectory for either of them, except that they would necessarily diverge. She pursed her lips, chiding herself to stay in the moment, the immediate task being a hearty vegetarian salad for four with a tuna fish option for Sarah.

The doorbell rang; Jenn wiped her hands and went to answer. In a moment, Sarah and Arun followed Jenn back into the kitchen. Sarah plopped down in the breakfast nook; Arun stood leaning in the doorway. Jenn cozied into him. Seeing the high color in Sarah's cheeks, Maggie put on the teakettle and sat opposite her.

Sarah's eyebrows arched. "It seems we have a difference of opinion. Arun and I agree there's more to a human than flesh and blood. There's something ineffable I call spirit. He says it's a life force, like an aura, you know, a ring of energy around someone's head, and it's just a matter of time before some hacker cracks the code."

Arun said, "Not exactly, Sarah." His cheeks bunched up in a broad Indian smile. He addressed Maggie. "I am trying to express my opinion that humankind will eventually develop a deeper respect for the mystery of life. I used the example of bees. Bees can perceive the electric field of a flower. It's like another color for them, I imagine. I told Sarah that I hope there is potential for people to perceive so many colors that they stand back in awe."

"Are you talking about *darshan*?" Maggie said.

"Ah, Maggie, you are very kind. Jenn told me about your studies. I have seen *darshan*; I have seen Indian people moved to tears by the sight of greatness. My grandparents talked about Gandhiji with such love, and my parents about Mandela. No, I mean something more earthly and achievable.

"And I say," Sarah cut in, "that we don't need to wait for some academic to write up auras. Spirit is in the holy books that have guided people for thousands of years."

Jenn said, "I thought you didn't hold with religious orthodoxy, Aunt Sarah."

"I don't. I don't feel constrained by dogma, any dogma. I do believe that the great religious teachers of the past have been moved by spirit. It's no coincidence that all the holy books say the same thing. Love God and you are saved. There's no need to get more complicated."

The kettle that had been burbling launched into a full scream. Jenn left Arun's side to turn it off. No one made a move for a cup.

Maggie said, "Sarah, it *is* complicated. So many things get in the way. Think of all the self-help books people buy. With cause."

"I tell you, I can see it in my clients. When people talk about complications they are just making excuses for their unwillingness to look at the truth of their lives."

Jenn interjected, "Maybe they're not unwilling. Maybe they don't know how."

"That's no excuse for not doing the hard work to learn. I thought I could ignore the great teachings. I did ignore them until now. And *now* I am fulfilled."

Jenn said, "That's how Arun and I want our clients to feel."

Arun said, "But it is difficult, especially in India, where so many do not have basic necessities. Clean water, an intact roof during the monsoon. That is why we align ourselves with the microfinance NGO. To provide the whole package, so to speak." Jenn stepped to his side, and he took her hand.

Maggie said, "We can continue the conversation over lunch. Do you want to wash up first? I need twenty minutes to get everything on the table."

Jenn blew her mother a kiss and led Arun out of the kitchen.

Sarah stared at Maggie. "Why did you cut me off? I didn't get to use my A game."

"You can argue with him later. I want you for myself." Maggie reached across the table to hold Sarah's hand. "Tell me what you mean about being fulfilled now. You've always seemed to be dug in and enjoying it. Far more than other people, including me."

Sarah's expression softened. "That's the way it looked.

I even believed it myself. Each time I made a life change, I thought I'd found the key. And I enjoyed the idea so much that I ignored how miserable it made me."

"You never talked about being miserable. You could have cried on my shoulder."

"I was too busy being busy. But the universe has finally brought me peace." Sarah leaned forward and lowered her voice. "Maybe it will bring me a man. Better than old Matthew—what a misguided choice that was."

Maggie pictured Sarah on the arm of her former husband, preening and smiling at a thousand watts. Each time they traveled, Sarah brought back acres of photos that looked like happily ever after. Until she began to find Matthew lacking, first in polish, then in gumption. Maggie had thought Matthew gutsy enough, if a little pale. When Sarah had confided her growing doubts, Maggie had said that Sarah had enough gumption for two. Sarah had replied that she wouldn't settle, and that was the end of that.

"And so?"

"Don't get excited. I'm not looking for a lover, although it would be nice to fuck now that I don't need contraception. No, now I have what I needed all along. It is such bliss to finally stop searching and curl up in God's love, whatever you want to call it."

Maggie wondered if Sarah heard the irony in her words. How could she be sure this life change wouldn't disappoint her as well? What a revelation—strong-minded Sarah had felt rudderless underneath! In comparison, Maggie thought, her own commitments looked solid. Her heart went out to her friend, suddenly transformed from heroic into ordinary, and pathetic, and sympathetic. She wanted to shake Sarah and comfort her at the same time.

"You sound a lot like Arun."

"Nope. Night and day. He makes excuses for people."

"Do you object because he's not Christian?"

"Of course not." Sarah sighed and withdrew her hand. "I have no truck with organized religion. I just don't trust him. He talks about electric fields and mysteries in the same breath. I think he's trying to suck up to you and Paul. To make Jenn think you approve of him. I'm sorry to say I do not." Sarah's face looked pinched.

"I've spent more time with him than you, and I have to say I think he's sincere. He's trying to do something old-fashioned in a modern way."

"Sell snake oil?"

Maggie laughed. "There's always a market for snake oil. No, he reminds me of a teacher I had in Sunday school, only more up-to-date." The teacher, Mr. Steede, used to quote Aldo Leopold to the class so fervently that Maggie, at twelve, felt embarrassed for him.

"How is he going to earn a living teaching Sunday school in India?"

"You sound like Paul. We'll never convince Jenn that he shouldn't try."

Jenn walked into the kitchen. "Did I hear my name? I came to help with lunch. Arun's Skyping with his folks."

Sarah said, "I meant to ask, how old is Arun?"

"Thirty-one. He seems older because he's wise."

Maggie rose to get lunch going. Months before, she'd assumed Arun was older and hadn't thought to ask. Foolish. His talk made more sense coming from a thirty-year-old than a forty-year-old.

"Does he call his parents often?" Sarah said.

"He's close to his folks. They're ophthalmologists. They

work in a big hospital and run a free clinic on the side in a poor neighborhood. I think they're his inspiration, although he says it's me." Jenn blushed. "What can I do, Mom?"

"Nothing yet. I'll need a steady hand at the cutting board in a minute." Jenn sat in the nook as Maggie gathered ingredients from the fridge.

Sarah said, "What do his parents think about his marrying an American?"

"We spent a week with them last spring. They like me. They sent Arun to school here, so I guess they were prepared." Jenn paused. "Aunt Sarah, you seem so uncomfortable around Arun. Will you tell me what's on your mind? I want you two to be friends."

"Oh, boy." Sarah leaned back and crossed arms over her chest. She looked at Jenn and her face softened. "I'll be straight with you, hon. Arun makes me uncomfortable because I think he's got the wrong idea about what people need to be happy. He can't build a business on shifting ground. I'm worried that he'll disappoint you."

"He's not building a business—*we* are. And we expect the ground to shift. It always does when you start something." Her voice lowered. "Arun and I agree about all the big things and most of the little things, Aunt Sarah. We match. I hope you will be able to see that."

"I hope so too sweetie." Sarah uncrossed her arms in a gesture that Maggie took for surrender. Temporary surrender. No doubt a tactic.

"It's my turn to go wash up." Sarah rose and headed for the stairs. "Fifteen minutes 'til lunch? Half an hour?"

"Fine. I'll call."

Maggie spread plastic tubs on the counter and lifted a chopping knife from the wood-block holder that had been a wedding present a million years earlier. Jenn approached, and Maggie pointed with the knife.

"All the veggies need to be chopped bite-sized. Keep the cooked and the raw separate for now, okay?"

Jenn nodded. She picked up tomatoes and took them to the sink. Rinsing, she talked over her shoulder. "Thank you for stopping the argument. I thought Aunt Sarah would like Arun. I don't know what's bugging her."

"She wants the best for you, according to her way of thinking."

"Yeah, I know. Like you and Dad. No one seems to see that I *have* the best according to *my* way of thinking. You're all watching Arun's every move, dissecting every word. It's like I'm invisible."

Maggie felt Jenn's hurt and sought to ease it. "I'm sorry. No one means to ignore you. We're just trying to understand Arun." She stepped beside Jenn. "Help me see you better."

Jenn dried the tomatoes with a dish towel and placed them on the counter next to her mother. "I'm not worried about money. You and Dad should know that I'm not irresponsible. If the NGO deal falls through, Arun and I will both get teaching jobs. We'll be fine. We know how to take care of ourselves and each other. But we also care about what we do in the world, and we won't stop until we get that right. Separately and together."

"You're so quiet around Arun that I never see the separate part. And you don't seem to be having fun."

Jenn looked surprised. "I'm fine. I'm trying to give all of you a chance to get to know Arun. You already know me."

"Fair enough."

Did she really know Jenn as well as she should? Could

she imagine Jenn's dreams? Would she like them if she could? Did she have the right to judge? Maggie promised herself to do a better job of focusing on her daughter and not on the distraction. She handed over the knife. "Chop, please. They took such a long walk they must be hungry."

Maggie went into the pantry to get a can of tuna, thinking hard. Jenn had said *they know how to take care of each other*. How wonderful that at twenty-six Jenn understood commitment, perhaps better than Sarah ever had. Maggie's heart swelled with pride, and something deep inside shifted: she saw Jenn as her own woman, with a moral compass she wouldn't lose, more sure of her direction than she herself had been when she first followed Paul. Yet Arun would take Jenn away. That god-awful fact dimmed the light.

TWENTY-THREE

A long marriage, Paul thought, conferred a few benefits. Without a word, they had adopted a truce. Maggie had nodded assent when he left early to escape the clamor of the houseguests. Here in the office, he'd have eight hours—nine if he skipped lunch—of blessed silence to lay out the slides for his presentation, to display the logic behind those gorgeous red and green curves. He opened PowerPoint and the data files. No need to make an outline. The structure of his argument would emerge naturally, as it always did when he concentrated on his science.

A knock on the door. Robert Stamford stood in the open doorway.

"May I come in?" Stamford's mouth bent in an odd little smile.

Paul did not invite him to sit in the folding chair beside the desk.

Stamford continued. "It seems there's a problem. I got a call from Martin Miller last night. Evidently he's been looking up your last few papers."

"If Miller has questions, he should call me, not you."

Stamford frowned and clasped hands in front of his chest. His head bobbed over a ridiculous yellow bow tie—a clown with clout. "That's the problem. He said it's a matter of concern for the hospital, and he doesn't want to confront you."

"Confront me? What are you talking about?" His gut began to tighten. He wanted Stamford gone.

"Evidently Hope Caldwell showed him some of your results. Martin says he discovered anomalies in the data. I suggested he contact you directly." He paused. "You are listed as second author on the papers he's questioning."

"Always good to advance the team."

"I know you are directing the experiments, but are you absolutely sure of your staff?"

"So that's why you interrogated Alicia the other day." His temper was rising.

"Hardly interrogation, Paul. I am trying to help."

"No you're not. You're trying to intimidate my employee and undermine me. How did Miller turn himself into your new favorite?" He heard the absurdity in his words, but he couldn't control them. Miller's audacity stunned him. Wait, he thought, was Hope behind this? He'd done nothing to her that deserved retribution.

Stamford raised hands in the shape of a tepee to his chin. "Paul, patience. We'll get to the bottom of it. I reported Martin's comments to the ethics board. Hospital policy, you know. They will want the facts from you and your researchers, and they'll straighten things out."

"I don't have time for your bureaucracy. I have a presentation to give." You meddling jackass, he thought.

"The chair is aware of your constraints. The committee

will respect your time. Please cooperate. It's to your advantage." Stamford took a step backward, as if recoiling from the tension in Paul's body.

Paul growled, "You should have come to me first."

"I followed policy. I'm coming to you now. I want to help."

"Like hell you do."

"I'll leave you to your work." Stamford took another step back. "I assure you, the board will clear up any misunderstandings." He nodded and turned on his heel.

Paul focused eyes on those red and green curves on the screen, but his brain did not cooperate. His arms and legs filled with electricity, demanding action. He stood, phoned Miller's lab, and asked for Hope. Told she was working from home, he made a rash decision. He'd take the subway and get to her place in twenty minutes, max. Telling Sandi he'd be back within the hour, he left.

In the underground, the clatter of the ricocheting trains soothed him. He boarded the 5; the rails screamed as it rounded bends. He admired the hard, hot, groaning steel—real power as compared to innuendo. His anger cooled, giving way to confidence that he could make Hope drop whatever game she and Miller were playing. She owed him big, after all.

He held the door to Hope's building open for an elderly woman on her way out. Piece of luck—no need to ring to be let in. He took the elevator to the fourteenth floor, rehearsing his opening lines. The hallway on fourteen smelled expensive: echoes of furniture polish, cut flowers, and other East Side indulgences. He knocked on the door. An eye appeared on the other side of the peek hole above the brass 14 C. In a moment, Hope opened the door to her tiny apartment, her face a question mark.

"This is unexpected." She gestured to the lone stool in the kitchenette. He entered and sat. She wore leggings and a tight T-shirt, with no makeup. Not pretty, but fabulous legs, hips, tits. She said, "There's some stale coffee." He shook his head no. She leaned against the wall across from him, eyes fixed on him.

The place looked different, messy. Clothes drooped from the edges of the two large canvases; a pile of books sat next to the unmade bed. She had added a reading lamp and a wing chair that looked like it could be one of her mother's antiques. Shoes lay in a jumble on the floor of the open closet. Text editor was open on a laptop sitting on the counter. So she lived here now, no new guy in the wings. Despite his better judgment, he felt gratified. "They said you're working from home. I expected to see a lab setup."

Hope shook her head. "I've been given editorial duties. Most of the others have English as a second language. Martin wants them published well. My very proper education comes in handy." She shrugged her strong shoulders.

"Disappointed?"

"Why are you here, Paul?"

He had planned to take an indirect approach, but need got the better of him. "I want to know why Martin Miller is complaining about me. What have you shown him?"

"Nothing. I haven't been asked to mount any experiments. Yet." She appeared confused. "I told him what we'd—what your lab's been doing, and I referred him to the current papers." She hugged herself, lifting fulsome breasts beneath the T-shirt.

"Then why did he call your old buddy Stamford?" He stood, frowning, unbelieving. Something didn't click. "What are you and Miller up to?"

She shot him a look of what . . . defiance? Desire? "I don't understand. I've hardly said a word to Martin. He's not hands-on in the lab like you."

"I'm told you like his style better." The memory of Miller's accusation rankled.

She shrugged again.

He lost his last shred of cool. "So if you're not sleeping with him, why did you leave me?" Dammit, he'd had no intention of going there. Picking at a sore that wouldn't heal.

"I told you. It looked like a good career move. I am serious about my future as a biologist, whatever you may think." She took two steps toward the house phone on the wall.

Electricity flooded his arms and legs again; he fought the urge to move. "Are you kidding? I *made* you a biologist. You were a dilettante."

Silent, she took another step.

"I don't know why you and Miller want to screw with me, but it won't work."

"You'd better go." She picked up the receiver.

He glared at her angry horse face. How could he have found her so attractive? "Good luck. You'll need it." He strode out.

He took the fire stairs down two flights, then stopped to catch his breath. He went to the elevator. He'd learned nothing. He kicked himself for coming to see her.

In the subway, replaying the encounter, an awful thought came to him. What if she were telling the truth? Miller was the kind of chilly, brainy guy who got on a high horse and rode. But why? His answers were right. The field would only benefit from his discoveries. He felt agitated, which unnerved him. He returned to the hospital on autopilot. As he walked through Sandi's office toward his own, she raised her questioning head. He waved her off. He wanted to burrow into the data; he wanted to be consoled by the mute certainty of the subcellular world, his muse and refuge for so long.

⋐◎ ◎⋑

He entered the kitchen through the mudroom, stepping into a cloud of frying onion. Arun stood with his back to him at the stove; Jenn sat in the nook chopping cilantro on a cutting board. She looked up, knife in the air.

"Hi, Dad. Nice to see you so early. We're giving Mom a break and cooking an Indian specialty."

"Where's your mother?" He looked around, anxiety barely controlled.

"In the living room with Aunt Sarah. Don't look so worried. We're roasting a chicken for the carnivores. You'll smell it any minute."

He parked his briefcase and entered the living room. Maggie sat on the couch, glass of pinot grigio in hand. Sarah, now a bloody teetotaler, sat opposite. He poured a bourbon at the sideboard and took a swig. Maggie turned toward him.

"You're early. I'm glad. Jenn and Arun are fussing over dinner. I trust we'll like it."

He gestured with the drink to the hallway. She placed her wineglass on the coffee table and followed him. He could see by the cut of her mouth that she was about to lecture.

"You look awful. Are you getting sick?"

He didn't want to explain: he wanted to vent. "Stamford is hounding my staff. I'm sick and tired of his interference."

She rolled her eyes like a teenager. "Oh, Paul. Robert

has a right to talk to your people. He's probably doing you a favor."

"Why do you say that?"

She lowered her voice. "Robert's been a good friend to this family. I trust him."

"That has no bearing on my work."

"I'm not going to fight with you. Let's try to have a civil dinner. Jenn won't live here much longer." She turned on her heel.

He escaped into the basement and powered up his machine. The office cubby smelled moldy despite the constant cranking of the dehumidifier. The papers and charts he had left in disarray on the desk lay curled and soggy. He hadn't the heart to sort them. He switched off the computer and mounted the steps. Maybe he should try to reach his brother. Lenny understood intimidation—used it in his business all the time.

From the hallway, he saw Arun seated on the living room love seat, with Jenn draped against him, opposite the women. Reluctantly, half hiding behind the bourbon in hand, he joined them.

Jenn said, "I hope you're hungry, Dad. We made a lot of food."

Arun said, "The chicken will be ready in less than half an hour. While it roasts, the flavors in my grandmother's best vegetable curry will blend. She would want me to serve it properly."

Sarah said, "Who did the cooking in your household in India?"

"When I was small, my grandmother and the cook fought over control of the kitchen. The food was very good as a result."

"So how did you learn to cook?"

"My father made me learn to prepare a few dishes before I came to America. To combat homesickness. It didn't work, but I discovered that I like to sauté. I like to transform onions into brown sauce, something Americans don't do but Indian cooks very often do."

Sarah pressed on. "What about your mother?"

"My mother deferred to her mother-in-law. She worked full time in a hospital near our home, so she was glad to honor tradition. My grandmother lived to be ninety. After she died, my mother bought a microwave oven." Arun smiled and winked at Jenn.

Sarah said, "Right on, sister."

Maggie laughed. "I don't imagine your parents eat ramen noodles all the time?"

Whiskey caught in the back of Paul's throat and he coughed. They all looked at him. He made a choking gesture and waved them on.

"My parents take most of their meals outside the home. They are devoted to their clinic. They seem to be delaying gratification until their retirement."

Paul cleared his acidic throat. "Is that what you expect my daughter to do? Wait forty years for some comfort?" He knew the women would turn on him, but he didn't give a damn. The fakir deserved to be challenged.

Arun answered, "The only thing I expect your daughter to do is speak for herself."

Jenn sat upright. "Haven't we been over this? You know I don't care about things. You and Mom gave me comfort, but I've seen the other side. I care about being of service. So does Arun. You should congratulate us on finding a way to live our values."

"Fine speech, my girl. What are you going to say when you're flat on your back with dysentery and there's no money to bribe the ambulance driver?"

Annoyance crept into her voice. "Some humane person will get me to the hospital in a pedicab. They do better in traffic anyway."

Arun said, "Your daughter has two wonderful qualities in equal proportion: compassion and the ability to get things done. My admiration for her knows no bounds."

Paul's stomach began to turn. Could be the liquor, could be the sycophantic talk. He leaned back to wait out a wave of nausea. "Well, we agree on something."

Jenn stood and said, "I'm going to check on the chicken." Arun and Maggie followed her out of the room. Sarah stayed behind. He suspected she would scold. Sure enough, she sat down next to him, shaking her head.

"I'm afraid you just blew an opportunity. There are many wonderful ways to be of service in this world. She doesn't have to follow him to India. I suggest you hush up and let me lead the conversation at dinner." She looked at him with arched brows.

He nodded, to be rid of her. The gall of the woman. In his own house. Bile threatened to rise above his epiglottis. He swallowed hard to push it down.

Sarah said, "You will thank me. I'm on your side, you know. I don't want them married. My reason is different from yours, not that it matters." She tapped his arm as if to reassure him. "You don't like his balls. I don't like his spirit—too secretive. Maggie is vacillating. Leave it to me." She rose and left the room, trailing perfume that smelled like rotten fruit.

If he weren't fighting with his gut, he'd protest. Both

women trying to shut him up. No dice. Time he took Jenn in hand and told her what to do. Every girl needs her father to define things for her. He'd get her alone later and straighten her out. Once and for all.

He farted and immediately felt better. His gut rumbled and relaxed. He took another sip, and his thoughts returned to Stamford's words of the morning. No one had challenged his science for a long time, not since graduate school, where carping was a matter of course. When he began getting grants for his specialty, they showed him grudging respect. They may not have liked him, but they admired his ability to invent new approaches to problems. Directing a lab felt great; he'd been pushing himself and his team to accomplish a miracle so sorely needed in biology, and eventually medicine. Miller's comment as reported gnawed at him. Miller, a superb technician, didn't play politics like so many of their colleagues. A creeping sensation around his head and tinnitus in his ears signaled a rise in blood pressure. He took another sip of bourbon to lower it.

Maggie called to him from the dining room saying that dinner would be on the table in ten minutes. He drained the whiskey glass and heaved himself out of the chair, heading for the bathroom to wash up. He'd eat the chicken. After dinner, in the basement, he'd try Irene's line. Irene understood the pressures he felt at the hospital. She would be sympathetic, although it had been a while.

TWENTY-FOUR

Last day on the job for Jenn, nine days until the wedding. Maggie pulled up in front of the law office, and Jenn got out of the car. Maggie promised to pick her up at four o'clock. Jenn blew a kiss and sailed into the building, long skirt swishing around her legs. After a minute, instead of going to the post office and supermarket as she'd told her houseguests she would, Maggie drove to Brian's place. She needed to explain her silence these past weeks. Brian had agreed to delay the start of his workday to hear her out.

She parked across the street from his condo and sat behind the wheel. Lying to Sarah and Arun had been easy. She'd left them sitting in their separate corners, wary of each other after the previous night's interchange. Nothing to be done about that bad blood. Something to be done about Brian. Her desire for uncomplicated sex had faded; she had found her juice again and had tired of the subterfuge. But she was grateful to him for warming her without making demands. They'd had a good time that winter. That was enough. She gathered her purse and phone and locked the car behind her.

He opened his door before she rang the bell.

"Here for a quickie?" He smirked, waving her in.

She refused to be baited. "Thanks for meeting me on short notice. I've a houseful of people and it's hard to get away." She sat in the rocker he had rescued and refinished, barricaded behind its wooden arms. Brian stood leaning against the living room wall, arms and ankles crossed in the lithe posture she'd found so attractive. Before the wedding took precedence. Before the sight of Jenn and Arun exulting in each other had cracked open her longing.

"I've been rude not calling back. I'm sorry."

"Why are you here now, Maggie? Want to make a date?"

"No. I came to apologize. And to explain."

"Explain why you've been wasting time? My time and your time?"

This was getting ugly. "I'm not wasting your time. And I don't have to account for mine."

"What do you expect me to do, sit by the phone and drop everything when you ring?"

"I don't expect you to do anything different than you always do."

"Then why aren't we doing what we always do?"

This was absurd. They had made each other no promises. He had said he was proud of making no demands. A false pride, now showing its true face. She didn't want to cater to another man's pride. In an instant, her heart resolved.

"Brian, it's time to call it off."

"Call it off? Like a dog on the hunt?"

She kept her voice even. "I'm sorry to disappoint you, but I don't want to waste your time. I'm not available now." Not quite true, but she wanted to preserve his dignity.

"I can wait a week until the light turns green." He grinned.

"I haven't toyed with you. Please don't toy with me now."

He unpeeled himself from the wall and sat on the coffee table directly in front of her. "What's the matter, Maggie? Lost your appetite for sex?"

If she reached out, she could stroke his face and neck. He'd been an accommodating lover, and she'd enjoyed learning his ways. When she had wanted to experiment with the tantric sex book one of her classmates had lent her, he had looked bemused but gone along. He'd said she was the only intellectual he'd ever fucked. At the height of their lust, he'd said he preferred her to younger women, who were demanding and judgmental. She'd thanked him for the compliment, disbelieving but pleased nonetheless. Her resolve wavered for a nanosecond.

"I don't want to run away from my problems at home." Not quite true, she thought, but face saving.

He flinched. "Is your husband coming after you?"

"This is not about Paul. This is about you and me. I can't pretend I'm happy sneaking around. I'm sorry."

He looked surprised. "Happy? Who said anything about happy? 'Horny' is the word. Horny you and horny me."

She'd taken the wrong tack. "Brian, I respect you. Please let me say good-bye with respect."

"Come off it. You feel guilty for ditching me, and you think pretty words will make it all right. You're such a tight ass, lady." He reached into a pocket for cigarettes, which he had refrained from smoking at her request.

She opened her mouth to protest, then closed it with a gnash. "You're right. My ass is tight. Too tight to hang with you. You are the master of loose." She felt light, buoyed up because these words were true.

He flicked on a lighter and took a deep drag. "Isn't that why you need me?"

"It's one of the things I *like* about you." Still true. She'd always thought opposites attracted because they complemented one another. She and Paul: steady versus brilliant, practical versus idealistic, responsible versus passionate. Together they'd formed a complete unit, able to accomplish anything. But the attraction was gone. She wanted a new deal, which felt both disturbing and exciting. And Brian wouldn't be part of it.

"So why are you turning your back on me?"

She searched for the right words. "I think we've both been opportunistic these past months. It couldn't last." Still true! She felt no recriminations and no regrets, thank goodness. The sex had helped weld her fractures together, and now she felt solid, ready to act. "Thanks for a good time."

"You're walking out of here just like that?"

"Yes."

He took another drag. "Got another guy in the wings?"

She shook her head no. "It's not about sex. You're a great lover, but I'm not interested anymore." True, for all she knew from her limited sample.

He exhaled through the nose, eyes narrowed. "Giving up sex will make you old."

"I am old." She watched something flicker across his face.

"What if I show up at your daughter's wedding?"

She stared at him, surprised by such peevishness. "Am I really that important to you?" A bit of bravado. If he did show, she could trust Jenn, and even Arun, to make the best of an awkward situation.

He took another drag. "You've never been important to me. You've been convenient."

"Well, sorry for the inconvenience." Angry now, at Brian for lashing out, at herself for answering, she turned away to retrieve her bag from the floor.

"Hey, hey. Got a rise out of you." He stood and walked slowly toward the door. "I guess you're leaving."

She rose, fished car keys out of her bag, and stepped to the door.

He grinned a lopsided grin. "How about a farewell quickie? See what you'll miss?"

She touched his lean, hard arm for a moment and left without looking back.

On the way to Pelham, she let the tears fall. Tears not for Brian but for the self she was when they met, the tentative woman made dry by too much waiting. So dry that Brian had appeared strong and virile, not merely accessible, unlike the husband who stayed away. But it had never been about Brian. It had been about the blood in her veins. And now it was hot, desirous, not for sex but for intimacy, the kind of heated, committed union her daughter talked about. When she watched Jenn address Arun tenderly, she felt a surge of love and optimism. Jenn might succeed where she had failed. Jenn deserved to succeed. She herself might get another chance. And if not, so be it.

Hardly any cars in the supermarket lot. It was too early for the homemakers now driving kids to school. Did she miss having a houseful of children and dogs? No. Was she too old to start again? Maybe. She pushed a cart slowly down the produce aisle, picking up onions and garlic to flavor the vegetarian dishes she now favored, and the potted meat aisle for cans of tuna to add to the omnivores' portions. She walked through the cloying stink of the detergents to the paper section to replenish her store of napkins and toilet tissue. In another week, the guests would be gone and everything would have changed, permanently. She and Paul would be alone; no, she would be alone, Paul at work. And then what? Sarah would say, "Spend time with your spirit." Maggie took comfort in Sarah's endless enthusiasm, if not her philosophy. It was time to confide in her; she would give back.

She unloaded the car in the driveway and brought bags in through the mudroom. The blinking light on the landline answering machine greeted her. A final salvo from Brian? She dialed in and heard her mother's voice asking for an urgent callback about the wedding. She unloaded the groceries and braced for a conversation with Claudia.

Ah, Claudia. At first Jenn's grandmother had objected to a backyard ceremony with a lay officiant as too informal. She meant too secular and inconsequential. When no one responded to her comments, she complained that the noon hour was inconvenient for those coming from a different time zone, like herself. Then she worried that the guest list—twenty family members and close friends—was too short. Maggie could imagine the chaos in her mother's mind, propriety and prejudice battling for control, as she prepared for the trip. Maggie wanted her parents, Jenn's only grandparents, to stand up for Jenn, but she hated walking on eggshells around them, especially when her own feelings were so volatile. She dialed, hoping no one would pick up. Claudia answered. Maggie took a breath.

"I got your message, Mom. We're all having dinner together Saturday after the rehearsal. I'll drive you. I made a reservation for you and Dad at the best hotel in New Rochelle, on us. It's ten minutes away, and they have an accessible suite for Dad." Her father, always a quiet man, had receded further as he had aged. Claudia took good care of him and complained bitterly.

"Do I need to dress for dinner?"

"Be comfortable. And bring a sweater. It gets cool at night."

"Don't tell me the dinner is outdoors too. Isn't that risky? It rains in New York in May."

"The dinner is at a restaurant, and we have a backup plan for the wedding." She couldn't resist a jab: "With a small wedding it's easy to be flexible." She counseled herself to hush. Claudia would hang up soon to keep the cost of the long-distance call to a minimum, even though it was Maggie's nickel.

"Will you pick us up at the airport on Friday?"

"Someone will, Jenn or Arun."

"I'd rather you did. I don't fancy meeting him that way."

"Okay, I'll pick you up. Gotta go. Bye, Mom. See you soon." She replaced the phone in its cradle, mentally reorchestrating her Friday to include a trip to LaGuardia. It had been years since her parents had visited Pelham. Traveling provoked anxiety in Claudia, although Maggie bent herself out of shape to minimize the inconveniences. Claudia's fairly mild commentary just then gave Maggie hope for a satisfactory outcome next week. She took a deep breath and went looking to see if her houseguests wanted lunch.

Sarah descended the stairs into the hallway, dressed for a jog. "Want to run with me? I'll wait for you to change."

"Sorry, I don't run anymore."

"Well, come walk with me. Your future son-in-law is fiddling with his computer. It's just us."

"Let me take you to the park. It's a good place to run."

Maggie put veggies in the fridge, tucked wallet and

keys into her pockets, and swung the front door closed behind them. She didn't lock it; Arun would have to deal with
an intruder in the unlikely event one appeared in midday
in their neighborhood. An hour alone with Sarah would be
the tonic she needed.

They drove down the gentle slope toward Willson's
Woods and the playground Jenn had frequented as a child.
Houses grew progressively smaller along the descent, but
their facades were tidy, sporting shrubs with pink or blue
or white blossoms. In a few weeks, a load of allergens
would permeate the suburban air, and she would suffer.
From time to time she had wondered if living in New York
City itself would have spared her hay fever. They'd stayed
in Pelham for the reliable public schools, for Jenn's sake,
and for her, to be close to friends and commitments. And
through inertia, truth be told.

Maggie parked the car on a side street. She stepped
next to Sarah on the ribbon of sidewalk that paralleled the
curb, noticing, as she had not earlier, that the sky was a
clear blue and the oak trees chartreuse with new growth.
Sarah walked fast; it felt good to stretch out beside her.
Maggie stopped to balance against a waist-high stone wall
to remove a pebble that had lodged under the strap of her
sandal. Sarah stopped and lifted herself atop the wall. She
patted the spot next to her. Maggie boosted herself onto
the wall. She felt for a moment like a schoolgirl at play with
her best friend, not the mother of a girl long graduated.

Sarah said, "I'm sorry to report that I've failed. My
little talk with our girl? I tried to be specific and persuasive.
She agreed with most of what I said, but she didn't connect
the dots."

"Join the club."

"I stopped just short of picking a fight. I finally said every fiber in my body told me he was wrong for her."

"And?"

"She patronized me. She said she could understand how odd he would seem in Los Angeles, but he fit perfectly in her world. I said you can lend money to the poor in LA. She said, 'No offense, Aunt Sarah, but I want nothing to do with the people who caused the Great Recession.' I was tempted to remind her that she liked her job at my former bank."

"I'm sorry."

"Don't apologize. I can take a counterpunch."

After a beat, Sarah continued. "I'm trying to accept the inevitable. But he pisses me off. Even today, and I'm a peaceful person."

"What happened today?" Maggie still hoped to somehow evade the inevitable. Paul seemed to think they would.

"We were talking about the godhead, and he said there's no such thing as the soul. Not exactly in those words, but that's what he implied. Thousands of years of wisdom down the drain, like that." She snapped her fingers. "He said when we die, the life we were fades away into the universe. Then he excused himself to go Skype. I wish he would talk straight with me. There's no valid reason for him to keep running away."

Maggie could sympathize with Arun's wanting to avoid a metaphysical showdown. Even in this new, beatific state, Sarah could be formidable. She nodded in response.

The two women continued to sit in the warm sun. Sarah pulled knees up to her chest and wrapped arms around them. Maggie dangled legs against the wall, idly bouncing her sandals against the rock. Birds called from the tall, old trees. A gift in an otherwise harried season. Maggie sighed.

Sarah said, "I'm sorry I let you down."

"You haven't. You're here." She paused, weighing the moment. "Nothing will be the same after Jenn leaves. I need a new life."

"Talk to me."

"It was so nice to have another adult around. We had our issues, but we also had fun. I enjoyed the class I took. We talked about it a lot. I could see myself doing more."

Sarah turned to look at her. "What are you not telling me?"

Maggie's chest tightened. Pinned, like a butterfly under a microscope, Sarah's eye at the top of the tube. "I had a lover for a little while. Younger, a carpenter. Just for the sex."

"It's never just for the sex. Tell me more."

"We met last fall. We ran into each other, literally. A fender bender. No one was hurt. I asked him to help me with video for the India course. The sex was convenient." The story felt hollow to her, as it must to Sarah.

"Why him, Mag? Why now?"

Maggie searched her conscience. "I think I wanted to test myself, to see if I could handle a different kind of guy. Someone uncomplicated."

"Ah, so you admit that complications are an excuse."

Maggie felt a flash of impatience. Sarah came off as such a know-it-all, even when her intentions were impeccable. "I called it off. The sex was good. But it stopped being important. I had too much else on my mind."

Sarah spoke quietly. "Does this mean you've given up on Paul?"

The very question she had been avoiding since Jenn introduced Arun into their lives. "I don't know. I'm holding my breath until May 20."

"What do you expect to happen then?"

An even tougher question.

Sarah prompted her. "Jenn's going to marry Arun and turn her back on Pelham. Not much left for you here."

"I know. But I don't know where else to go." What a stupid thing to say, and to Sarah, who lived in such moral clarity. The conversation hurt more than anticipated. She needed to stop. "Maybe I'll be inspired. Isn't that what you mean by 'spirit'?"

"Nice finesse, my dear. I can wait until you want to talk." Sarah pushed off the wall and trotted downhill, calling over her shoulder. "Last one to the swings is a rotten egg."

Maggie followed, walking slowly, trying to think. Brian had let her go without a fight; he must have known what she was going to say when he opened his door. That was good, wasn't it? Yet she felt so low. Paul's dyspeptic face last night came to mind. Yes, she had been disloyal, not to his present person but to the Paul she carried in her girlish heart: a strong man, an independent thinker, a crusader for the highest of causes, the loving father of her child. That Paul no longer existed and could not be conjured by any effort on her part. What would it take to see past him?

She entered the underpass that led to the park and began to trot toward the playground, her sandals slipping on the young grass. She'd spend fifteen minutes getting dizzy with Sarah on the swings before returning home to prepare their lunch. She welcomed the chore; her best ideas emerged when she did mindless things like mince parsley or vacuum. She could use a flotilla of good ideas.

❦ ❦

That night, in the shower, Brian's parting words echoed in her head. They slid away without causing pain. If only she could say the same about Paul's.

TWENTY-FIVE

They sat beside each other on the 7:29 to Grand Central. Paul had bought coffee and tea from the vendor at the Pelham station just before they'd boarded. As the train picked up speed, he sipped the hot, black brew; Jenn gazed out the window, waiting for her tea to cool. Last night, she'd asked to ride along with him, since she planned to shop for wedding rings in the city. He wondered if her making this purchase at the last minute signaled cold feet. At any rate, this was his chance: twenty-five minutes in which to stop her from marrying the jackass.

"How come you're buying rings by yourself?"

"Arun's on the phone with India. It will take hours to straighten out our travel. When I see something I like, I'll text him. We very rarely disagree." She took a tentative sip.

"Yeah, but he shouldn't leave you holding the bag. Not a good sign."

"Dad, this is no biggie. We already took care of the marriage license."

"Why don't you shop with him in White Plains?"

"Because the city has more variety at half the price."
She took a sip through the hole in the plastic cup lid.

In less than a week this creature—she who had beguiled him since babyhood—planned to slink away to sleep beside a snake. Something inside his chest screamed no. He wanted Jenn to take her time, to learn about what makes men great, to find a man whom he could respect and who would keep her safe. Safe from heartache, safe from boredom. Safe from herself. All these years, he'd encouraged her adventurous spirit. Maybe too much, given her choice of fiancé. Now he would rescue her from her impulse, and eventually she'd thank him. He had planned his attack. He drained his coffee and took her free hand in his. "Tell me, are you absolutely sure you're doing the right thing?"

She looked at him through narrowed eyes. "What are you trying to say?"

"Sometimes people get so wrapped up in a plan that the plan takes over, and they lose track of how they really feel. Or they want out, but they're afraid to disappoint the world, or they're embarrassed about changing their mind. Does this apply to you?"

Her face relaxed. "That's sweet of you. No, I don't want to back out of marrying Arun. Everything that's happened has strengthened my resolve."

"You shouldn't need resolve at this stage. You should feel 100 percent positive."

She withdrew her hand. "I am as positive as I need to be. Haven't you always said, as a scientist, that no one can ever be 100 percent sure of anything?"

He nodded, acknowledging her parry. "Figure of speech. I want to be sure that you know you can call it off. And you should think about it now, not a month from now when you're sweltering in India."

Jenn flicked her hand. "Dad, I've been thinking about it nonstop for almost a year. Traveling in India is hard, especially if you're trying to find reliable collaborators. Every time we hit a bump, Arun and I had the same reactions. After a while, I said to myself, wow, I could spend my life with this guy. It took him another six months to come to the same conclusion." She beamed at something invisible to him.

"What about the physical? Sex is the basis of marriage." He hadn't wanted to go there, but she needed shaking up.

Her eyes opened wide. "Is this about the birds and the bees? Already talked to Mom." She smiled an inward smile. He saw her flush as desire flowed through her. Goddamn hormones.

"You don't have to go to India to get laid." Too belligerent, but he couldn't stomach the idea of Arun's pudgy hands on her flesh.

Jenn faced him squarely. "I'm going to India to help my future husband do important work that he is uniquely qualified to do. The way Mom supported you."

"Your mother is a lonely woman."

"That's your fault as much as hers." She raised the tea to her lips and stared him down.

Jesus, he thought, she's tough. He couldn't keep his voice down. "I don't want you following him. I want you doing your own thing."

She spoke slowly. "I *am* doing my thing. With a partner I adore. Wish me well." Her face had that arch, cold look that he remembered from the awful days when she went to California to recover. As if he were too impossibly dull to understand.

"If you want to take care of the needy, you can work for a nonprofit here."

"We're not taking care of anyone; we're building an organization so people can take care of themselves. India is ripe for it, more than the U.S."

"That's prejudice."

"Dad, we've been over this. It's outside your area of expertise."

"Just think about what I said. It's not too late." He didn't trust himself to say more. He'd give her space and reopen the subject that evening.

Her voice softened. "I will. I always do." She busied herself removing the lid from her cup and jiggling the tea bag.

He pulled his briefcase onto his lap and extracted a printout, pretending to read. Despite the monumental frustration, he felt a touch of pride at the strength of her. His girl.

Outside the windows, tall stone walls blocked the view of the Bronx as the train lurched ahead. Nothing to distract or disturb commuters—no derelict buildings, no garbage, no dark people—all the way into the gleaming heart of Manhattan. And Jenn couldn't wait to immerse herself in the detritus of the human race. The filth, the disease, the stench of the downtrodden. He'd stop her, one way or another, that night.

⁂

When he opened the office door, Sandi frowned at him. "Alicia is in a tizzy again."

"Stamford been here?" He primed for a fight.

"She's running around collecting supplies. She says she needs to go off campus for the next few days. She looks awful, more wound up than I've ever seen. Talk to her." Sandi pointed to the wet lab.

He found Alicia bent over a notebook, two colors of highlighter clutched in her left hand, folders and reagents cluttering the countertop in front of her. Her unbuttoned lab coat flared at her sides. She looked up at him with a tightly drawn face.

He feigned a casual tone. "What's up?"

"I have to go to Dr. Miller's lab to set up the last two experiments. They want to see how we did them." She had bent forward so far that her chest nearly touched the notebook.

"No you don't. You don't work for Martin Miller. You work for me. Stay here and put that stuff away."

"I have to go. I got a letter from the hospital ethics board. They copied you." She began to sob and reached into a pocket to extract a crumpled tissue.

He could have burst with impatience. He stepped forward and wrapped arms around her shoulders—no matter if Sandi saw them through the open doorway—to comfort her. "Take it easy. I don't think anyone can compel you to do anything outside your job." He hoped to hell that was true.

She leaned into him, sniffling, dabbing at her cheeks. "What if they find discrepancies? They'll question my dissertation."

He could feel her trembling. He willed her calm.

In a tiny voice Alicia said, "I'll never get another job."

"You won't need one. I'll take care of everything. Now, either get to work or go home until you've calmed down. We've got big stuff to do." She quieted. He released her. She stuck the tissue into the pocket of her lab coat and began to lift the folders from the countertop, tucking them into a tote. He watched, examining the reagents, understanding which experiments she had in mind. "I'll put the bottles away. You carry on as planned, okay?" She nodded, stood up, slung the tote over her inward-curving shoulder, a defensive shoulder protecting an inadequate heart. He willed her courage. She walked out of the lab. He gathered the reagent bottles to return them to the refrigerator in the anteroom. After the new work was published, he'd have enough clout to get a bigger lab suite, big enough to house the refrigerators in a more convenient place, and two postdocs and state-of-the-art equipment. A new era for his team.

The offending letter lay on top of the pile of paper on his desk. He supposed Sandi had read it when she had placed it there. Didn't frighten her, a mature woman he could count on, salt of the earth. He fished readers out of the drawer and scanned the page. The board had asked Miller to replicate two crucial experiments that Alicia had performed under Paul's direction. The board required her to cooperate, not to do the work. Alicia had misconstrued the letter; what else would she screw up in her current state? Thinking that Stamford could end the mess he'd started, he picked up the phone. Halfway through punching in Stamford's extension, he clicked off and phoned Maggie instead. Stamford could ignore him, but Maggie had a way of getting Stamford's attention. Whenever she invited him to something, he came running. She answered immediately.

"How was the train ride?"

"Normal."

"What did you say to Jenn?"

He condensed the story: "I gave her an out. She's gonna think about what I said. I'll check in with her tonight."

"You're running out of time."

"I know, I know. Listen, I need you to do something. I need you to call your friend Robert Stamford and get him to withdraw a complaint he made to the ethics board about Alicia's work. He scared her silly, and with the conference coming up, I can't afford to have her distracted."

There was a long pause. "What's the matter?"

"Martin Miller got a hold of some of our papers and made comments to Stamford that your buddy blew up into a case for the ethics board. Alicia is first author and she's freaking out. She's ready to dump her career over a bunch of nits."

"If it's a question of nits, you don't have a problem."

He hated that superior tone, as if only an idiot would contradict her. "Can't you just do what I ask?"

She said something muffled to someone else and then spoke quietly to him. "Has Alicia tampered with the evidence?"

"Goddammit, I'm making history!" He wanted to throw the phone at the wall.

She said something to someone else, and then back to him: "I've got to go. We'll discuss this tonight. After your talk with Jenn."

He cut off the call before she could, infuriated at the delay. Did she not get it, or was she holding him hostage to her priorities? She could be such a bitch.

What else could he do to buy a couple of weeks? After his presentation at the conference, no one would bother picking nits. No scientist's work was unassailable. In fact, you were supposed to assail every idea to separate the dumb-ass from the genius. Ideas mattered, big ideas that changed the course of progress for everyone, not dotted i's and crossed t's, the province of the second rate. Ever since graduate school, he'd disdained the plodders, especially after reading how Barbara McClintock had stood genetics on its ear. By examining generations of corn plants in an idiosyncratic way, she was able to assert, against prevailing opinion, that parts of genes could move around in the chromosomal complement, and that the instructions for that movement came from the living cell itself and perhaps from its environment. Her work was hard to understand and her colleagues ignored her for decades, until they couldn't anymore. She won the Nobel Prize at age eighty-two.

Back then, McClintock's story confirmed everything he believed about the importance of the big picture and sticking with your intuition. He'd prided himself on doing "McClintock science" all these years. Yeah, he wanted colleagues to adopt his ideas and apply them to different kinds of tumors, and to medicine—he couldn't possibly do all that work himself—but first he had to shake them out of their received knowledge, impress upon them the value of his voice. So when the data Alicia produced hadn't yelled loud enough to galvanize attention, he'd turned up the volume a bit. Alicia was too timid to do McClintock science; she needed to be led, and she'd accepted his guidance without a murmur. But now Stamford had her in his sights. And she was weak, dangerously weak. He shuddered at the thought of Stamford pushing her to reveal the minor adjustments they'd made. Stamford would jump to the wrong conclusions, and she wouldn't be able to defend them. His heart began to pound.

He strode into the next office where Sandi sat at her desk. "I need you to take care of Alicia. Now. Go find her and take her home. No, take her to your house. She's hysterical and she needs to be watched."

Sandi bent slowly to open the bottom drawer, where she stored her purse. "She looks okay now. Whatever you said seems to have helped." She rooted in the drawer, put purse in lap. "Are you sure you want me to leave the office?" She didn't rise.

"Go find her and take her away."

"And after she calms down, then what? Should I bring her back?" She didn't move.

"No. Stay with her until I call you." Dammit, he shouldn't have to explain. "You could put her up for the night."

"I could." She kept sitting. "Is it necessary?" She folded hands over her purse and looked up at him, no urgency in her face. He calmed a notch.

"Not necessary. Desirable. Will you please take her to your place for a few hours? I'll phone when I figure out the rest." She rose slowly. She bent over her desk to fuss with her computer. "Here's today's calendar." She straightened and searched in her purse, removing keys. "We'll be back after lunch. You're buying."

"Wait for my call. I'm counting on you."

She smiled. "What else is new?" At the door, transferring purse and keys from one hand to the other, she took off the perpetual blue smock and hung it on the plastic hook she'd installed. "Give me a hint about what's on Alicia's mind, so I can be a good influence."

He hesitated. Sandi needed to know. "She's worried about mistakes in the two papers Stamford wants checked. She thinks her thesis is in danger. She's blown it out of proportion. You know she doesn't understand office politics. We've gotta stop her from doing anything foolish."

"What foolish thing could she do?"

"Just take care of her."

Sandi's brow furrowed. "Okay, I'll talk to her." She ambled into the wet lab.

He shut himself in his office. The only solution was to keep Alicia away from Stamford until Maggie could get to him. Maggie was his secret weapon. He would call her again and get her to come to the hospital if necessary. How could she refuse when so much was at stake? His last chance to grab the brass ring, and he wasn't going to miss it. He booted his computer to reread the two papers and put on his armor. He forced himself to focus, forcing each sentence to permeate his brain. His knowledge of cancer biology was so well structured and so profound that, he believed, an unassailable explanation of the adjustments they'd made would emerge from its amassed depths.

TWENTY-SIX

Maggie put the phone down, exasperated. Paul had been hounding her to call Robert for two days. It made no sense. Robert had every right to talk to Paul's staff. She *had* called, as requested, but had not reached him. Just now she'd heard an unusual note of panic in Paul's voice. She'd deal with his insistence later; the wedding was scheduled for Sunday morning, the bride and groom would fly off to another continent Monday, and she had a lot to do today, Friday, including picking her parents up at LaGuardia, for which she'd be late if she didn't hustle.

Jenn, upstairs, writing place cards and folding origami table decorations, had seemed relaxed at lunch. Arun, now pacing overhead and mumbling, presumably rehearsing his vows, had seemed nervous, speaking in little bursts, with a look of terror on his face that was oddly endearing. Downstairs, all systems were go: the paperwork was ready, and two simple matching rings lay waiting on the mantelpiece. The retired judge who would officiate, a good friend of

Jenn's boss and a casual acquaintance of Maggie's, would come to rehearse on Saturday after the canopy tent went up and Maggie had the catering in hand. She sighed, resigned, prepared to host the modest, symbol-filled affair Jenn wanted. No one had been able to dissuade Jenn—not Sarah, not Paul, not she herself. She did not understand Arun as a man apart from her daughter, but she wanted to make the most of the union, for Jenn's sake, and for peace of mind. She wrote herself a Post-it for tomorrow: buy flowers at the farmer's market, charge the camera. She called upstairs that she was leaving the house.

In the car, sticking the note to the dashboard, backing down the driveway, she mentally reviewed the RSVPs: a few high school friends of Jenn's who still lived nearby; a few close family friends who had watched Jenn grow up; and relatives: Arun's cousin from New Jersey and her husband, who would stand in for his parents, and Paul's brother, now divorced for the second time. She'd sent him an invitation pro forma and had been surprised at the instant reply. He must need something from Paul, she thought, and he's coming to plead in person instead of long distance. For reasons she never fathomed, Paul jumped to attention for his older brother. Given Paul's current frantic preoccupation with work though, Lenny might go home empty-handed, which might not be a bad thing.

Paul, Paul, Paul. Got hung up at work and stopped talking to Jenn just when he could have done the most good. When he'd confessed to Maggie that the promised ultimate conversation had slipped his mind, she'd gotten furious. It might not have made a difference, but it should have happened. Her fury faded into deep disappointment, a disappointment, she felt, from which she would not re-

cover. She could and did overlook so many of his little neg-
ligent actions. But not now, when their life was on the cusp
of change and Jenn's well-being was at stake. She shook her
head to clear her mind.

On the Whitestone Bridge driving onto Long Island,
she saw gray cumulous clouds massed in the distant sky.
If her parents' plane experienced turbulence coming into
LaGuardia, Claudia would worry about the weather, out
loud, all weekend. Maggie braced herself to absorb that
worry, and last night's dream appeared in her mind's eye.
In the first segment, she's trying to phone Jenn, and she sees
that she has Jenn's phone in her own purse, along with a
bunch of other electronic stuff. The message is urgent, so
she runs to find her. Jenn is unperturbed, having handled
the emergency her own way. In the second segment, she's
back in Michigan and her old boss, Mr. Greenberg, is re-
arranging the furniture in the office, but it's a bedroom.
Greenberg pushes the cots together so eight people can
sleep in a space for six. He's proud of his cleverness, and so
is she. The third segment, and she always dreamed in three
segments, is fuzzy, further back in time, before Greenberg,
before Paul . . . maybe Girl Scout camp, where she first
learned about sex. She isn't in the dream, she's watching
from afar. The scouting unit doesn't need her. On waking she had thought the dream peculiar but inconsequential. Now she wondered if, and how, it connected to her
parents' arrival. As if there would be time this weekend to
revisit the past. The future demanded all her energy, short
and long term, Jenn's and her own.

Overhead, green-and-white highway signs pointed toward airport arrivals. She followed a circuitous route to
the parking lot and looked for an accessible slot. No handi-

capped emblem on her car, so she'd have to chance a ticket. Most likely, the car wouldn't be towed. She locked up and hastened inside to wait at a security barrier for the third time in three weeks.

Her parents' last visit to Pelham, for Jenn's high school graduation, had been pleasant enough. They'd talked about college and the importance of being well rounded, by which Claudia meant "traditional." Her parents had skipped the party Maggie threw for Jenn's college graduation because Roger had been unwell. Maggie visited them afterward, bringing photos and news. Of course Claudia objected to Jenn's living in Brooklyn. Later she objected to her leaving Brooklyn to travel. Claudia would have so much to object to on this visit. Maggie could only hope her mother's desire to act the proper grandmother would keep her civil.

In the stream of people passing out of the secure zone, she spotted her parents slowly advancing. A gate attendant pushed her father in a wheelchair, and Claudia walked next to him. She looked shorter, grayer than remembered, and she lumbered, as if burdened by more than the jacket and shopping bag she carried. Maggie embraced her parents and asked if she needed to hire a wheelchair for the visit. Claudia said no; Roger could walk but he was too slow. She handed Maggie a luggage receipt, saying they'd wait at the baggage claim doors while Maggie collected their suitcase, the flowered one, and Roger could walk to the car. Maggie did as bidden.

They settled into the Prius, Roger up front. He had lost some hearing, which made it hard to talk over the sounds of traffic. Maggie previewed the weekend schedule without detail. Roger nodded and smiled in a way that indicated he wasn't following. They said little all the way to New Rochelle. After they had checked into the hotel and the handicapped suite had passed muster, Roger excused himself for a nap. Claudia wanted the particulars about the wedding weekend. The two women seated themselves in the suite living room, and Maggie began to describe Saturday's rehearsal dinner. Claudia interrupted.

"When is the young man going to pay us a visit? He owes us that courtesy."

Of course you want him to come to you, Maggie thought, and you're quite right. "When would you like to see him? I can drive him over here this evening, if you're not too tired. Tomorrow morning is also open. We need the afternoon to set up."

"Yes, this evening. We eat early, but it's an hour later here. So bring him at eight. Tell me, what do you think of him?"

How could she answer and preserve the peace? "He's hard to get to know. Very polite. He and Jenn are nice to each other."

"Nice doesn't make a marriage." Claudia took a checkbook and pen from her purse.

"She's in love. He comes from a different culture; he says things that I interpret to mean he's in love." If Claudia would buy the cultural differences argument, the visit might succeed.

"Humph." Claudia placed the checkbook on the coffee table and closed her purse beside it. "I'm going to check on your father. See you at eight."

Maggie brushed her mother's cheek with her lips. "I'll phone if there's a problem." She let herself out of the suite.

Driving back to Pelham, she twisted in her skin. To defuse her mother's prejudice, she would manipulate the conversation, and she might find herself saying things she didn't believe. Like attributing Arun's reticence to his Indian heritage. She felt a twinge of defeat. Two hours with her mother had rendered her arch and artificial. What a pity she had to pay the price for a grandparent's blessing.

⚬⚭ ⚮⚯

Maggie knocked on the suite door; Jenn and Arun stood in the hallway behind her. Jenn had insisted on coming along, and Maggie welcomed the diversion. Claudia, in a fresh seersucker pantsuit, opened the door and invited them in. Two chairs had been drawn close to the couch; Roger sat in one of them. Jenn pecked her grandmother's cheek and rushed to her grandfather to hug him. The old man's eyes lit up and he raised both hands to hold her face. Maggie observed, once again, how affectionately he treated Jenn. During her own childhood, he had been a benign but distant presence.

Claudia sat in the inquisitor's chair, and the three of them squeezed onto the couch, Jenn in the middle. The upholstery scratched Maggie's calves. Claudia disliked air-conditioning, and the room felt stuffy. Faint music played behind a wall. She hoped her parents would be comfortable in New Rochelle's best hotel, and in the present company.

Claudia spoke. "Tell us about yourself, young man."

Arun sat straighter. He'd worn a short-sleeved shirt and tie—first tie Maggie had seen on him.

"I am thirty-one and an American citizen. I was born in India and educated in the United States. I met your granddaughter nearly two years ago in India when she visited the school where I was working. She appreciated my methods, and she traveled with me to share them with many other schools. We learned to love each other, and she has done me the great honor of agreeing to be my wife."

Maggie had never heard Arun speak so concisely. She hoped her mother couldn't read surprise on her face.

Claudia said, "How do you expect to make a living?"

"We share a philosophy of service. We intend to start a school and then a chain of schools. And we hope to raise children who will have perfect temperaments and wonderful curly hair." He and Jenn looked smiles at each other. She took his hand.

Jenn said, "We'll probably live in India because there's more need there. But we'll come back here to visit. Those perfect children will go to college here, for sure."

Claudia frowned. "You want to be schoolteachers in India? You'll never be able to afford college."

Jenn said, "Grandma, we'll find a way. We're resourceful."

Arun said, "I hope you will consider coming to our Indian wedding in July and meeting my parents. I think you will have more confidence in our prospects in the context of India. It would be my parents' pleasure to host you."

Claudia's face softened a fraction. "We don't travel due to my husband's health." She tilted her head toward Roger but kept eyes on Arun. "So your parents are wealthy?"

Maggie said, "Mother!"

Arun nodded and said, "My parents are ophthalmologists who run a clinic that serves many people free of charge. They are not wealthy but they are comfortable, and family is important to them. They want to show you that they will treat Jennifer as their own."

For an instant, Claudia seemed nonplussed. She rearranged her body on the chair. "Why didn't your parents come here?"

"It is a difficult time of year to leave the clinic, but Jenn wanted to marry on her birthday. My relatives have been planning the Hindu wedding for months, and they worry still that they don't have enough time." He looked at Jenn. "I will be happy to marry Jenn as often as she likes."

Jenn said, "Twice will be enough for now." To her grandmother, "I am so glad you're here. It means a lot to me." She turned to her grandfather. "Grandpa, did you hear?"

The old man shook his head no. In a whispery voice he said, "Good luck, honey."

Claudia ignored him. "Will you raise your children as Hindus? I warn you, that would disturb my husband and me."

"No, I respect Hindu tradition, as I do Christian tradition, but I do not observe. Jenn and I have discussed this, of course. We are in agreement that we will cultivate our children's spiritual lives until they are old enough to take full custody of them. We will do as Jenn's parents did. And mine."

Roger's chin drooped to his chest. Grasping the opportunity, Maggie said, "Dad's falling asleep. Maybe we should go." She stood. "I'll pick you up tomorrow at five. If you need anything, call my cell." The others rose. Jenn kissed both grandparents. Arun offered a handshake. Maggie opened the suite door, and Jenn and Arun stepped into the hall. Claudia called as Maggie was about to follow them.

"Margaret, come here for a minute."

Maggie told Jenn that she'd meet them at the car and turned back.

Claudia stood beside Roger's chair. "She reminds me of you. Stars in her eyes for a smooth talker. I suppose you approve?"

She needed caution. "Actually, I'm not comfortable with the marriage."

"Then why don't you object?"

"On what grounds?"

"He's a foreigner, and he'll never make a decent living."

"He's an American, and Jenn wants to do the same kind of work. It's not my place to judge."

"I thought you'd say something like that." She slumped, looking limp and old, like her husband. "I won't contradict you. She's like you, and you turned out all right in the end." She reached into the purse leaning on the chair leg at her feet and withdrew a check. "Here."

Five hundred dollars, to Jennifer Adler. Claudia's blessing, prepared in advance. Would it have been offered regardless of Arun's words? "Thank you. I'll give it to Jenn after the ceremony. She will be delighted."

Maggie pecked her mother's cheek and said good night. She slipped into the empty hallway as reactions tumbled through her. Why were encounters with her mother never simple? *I thought you'd say something like that.* Claudia meant that they lived in different moral worlds and that, by implication, Maggie's was wanting. *I won't contradict you*—meaning she would go along with the wedding nonetheless. She would be charitable, not tight lipped and long suffering as she had been at Maggie's wedding so many years before. Was handing over the check an apology of sorts? Well, Jenn would be happy, the ultimate goal. *You turned out all right in the end.* Maggie could not remember the last time her mother had praised her, and it thrilled her, and she hated the fact that it did. She had struggled so long to remain indifferent to her mother's sallies. She thought she'd grown independent of a mother's love. But not so. *She's like you* . . . No, at twenty-six Jenn was far more self-possessed. Did Claudia mean that both generations' choice of mate disappointed her? If so, Maggie said mentally to her mother, I won't let you steal an ounce of joy from Jenn, not now, not ever. She's going her own way, and you will not demean her. She's not me.

The cool night air felt good on her face. She saw the young couple leaning against her car, Arun's mouth close to Jenn's ear. She unlocked the car from a distance, and Jenn pushed Arun into the front passenger seat. Eyes down, Maggie went about the business of getting the car started and on the road. As she turned onto Webster Avenue, Arun said, "Do you think that your mother is satisfied? I followed Jenn's instructions to be specific."

"Did your parents really offer to bring them to India?"

"Not in so many words. But they have said many times that they want to unite our two families. I interpreted the situation for them. I am absolutely sure they would agree. You will like them, Maggie. They are kindred spirits."

"What do you mean?"

"It has been my pleasure to get to know you these last few weeks. You are like my mother: you get things done without fuss, and you put other people first. I admire you."

"You flatter me." She distrusted his words, distrusted her mother-bruised ability to understand.

"If I had said this when we first met, it would have been flattery. But now it's truth."

"Did you tell my mother the truth?"

Arun drew back as if offended. "I am sorry if my method displeased you, but I represented my parents' interests faithfully. Truth has many dimensions, I have found."

"To answer your question, I think my mother is satisfied tonight. I don't predict tomorrow." Wanting the conversation to end, she made a show of changing lanes.

Jenn, leaning in from the backseat, said, "Fair enough. Thanks for taking us to see them, Mom." She leaned back. Arun swiveled to look at her. After a beat, he faced front and hunkered into the seat. They rolled quietly down Webster, peaceful this time of night.

Maggie thought that Arun had succeeded with Claudia. He'd been more forthcoming than she'd expected . . . because he had followed Jenn's instructions? Perhaps he was more malleable than he seemed, certainly toward Jenn if not the rest of the world. Still, she didn't trust him. She shook herself mentally, reminding herself to pay attention to the road. The next forty-eight hours would unfold regardless of her cares. Time had a way of creating wounds as well as healing them.

⚬⚬ ⚬⚬

Maggie turned off the light in the kitchen and prepared to mount the stairs. Passing the living room, she saw Arun alone, bent over a glowing computer screen. His face was knotted in concentration. She paused on the threshold, then seized the moment. "May I interrupt? I've been meaning to ask you a question about your work."

Arun punched buttons and closed the machine. "Of course. What would you like to know?"

"Jenn has only talked in generalities. What precisely do you do?"

"Our goal is to teach habits of mind from an Eastern perspective that can be beneficial to young people who need to figure out where they belong in global consumer culture. They must learn to look inside, and to nature, for self-satisfaction. They won't learn how to lead a good life from video and film."

"Yes, but how does that relate to microfinance?"

Arun leaned back and crossed his legs; his face was open. "When we started working with kids in Delhi, we saw that we had to work with their families too, or our efforts would be contradicted. Especially the mothers, who have little schooling and no sense of possibilities. The microfinance organizations give these women a way to make money, and that gives them power. They use it to help their children first, before they get a new sari, before they allow their husbands to squander it. When we can work with the whole family, then we make great strides."

"How do you do it?"

"In many small ways. Like your therapy dog. We are present to redirect their thinking when challenges arise. We start with the mother. When she develops confidence, then she wants to send her children to our school. If all goes well, she uses more of our services, and then we educate the husband. Sexual abuse is rampant in India too. Some men do not understand the motives for their actions, but we have ways to enlighten them."

"You keep saying 'we.' What does Jenn do? She doesn't know India."

Arun clasped hands in front of his heart. "Jenn is my inspiration. Her compassion is so deep and pure, she can talk with anyone. I watch her and I am guided by her. We are developing this practice together. You must come see our model in action."

"Perhaps I will." She stepped toward the stairs. "Good night."

As she changed out of her clothes and into a nightshirt, she thought that, to be fair, some of what Arun said made sense. At the shelter, she had often wanted to get at the kids' mothers, either to hug them or smack sense into them, but it wasn't protocol. She tried to imagine what sex education looked like in the Indian context. The course she had taken didn't help; everything about India, including various theories about retaining semen, seemed maddeningly complex. Perhaps Arun really did take cues from Jenn, who could be single-minded and powerful, like her father at his best. She might have to see for herself to set her mind, and her heart, at ease.

As she slipped between the bedclothes, Paul appeared on the threshold looking drained.

"I want to kill him."

She sat up to hear him out.

"I said if he really loved Jenn, he wouldn't make her live in poverty. Son of a bitch laughed in my face and said, 'Too little, too late.' I swear he wanted me to hit him. Prove I'm a bastard. I will stop this farce."

"No, you won't. Not on the eve of the wedding."

"She's got to see what a mistake he is."

"She's made her choice. Live with it."

"How can you say that?"

"She's a grown woman. I choose to trust her. You should too. Maybe her world is wider than ours was. Or just different. He's right, it's too late."

"I don't get it. Yesterday you hated him."

"That was last month. I'm moving on. Are you coming to bed?"

Paul turned on his heel and disappeared. She turned off the light and slid beneath the covers. Yes, she could learn to live with Jenn's decision. But could she continue to live with Paul's incompetence as a father? And a husband? Eyes closed, she waited for sleep.

TWENTY-SEVEN

Lenny squinted out the window at the practice putting green and the first tee beyond it. His bifocal sunglasses lay on the table in front of him. Paul thought the shirt with wide pink stripes might have looked good on a younger man, but it made Lenny, with florid face and potbelly, look clownish. No matter; his brother would be on his side. When the waiter came round, they ordered draft beer. At four o'clock on Saturday, they had the club restaurant to themselves.

Lenny had shown up at the house just after lunch, smiling and making small talk about the wedding. He had slapped Arun on the back and chucked Jenn under the chin. He'd bussed Maggie and Sarah, whom he didn't know, and asked about the in-laws. When Paul suggested a beer at the club, he jumped at the idea, saying how good it would be to catch up with his little bro. Maggie told them to make it back by five thirty for the rehearsal. Maggie had never warmed to Lenny. She criticized his extrava-

gance and his divorces. Paul loved Lenny; Lenny understood how far Paul had come.

The waiter brought two beers and a bowl of peanuts.
Lenny's wide fist covered the bowl as he scooped up a
handful. He threw a bunch of nuts into his mouth. Chewing, he said, "Didn't have time to get lunch. Not that I need
it." Lenny patted his belly with the other hand. "This will
tide me over. I like this place. Been a member long?"

"I don't come here anymore. Maggie keeps the membership for her women's things."

"You could've had the wedding here."

"Jenn said she wanted the backyard because it symboliz-
es family. Maggie was all over it. Listen, Len, I need advice."

Lenny put the remaining nuts back in the bowl and
licked his fingers. "Nothing you can do. Just roll with it, and
hope there are no kids before the divorce. My daughter didn't
learn anything from me. She made the same mistakes."

"It's not about Jenn. It's work." He swallowed the bad
taste in his mouth. "I'm the victim of a witch hunt."

Lenny's face sobered up. "What are you talking about?"

"The hospital provost got a call from a competitor of
mine questioning some of my results. Important results. More
than important—groundbreaking. He started an investiga-
tion, and he's picking on my research associate. He'll rattle
her into saying something damaging, and I need to stop him."
Lenny didn't know science, but he understood backbiting.

Lenny leaned in. "Why's he after you?"

"He's jealous. We overlapped in graduate school. He
can't stand the fact that I'm doing great science while he
pushes paper and sucks up to the rich. I think Maggie could
get to him, but she won't. Do you think I should get an
injunction?" He leaned over his untouched beer.

"Have you got anything on him?"

"No. He signs off on my budget."

Lenny sat back. "Wait a minute. You say your wife can stop him? Get her to do it. Simple is best."

"She won't. Too busy with the wedding." The excuse sounded as lame to him as it must to Lenny. His throat was closing up.

"Did you tell her he's screwing you?"

"She takes his side. Has done for years."

Lenny smirked. "Is something going on between them? Not that I would blame her. God knows you've taken your share of liberties."

Paul's mind spun as his throat squeezed tighter. Maggie was too straitlaced, and Stamford too repulsive. And you never saw him with a woman. But why did she make allowances for him whenever he interfered?

"No. Maggie's angry about other stuff, so she's taking it out on me now," which, he told himself, was the likely explanation. Likely, but not proven. He recalled Maggie and Stamford getting cozy at hospital parties. She called him Robert, the name rolling off her tongue so easily. His chest contracted.

"I see," Lenny said. "Well, take it from me. If you get a lawyer involved, it'll cost you plenty. It's like going to war, believe me, and it'll take years. This is the voice of experience talking. You're better off negotiating."

"You can't negotiate science."

"You can negotiate anything. Want me to try?" Lenny opened his hands wide as if receiving a blessing.

Paul recalled the times Lenny had negotiated successfully for him: getting a loan over and above the GI Bill, keeping their father out of his way until the old man's liver exploded, helping him get out of a sticky affair at Michigan before Maggie arrived. And then, the big one: it was Lenny who coached him, behind the scenes, when Stamford first approached about bringing his lab into the hospital. Lenny practically forced Paul to demand an unprecedented subsidy for the whole team. He had Lenny to thank for years of breathing room. Breathing room now in jeopardy. No, Lenny could take Stamford out in a fistfight, but not in a battle of words. Yeah, he was right about the legal route—too slow. With the conference four weeks away, Maggie had to help, for Chrissake. He needed her more than ever before. "No, I'll handle it. Monday after everyone's gone, I'll get Maggie in gear, one way or another."

Lenny closed his big, square hands around his beer glass. "I can help, you know. You can count on me."

For a long two seconds, he thought Lenny might have a magic touch. Then he snapped back to reality. He'd have to be crazy to think Lenny could handle Stamford. Or utterly desperate, which was not the case.

Lenny took a swig of his beer. "If it makes you feel better, I've got issues too." He took another swig and wiped his mouth with the back of his hand.

A burst of clatter came from the far end of the room. A waiter had dropped a tray of dishes, which scattered and broke on the terrazzo.

"That poor son of a bitch just lost a paycheck," Lenny said. "Sometimes I think it would be nice to have a regular job instead of running a business. My biggest customer can't pay me because his money's tied up in the Middle East. Why anyone would deal with Arabs I don't know." He took another swig.

Paul felt the hustle coming; he took two deep breaths to loosen his chest.

Lenny said, "Now I'm short because he's stupid. All my cash is locked away. CDs and such. I need some capital to get past Ramadan, if you can believe it."

Paul winced; Lenny's timing sucked. He could hear Maggie's "I told you so" already. Over the years Lenny had gravitated from one marginal import–export business to another, each time starting with big talk and winding up on the outs with an "idiot partner" and hurting for cash. Paul had helped a couple of times; Lenny hadn't paid him back, promising more when the next deal came through. Maggie nagged him to collect, but he didn't sweat nickels and dimes. Lenny was Lenny, the only blood relative who'd protected him from a hostile world.

"How much do you need?"

"Five thousand. My guy says he'll get paid by the end of the summer. I'll pay you back as soon as I see his check."

Paul shook his head. "You won't."

Lenny lowered the beer glass, a hurt look on his face. "If you help me over this hump, I'll never have to ask you for another dime. I'll be done with alimony in six months, and I'll pay you back, with interest. What do you say?"

The pressure in his chest mounted. Heart attack? Panic attack? Or disgust at Lenny's cupidity? His entire career was at stake and Lenny whined over five grand. He couldn't trust Lenny to put him first for five minutes. The Lenny of his youth, Batman to his Robin, had transformed into a fat, selfish clown. Fear flooded through him: Lenny couldn't help. Maggie wouldn't help. He needed another strategy. "Let's go. They're waiting." He signaled for the waiter. His chest burned, no remedy in sight.

The elderly judge stood on a wooden platform that had been set up at the back of the lawn against the hedges that bounded the property. Two oriental screens at the rear of the platform were draped with branches of lilac blooms, and three rows of wooden folding chairs sat on the grass facing the platform. Three round tables stood on the grass close to the house beneath a yellow-and-white-striped canopy, and the caterer's kitchen equipment waited on the patio. Arun and his parent surrogates were chatting with the judge when Paul and Lenny arrived. Paul spotted Maggie and Jenn hovering over one of the tables, covered with cut flowers and an array of vases and bowls. Maggie saw him, checked her watch, and shot him a dirty look. It was five thirty on the dot. He wanted a bourbon, but he didn't want to cross her.

Jenn flounced over in a filmy dress to peck his cheek. "In the nick of time, Dad. The judge is ready to begin the rehearsal."

"You look pretty," Lenny said.

Jenn blushed. "Thank you. I'm nervous and it makes me pink." She laughed and took his arm. "Come meet Arun's aunt and uncle. Uncle to uncle. Actually they're second cousins, but he calls them aunt and uncle." She led him toward the rear of the lawn.

Paul stepped to Maggie's side. She placed a stem of iris in a tall vase and wiped her hands on a towel. She said, "How's Lenny?"

"He needs five thousand dollars."

"That's our Lenny. What are you going to do?"

"If I have a job next week, I'll give it to him." He hadn't meant to bait her, but he couldn't help himself. Monday yawned a year away.

"What do you mean?"

"I told you Stamford's out to get me. The Alicia thing is an excuse. Because after the conference he won't be able to hold me back. No one will."

She shook her head. "You're off base. Look, Jenn's beckoning."

"Why won't you listen to me?"

"Take it up with Robert tomorrow. I don't want to be in the middle."

"He's coming to the wedding?" An ugly thought flashed through him, an image of Maggie naked, wrapped around the man he most detested.

She addressed him as if he were a child. "I told you he's coming. And Sandi. They've both done me a thousand favors. Robert and Jenn made friends when she broke her leg. You were out of town and he helped me, remember? Jenn wanted to invite them, and I agreed."

His chest was so tight that he could hardly breathe. He felt violated; Stamford would come kiss his daughter—and maybe his wife—and eat his food while plotting his ruin. This should not happen. He'd stop it from happening.

Jenn called to him from the edge of the lawn. He felt sick, but Jenn expected him to perform. Arun separated himself from the knot of people gathered in front of the judge and approached, hand outstretched. Paul's craw overflowed with disgust. "Don't touch me!" He stopped short. "I don't want any part of this."

Maggie stepped between him and Arun. She growled low at him, "Do not embarrass your daughter."

"Everything is coming apart and you worry about embarrassment." He hated her.

"Shape up. Now," she hissed.

He saw Jenn watching, pain on her face. His heart split open. Maggie took his arm and pulled him toward the others. He followed her lead.

In front of the judge, he listened for instructions through a haze of misery. He stood, he sat, he walked where indicated; he followed them into the house; he served drinks. When alone in the kitchen, he smashed his hand into the yellow tile for relief; it was temporary. In the restaurant, he sat through dinner next to his father-in-law, equally deaf and silent; he did not finish the steak with zero taste. Jenn stared at him, lips pursed like her mother; he looked away. Willing himself numb, he drove Jenn and Arun and Sarah home while ignoring their talk. He poured a drink and descended into the Lair to wait for Maggie to return from ferrying her parents to the hotel. The bourbon burned his throat.

Seated in the tattered chair at his desk, he pictured Alicia—lab coat unfastened, hair disheveled, crumpled handkerchief in hand—in the hospital boardroom, sitting across that slab of a table from the committee, whoever the hell they were, Stamford egging her on. She wouldn't be able to explain the extrapolations they'd done. She'd cry, branding him a cheat. Stamford would call him a fraud and broadcast it everywhere. Thirty years' work obliterated just like that. He'd be ridiculed and shunned. He felt dizzy and saliva filled his mouth.

Muffled sounds penetrated the ceiling from the kitchen overhead. Maggie. Should he come clean? Let her know how vulnerable he was—no, how vulnerable they were? Her own comfortable life depended on his success. Maybe then she'd persuade Stamford to lay off. Or bribe him. A disgusting picture formed in his mind's eye and he shut it down. No, if he laid it all out, Maggie would turn judgmental and mock him. It was up to him to find a way to neutralize the bastard. Pronto. He closed his eyes, also burning. Tomorrow would be torture. He remembered that there was some oxycodone in the medicine cabinet. It had been three years since his hernia surgery, but the stuff should still work.

TWENTY-EIGHT

Sunday, eleven o'clock, partly cloudy and cool. In the soft light, the backyard looked serene: bright, new grass; dark green hedges sporting light green growth; pots of pink and white flowers lining the wooden platform and rows of wooden folding chairs. Most of the guests were milling near the bar under the canopy, sipping mimosas and circling the bridal couple, who mingled with them although the ceremony had not yet begun. Jenn wore a long, white Indian cotton dress and, around her shoulders, a shawl of sari cloth, lavender threaded with gold. Arun stood close to her, beaming, in a blue suit with a lavender tie. The lilac bush bloomed lavender with darker purple buds, promising more new life in the Adler garden.

Maggie conversed with the caterer on the patio. Sarah stood near the patio door, which was decorated with lilacs, to take photos of arriving guests. Lenny helped the bartender serve drinks, inviting toasts to the bride. A string trio played Mozart in the far corner of the backyard. Seated together in the front row of folding chairs, Roger and Claudia chatted with the elderly judge. Arun's cousins talked to another Indian couple in sari and Nehru jacket.

Paul roamed the yard, tension written on his face.

When Robert Stamford appeared in the doorway, Paul loped over to him. Robert extended his hand, smiling. "Congratulations. She's such a lovely girl."

"I don't know how you can show up here."

Stamford looked taken aback. "Maggie asked me to come."

"How can you come to my daughter's wedding when you're pulling the rug out from under me!"

"What are you saying?"

"You're investigating my lab just because a competitor asked questions. That's sabotage, and I'm going to fight back." Paul's face reddened and he drew himself taller, towering over Robert Stamford.

"Paul, you exaggerate. We're doing a pro forma inquiry into an allegation. When we replicate Alicia's work, that will be the end of it."

"Alicia's work you say. You know very well that I'm the target. And if she made a few errors, it will damage me, not you. You pretend you're protecting the hospital, but you're really out to kill creativity. You will regret this."

"You misunderstand. I support your work, always have. I will do everything I can to clear up the allegation." Stamford lowered his voice. "You mention errors. Is there something I should know?"

"I am not going to sell out my research staff. You need to stop the charade. I will raise a stink if you don't. The fat cats you care about will react."

"Tell me about the errors. I need to know the extent of them so I can protect you and your staff."

"Protect? You mean eviscerate."

"Paul, be logical. Why would I want to damage you? Your lab makes an important contribution to the hospital."

"The hospital. Keep this up and the hospital will suffer."

Stamford stopped smiling. "You can't threaten me. If need be, I will rescind your overhead and use it to undo your so-called errors. Whatever happens between you and me won't affect the hospital one iota."

Maggie appeared at Paul's side. "Gentlemen, please. This is Jenn's day. Robert, come meet the groom." She took his arm and led him away.

Paul glowered after them. He tramped over to Lenny at the bar under the canopy. Lenny looked at his face and reached past the bartender to fill a tall glass with champagne. He offered it to his brother, saying, "That the guy giving you agita?"

Paul downed the bubbly. "Yeah. I let him know I'm going to fight. He'll think twice. Scandal's bad for fund-raising."

"Pretty poor specimen. Maggie'll come back to you." Lenny elbowed Paul in the ribs.

"You son of a bitch. Forget about Maggie. This is my fight." His voice had risen way above polite.

"Easy there. I'm busting your chops."

Arun detached himself from Jenn's side and approached the brothers. "Paul, may I escort you to your place? I believe we're nearly ready to begin."

"No, you may not. I'm enjoying a talk with my brother here."

"Please, for Jenn's sake. She is concerned about you."

"If she were truly concerned about me she wouldn't marry you."

Arun spoke calmly. "I look forward to the day when

Jenn's extraordinary happiness makes you retract that statement."

Lenny stepped between them. "Hey, hey. No hard feelings today." Addressing Arun, "Tell Jenn not to worry. She can count on Uncle Lenny."

Arun nodded and turned away. Lenny took the glass from Paul's hand and poured a refill, saying, "This is your last one until after the ceremony. You want to be able to see your daughter do her thing. Then you can get stupid drunk. Not that I'm recommending it."

Paul took a swig, then laid the glass on the bar. "I won't get drunk. I have a fight on my hands. Not just with him," tipping his head toward Arun's receding figure.

"You're the man," Lenny said, clapping him on the back.

Sarah crossed the lawn to Maggie and gestured with the camera in her hand—evidently the last guests had arrived. Maggie moved among the rows of chairs and spoke to the judge. She signaled to Paul to join her. Head down, he trudged toward her, Lenny following. They took seats in the front row.

The judge shook hands with Claudia and Roger and, moving slowly, stepped up onto the platform. When he had settled himself facing the gathering, the musicians segued from divertimento in E-flat into the wedding march. Guests picked up their heads like a flock of birds on alert and seated themselves with a shiver of excitement. Jenn and Arun stepped onto the platform in front of the judge and faced each other. Everyone could see them in profile, a little smile playing on Jenn's lips, Arun grinning so broadly that his round eyes looked like slits. Arun extended both hands and Jenn took them in hers. Maggie stepped onto the platform beside Jenn, and Arun's cousin, Megha, stood beside him. The music stopped and the judge cleared his throat. A hush fell over the guests; in the momentary silence, a bird chirped and a neighbor's child called.

The judge removed a slip of paper from his pocket and looked over the top of his glasses at the couple and then the seated guests. He explained that the state of New York had vested in him the power to unite a couple in matrimony, but not to secure their happiness. The latter depended on the couple themselves, and this couple had something to pledge to each other in that regard. Taking the cue, Maggie stepped forward and wrapped a wide purple ribbon around Jenn's left hand in Arun's right; Megha wrapped another ribbon around their other joined hands. Maggie and Megha stepped off the platform, taking seats next to their husbands. Maggie grasped Paul's arm and leaned into him, as if to press him more solidly into his chair. The judge invited the bride and groom to avow their love.

Jenn spoke first in a firm, clear voice: "Since the day we met, I have enjoyed your strength and your kindness. You are my best friend. I will love you and honor you all my life."

Arun replied too quickly, obviously nervous: "Since the day we met, I have delighted in your spirit and your compassion. You are my greatest gift. I will love you and honor you all of my life."

Maggie wondered if any promise could last a lifetime. At twenty-six, she had thought her promise to Paul would. She no longer loved the blustering, sulking male animal sitting beside her, but she still loved the brilliant youth he had been, or the picture in her mind of that youth. Or perhaps it was nostalgia for her own youth that aroused her tenderness. What would Jenn reflect on thirty years from now?

Thirty years yielded so many trials. She had to trust Jenn to manage them competently and, she hoped, with loving support. She did not judge, which, she realized, made her different from her mother in the same shoes. And she could not predict. Arun remained indecipherable to her, but the obvious bond between him and Jenn demanded respect.

Arun: "I promise to inspire and encourage you to live a life of devotion and learning."

Jenn: "I promise to celebrate with you and to help you achieve your goals."

There was a time, Maggie thought, when she would have thought those words perfect. Today she bridled against the asymmetry. Arun expected Jenn to lead a life of devotion. To him? To his strange ideas? And Jenn promised to serve his goals. What would happen when his goals contradicted her needs? Could Jenn pull Arun around to her way of thinking? If Maggie asked her directly, Jenn would flick her hand and say, "No problem. We want the same things." Maggie sighed; there was no antidote to youth.

Jenn: "I will cherish you in good times and in hard times, and I will see you through."

Arun: "I will nurture you in sickness and in health and share blessings even when they are scarce."

The words took Paul back to his own wedding, when an innocent Maggie had promised to stick with him for better or worse. She wasn't delivering, and it infuriated him. She had been steadfast in her support before, or so he'd thought, until Lenny poisoned his head. Maybe if he told her the whole story, the real story about Alicia and his extrapolations, she'd come through. Or would she scorn him? Revealing all was too risky. He'd fight Stamford on his own.

Arun: "I want to raise a family with you and to savor the happiness and share the cares."

Jenn: "I want to observe the traditions that are meaningful to us and to create new ones together."

So, Paul thought, the fakir promises to do housework, the faker. God, he wished he could take him on—smash that smug face, knee those offending balls—and obliterate this nightmare. Every time he had wanted to argue with Arun these past weeks, Maggie or Sarah had interfered. And then Alicia freaked and he got distracted. So Jenn would be stuck with a hypocrite who would steal the bloom from her rose. With a pang, he felt abandoned by the child into whom he had poured such affection and whose companionship had elevated his days. Jenn's future pain would be his pain. He couldn't bear the ceremony any longer. If not for Maggie's insistent arm, he would have slipped away.

The judge reached into his pocket and pulled out a ring box. Jenn nodded to him and he mumbled, "Ah, yes." He replaced the box and unwrapped the ribbons binding the couple's hands. Stuffing ribbons into his other pocket, he told the assembled body that Jenn and Arun had chosen rings to symbolize everlasting commitment to each other. He took out the box and offered it to the bride and groom in turn.

Jenn, sliding the ring on Arun's finger: "You bring me joy. I am your wife."

Arun, sliding the ring on Jenn's finger: "You bring me wonder. I am your husband."

The judge said husband and wife could seal the marriage with a kiss. Jenn stepped into Arun's arms, and they kissed to applause. They stepped off the platform and their guests clustered around to wish them well. Maggie released

Paul's arm and he bolted. The string trio began to play, and the caterer's people sprang into action on the patio. Lunch smells began to waft toward the guests.

Maggie stood to the side of the circle around Jenn and Arun, watching her radiant daughter and the now relaxed groom. Sarah approached and hugged her; Maggie held Sarah tight, swallowing the lump in her throat that presaged tears. It was hard to say good-bye to Jenn's childhood without confidence that Jenn's womanhood would be fulfilling. And then, with Jenn truly gone, what next for her?

She murmured to Sarah, "I think I need to go to the wedding in Bangalore."

"I'll go with you."

They dropped arms. On impulse Maggie said, "Can you take a month off and travel around India with me?"

"I can take six months off and travel around the world with you. I'll Skype my clients. No big deal. I've wanted to go on safari in the Serengeti for years! We need to start planning."

"Sarah, just India."

"I'll present you with one-, two-, and six-month options. This was meant to be." Sarah kissed her cheek and slipped away, camera raised in hand.

As she moved toward the patio to supervise the buffet, Maggie thought about Bangalore. How much would a trip to India cost? Did she have enough saved or would she need Paul's help? Would he cooperate? She would not give him a choice. She wanted to see Jenn and Arun in the context in which they'd grow, and she needed time away from routine. Time to feel into the corners of her soul's pantry and handle the bits of pottery nestled there, see what they held. She felt as if she'd opened a door and let in light and air that made dust rise, dust she had to see clear.

She saw her mother easing her father into a chair at one of the luncheon tables and stepped quickly to them. "Why don't you sit, Mom? I'll bring you and Dad plates."

Claudia shook her head no and placed her bag on the seat next to her husband. "I need to keep moving. It was a nice ceremony, better than I expected. Jenn looks to be in love, God bless her."

Maggie heard the righteous undertone in "God bless her" and pretended not to. "Why don't you tell her so? It will make her happy." It felt odd to be manipulating her mother, but Jenn's feelings were more important. So important that she felt no guilt. Her mother looked small, leaning on the chair back, wearing a white sweater over her floral print in case of rain. Grandmother and grand-daughter, separated by so much more than years. Claudia had worshipped convention; Jenn wanted to create a new world order. Maggie empathized with both of them; she'd been both of them. But she was someone different now, someone with dimensions she intended to explore.

She scanned the backyard. A few well-wishers still surrounded the bride and groom; a line had formed at the buffet; Sarah snapped pictures; Paul and Robert Stamford were nowhere to be found. "Excuse me," she said to her mother. She went scouting.

She saw Paul on the patio threshold, his face a storm cloud, a white envelope in his hand. He met her gaze. They approached each other.

"This is for Jenn," he said, brandishing the envelope. "Your buddy Stamford wants to buy me off."

"Where is Robert?"

"He left. Do you miss him?"

"Did you kick him out, for no good reason?"

"Haven't you given me good reason?"

"Oh, don't be silly. I made friends with Robert for your sake. He's admired me from a distance for years, but that's all."

"And you encouraged him?"

"I am not going to argue with you. Make peace with your daughter's wedding." She snatched the envelope and turned on her heel. He caught her arm.

"Where are you going?"

"I have a party to attend to."

"Always work to do when I want you."

"No, my work is done." Almost done, she thought, my work as a mother is almost done. She decided to tell him. "I'm going to Jenn's wedding in India. Sarah's going too. We'll stay for a while. I want to see our daughter and son-in-law in action."

He looked stunned. "What about me?"

"You can go if you like."

"You can't leave me now. This is my best shot!"

"Oh, your conference. Good luck. Call and tell me all about it." She pulled out of his grasp. "I don't know when I'll be back."

He watched her circulate among the diners, so attentive to everyone but him. And Jenn, flitting from table to table, hugs and kisses for everyone but him. This, the bosom of his family, should be warm and soothing, but he felt battered and alone. He scanned the party for a friendly face. Lenny stood with Arun, glad-handing: too noisy. The neighbors, Ellen and Joel: too remote. He spotted Sandi at the far end of the tables, and she waved. He strode to her.

"You should be proud of your daughter," Sandi said, offering him the empty chair beside her. "She's a fine young woman. Makes up her own mind."

He sat. Sandi looked odd in a purple dress, with spots of rouge on her cheekbones and red lipstick that made her face look like a Kewpie doll's. He never thought of her as female, yet here was proof. Makeup or no, she exuded calm. He could count on her.

"She's going to marry him again in India in July."

"Sounds like fun. I'll watch over the lab for you."

"Not going. Too much happening here."

"Speaking of business, you do remember that Alicia's camped out in my condo? She seems okay, ditsy as usual. Do you still want me to keep her?"

"I'll come over this evening and talk to her. Stamford may have cooled down. I gave him a talking to. I think the problem will clear up."

"Of course it will," Sandi said, punching his shoulder with the knuckles of her strong right hand.

He hadn't the slightest idea whether his threat of scandal would work. Sandi's confidence in his ability to keep the enterprise going calmed him some. He'd been able to pull it together for the past twenty years, and past is prologue, isn't it? Doubt clawed at his heart and soured his stomach. The threat this time was different: he could be ruined and the world could lose something invaluable. He poured a glass of wine from the carafe on the table in front of Sandi and drank, building up the burn in his chest. Sandi would stand by him. And there was always Irene.

✦ ✦

Five o'clock, evening chill in the air. Alone in the backyard, Maggie waited for the tent company to come pick up their wares. Jenn and Arun had taken Maggie's car to follow his cousins to New Jersey for supper. Lenny had given Sarah a lift to the airport, and when Maggie returned from dropping off her parents at their hotel, Paul had gone for a walk. Except for the lilac branches piled in a corner, the backyard looked as it had before the wedding: spring green with a touch of white and pink.

Maggie sat in the blessed calm, feeling satisfied. The wedding had gone smoothly; people seemed to enjoy the party, and she and Sarah had a plan. Or the beginning of a plan. Sarah would want to hit all the famous must-sees on the Indian subcontinent. Maggie wanted something simpler and harder to achieve. Yes, she wanted to observe Arun and Jenn in context so she could understand their work. But even more, she wanted to shock herself back into gear, free of Paul and Pelham and her usual preoccupations. India, she expected, would be fertile and chaotic, like a primordial soup from which animating impulses emerge. She crossed arms and hugged herself against the chill and in anticipation.

Paul appeared on the patio, looking haggard. He sidled up to Maggie.

"So when are you leaving?" He positioned a patio chair next to hers.

"Probably in a week. Sarah's working with a travel agent. They'll confirm flights in a couple of days."

"Can't you wait until after the conference?"

"Too late. I want to get there well before the wedding. Besides, you don't need me."

"I need you to get Stamford to lay off."

"I talked to Robert before the ceremony, after you two argued. He said it was out of his hands. You have to get the person who made the allegation to withdraw it. He said he agreed the timing is unfortunate, but he had no choice. He didn't seem concerned, given the quality of your work."

"So he won't lift a finger, not even for you?"

Maggie shook her head no and looked away. She felt sorry for him, alone in his needless jealousy. But she wouldn't stay to nurse him, and she wouldn't come back to him. He'd alienated his daughter and blown their partnership. She deserved better.

A glimpse of life after India, because surely she'd return, began to form. It was vague, more a sensation than an image. She'd move into the city, get an accounting job, perhaps go back to school. She could redo her adolescence with abandon this time, welcoming diversions, savoring the flavors.

And what of Paul? She pictured him trudging into the lab unkempt, having spent the night on Tim's couch or in some woman's bed. For all his vaunted independence, he didn't like to sleep alone. He looked diminished, pathetic in his protest against Robert. She felt pity, nothing more.

In the silence, Paul recalled his past interactions with his accuser. Miller had always been cordial until Hope stole his techniques. Could he wangle some help from Hope, or was that bridge burned? He still didn't understand what had gone wrong with her.

"Don't go," he said to his wife.

"Is there anything specific you need me to do before I leave?"

"When are you coming back?"

"You realize I'm not coming back, to you. You'll have a hard time at first, but you'll be fine. Someone will take my place."

The men from the tent company appeared in the driveway. Maggie pressed his hand and got up to greet them.

Alone on the patio, he shivered in the evening chill. Maggie's news sank into him as Stamford's words whirled through his head. Miller was such a fucking stickler for protocol, worse than Maggie. Maybe if he told Maggie, she'd stay and help him. But he would have to tell her everything to make her stay. Then the look on her face would crush him. He remembered the admiration he used to see there. No, he wouldn't debase himself. He'd go it alone. The prospect made him nauseous.

He went into the mudroom to get his jacket. Thirty-five minutes to drive to Sandi's place in Parkchester. He'd call Maggie from the car and tell her not to expect him. If Irene wouldn't take him in, he'd sleep on a cot at the hospital. Used to do that a lot in the old days, when his experiments were so damn exciting and he didn't have staff to handle the mundane stuff. He thought about how much had changed since then. And then defeat sliced through him—he would have to let Stamford control the most important thing he'd ever done or could ever do. His chest contracted and the old hunger rose up. He wanted to start again. He wanted freedom to work his own way. He wanted Jenn to come back. He wanted Maggie to stay. He had run out of luck. He wanted more.

ACKNOWLEDGEMENTS

I am grateful to the many people who provided wisdom and support, especially Pam Hait and Carol Test, superb editors both. Thanks also to Jana Bommersback, Susan Freeman, Barbara Grinell, Glenn Hait, Emily Hinchman, Dominique Hoelzinger, Rachelle Marmor, Lisa Miller, Marilyn Millman, Jim Sallis, Ellie Sutter, Lois Zachary, and my patient husband, Tom Johnson.

ABOUT THE AUTHOR

photo © Scott Foust, Image Industry

Toward the end of her forty-year career as a creator of science museums, Sheila Grinell began to write fiction. *Appetite* is her debut novel. Born in a taxi in Manhattan, she studied at the Bronx High School of Science, Harvard University, and the University of California, Berkeley. She lives in Phoenix with her husband and dog. To learn more, visit sheilagrinell.com.

Selected Titles from She Writes Press

She Writes Press is an independent publishing
company founded to serve women writers everywhere.
Visit us at www.shewritespress.com.

Stella Rose by Tammy Flanders Hetrick. $16.95, 978-1-63152-921-4. When her dying best friend asks her to take care of her sixteen-year-old daughter, Abby says yes—but as she grapples with raising a grieving teenager, she realizes she didn't know her best friend as well as she thought she did.

The Geometry of Love by Jessica Levine. $16.95, 978-1-938314-62-9. Torn between her need for stability and her desire for independence, an aspiring poets grapples with questions of artistic inspiration, erotic love, and infidelity.

Shelter Us by Laura Diamond. $16.95, 978-1-63152-970-2. Lawyer-turned-stay-at-home-mom Sarah Shaw is still struggling to find a steady happiness after the death of her infant daughter when she meets a young homeless mother and toddler she can't get out of her mind—and becomes determined to rescue them.

Things Unsaid by Diana Y. Paul. $16.95, 978-1-63152-812-5. A family saga of three generations fighting over money and obligation—and a tale of survival, resilience, and recovery.

Again and Again by Ellen Bravo. $16.95, 978-1-63152-939-9. When the man who raped her roommate in college becomes a Senate candidate, women's rights leader Deborah Borenstein must make a choice—one that could determine control of the Senate, the course of a friendship, and the fate of a marriage.

Play for Me by Céline Keating. $16.95, 978-1-63152-972-6. Middle-aged Lily impulsively joins a touring folk-rock band, leaving her job and marriage behind in an attempt to find a second chance at life, passion, and art.